THE DEVIL'S ACRE

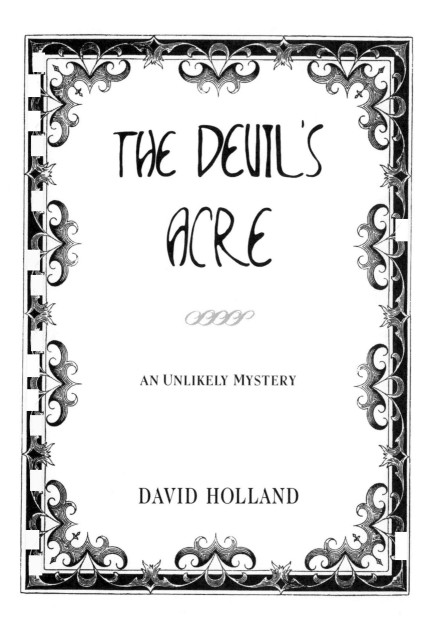

THE DEVIL'S ACRE

AN UNLIKELY MYSTERY

DAVID HOLLAND

THOMAS DUNNE BOOKS
ST. MARTIN'S MINOTAUR ⚔ NEW YORK

THOMAS DUNNE BOOKS.
An imprint of St. Martin's Press.

THE DEVIL'S ACRE. Copyright © 2003 by David Holland. All rights
reserved. Printed in the United States of America. No part of this book
may be used or reproduced in any manner whatsoever without written
permission except in the case of brief quotations embodied in critical
articles or reviews. For information, address St. Martin's Press, 175
Fifth Avenue, New York, N.Y. 10010.

www.minotaurbooks.com

Library of Congress Cataloging-in-Publication Data

Holland, David, 1959–
    The Devil's Acre / David Holland.—1st ed.
        p. cm.
    ISBN 0-312-31866-9
    1. London (England)—Fiction.   2. Philanthropists—Fiction.
3. Clergy—Fiction.   I. Title.

PS3558.O3482D47   2003
813'.54—dc21

                                                    2003046875

First Edition: December 2003

10 9 8 7 6 5 4 3 2 1

To Joe and Roxie and Kim and Natasha,
two of whom are people

THE DEVIL'S ACRE

CHAPTER I

"VAGES!"

D arkness fell on London, easing its inky fingers along the dust and filth of the streets of Westminster. Throughout the daylight hours (if that can be called day that only sees the sun through a thick and virulent haze), the city had been engulfed in a flood of noise, the surge of activity, the human neap and ebb of commerce swirling past houses and storefronts, up and down lanes, swamping market stalls and shops, pulsing to the frantic rhythm of a million hearts' desires. June was creeping toward July upon a fetid wind, and the very air that day had held an unwholesome flavor of grit and decay that made the whores on the street smack their painted lips and gentlemen cluck desultorily to themselves. Even the blackened sweeps found the outside air no less oppressive than that within their suffocating world. It had been, as many reported that night, cringing in their homes with a shake of the head and a woeful gaze, "a particular London-y day."

The crowds were gone now, and even the watch had left the streets abandoned to the dark. Yet the flavor remained to taint the breeze blowing up from the Thames. Like a woolen blanket left too long out-of-doors, the wind laid a thick, wet heat over the city that drove away all comfort. Such palpable weather might have led one to believe that night itself could congeal into a solid form, the shadows taking shape and substance to pass unseen through the streets of Westminster, past Abbey and Cathedral, Palace and Hall. The washing of the waves against the filth-encrusted banks of the Thames might have sounded like the steady plod of hooves pulling their weary weight along the earth. The lazy moaning of the wind over chimney pipes might have sounded like the creak of a carriage lumbering along. On such a night as this, who knows what one might imagine to inhabit the darkness?

A coach was making toward the river in fact, not fancy. Moving past buildings that were merely dark smudges upon a dark canvas, guided only by the sound of the sluggish waters, a black coach behind a black horse made a somber procession down, down into the lowest quarter of Westminster. The momentary flash of sulfur, the striking of a match, revealed two figures atop the box. One leaned forward in a black cloak, upright and alert as he clasped the reins. The other lolled beside him in a dirty shirt and no collar, a rounded hat with a dented crown balanced upon his knees, a blunt cigar clenched tight in his teeth. He leered out at the night from a single bright eye, the other being dead and milky white like the underbelly of a fish where a jagged scar creased his face. This fish-eyed man waved the match flame back to darkness, puffing easily so that the cigar's fiery tip glowed with each slow drag as he fanned himself lazily with his hat.

Suddenly he leaned forward and grasped the reins, pulling the horse to a complaisant halt.

"Ssst!" he hissed to his companion, and listened. For a tense moment his one eye peered into the blackness, and nothing but the blackness looked back. "Close on by the place, I'd vager." He spoke with a thin, whispery voice in the thick accent of the streets.

"Then get down and lead the rest of the way," the cloaked man commanded.

The other turned his one eye upon his partner with a look of cold calculation, but only for an instant, and then a smile of genial camaraderie graced his stubbled chin. With a flourish he popped the hat onto his head. "Right you are, Mistah Vick," he crowed, and leaped down into the dust.

Taking the bridle, he led horse, coach, and all for another several dozen yards, before coming to a stop.

"Are we close?" the cloaked man asked from his perch above, unable to penetrate the black.

"The vaters is lickin' my boots as ve speak."

"Is the boat by?"

"Right 'ere as I said it vould be." The soft sound of a boot knocking against damp wood confirmed the fish-eyed fellow in his answer.

The cloaked man waited grudgingly for a moment, then descended the box and walked toward the other until his own boots splashed in the wash of the river. He was shorter than his companion by half a head, though his formality added a certain presence to his stature. "All right," he admitted at last, tying the horse to a rotting post. "Go get it."

The fish-eyed man took the cigar from between his teeth and snuffed it against the top of the post. Placing the twisted weed in his pocket for later, he gave a nod and a horrid wink, then strolled back to the coach, reached inside, and emerged cradling a heavy sack. This he carried in his arms down to the water before dropping it into the bottom of the boat with a dull thud.

"Quiet!"

The fish-eyed man grinned rudely in response to this harsh command, but said nothing. He merely bent to gather stones from the shore, dropping them into the sack's gaping mouth.

"What are you about?" the cloaked man demanded, passing a hand across his sweated brow. "Hurry!"

"A little assurance," the other answered, not ceasing in his labors. "Vouldn't like to see this'n pop up in a for'night to go peachin' on us." He chuckled at the thought, and continued to add weight to the sack, testing the heft of it occasionally until he was satisfied.

Producing a length of rope from somewhere unseen, he tied up the package into a lumpy, shapeless, but governable bundle. Even then he was not quite finished with his ministrations, for he suddenly pulled a knife from his boot, a thin stiletto.

"Here!" the cloaked man uttered in surprise, taking an involuntary step backward into the water. "What's this?"

"More assurance," the fish-eyed man clucked, and cut a few slits in the sack. "A bit o' wentilation. To let the airs escape." He leered at his companion. "Bubble, bubble, eh, Mistah Vick?"

The cloaked man shuddered. "You know your business well."

His partner in these proceedings stood up with a groan. "They say it's visdom in a man as knows as much," he asserted with a sage look. Setting one foot into the boat, he steadied it while the cloaked man stepped in and sat as far from the sack as he could position himself. "Aye, they say it's a vise chap knows 'is own business," the other repeated, pushing off smoothly and taking the oars.

The boat flew silently into the night, setting barely a ripple across the flowing surface of the Thames. "Labor and vages, that's all it amounts to these days," the man went on, quite as though he were at home before his hearth instead of pulling across a river of darkness. "A family as kep' at farmin' for ten generations gives it all up so as to labor in the city and earn better vages. And vhat's the end? Only pain and 'ardship from not knowin' their business."

"Hush, can't you, man?"

"You sees vhat I'm gettin' at?" the fish-eyed man went on, oblivious to the importunate request. "The trick to livin' a fine life, as it were, the sort o' life your master lives, is to do the least labor for the best vages. See? And that comes o' knowin' your own business, as I said."

The other man produced a green kerchief from within the folds of his cloak and began to mop the streaming sweat from his face. Yet he made no move to discard his heavy garment, pulling it tighter about his throat, as though he could protect himself from some contagion on the wind. "It's a vile business," he whispered in disgust, peering into the blank face of the water.

"That it is, that it is. Wile and shameful." The fish-eyed fellow grinned. "O' course, for the right vages, a man might never be forced to it again."

"You'll get your wages," the cloaked man snapped.

"But you see, there's vages, and then there's *vages*." The oarsman paused in the easy flow of his narration and glared with a bright eye and a livid scar at his cloaked companion, demanding attention.

Slowly, the cloaked man ceased his mopping and returned the fellow's stare. "Go on," he muttered.

The fish-eyed man stopped rowing and let the boat drift into the stream of the river. "Your master knows 'is business, Mistah Vick. Vell, ve knows 'is business, too. Vages might be had o' such knowledge. Fine vages."

The cloaked man seemed confused by this observation at first, then affronted, and finally he leaned back in the boat and fell deep within himself. His fish-eyed partner was silent now, letting the lapping waves against the hull do his work for him.

At last, the cloaked man spoke. "My master places great trust in me."

"O' course 'e do. That's vhy you makes such 'igh vages. And that's vhy you finds yourself 'ere this night vith me, attendin' to 'is business. The thing to ask yourself is, can 'igher vages be got from such trust as 'e places in you, eh, Mistah Vick?"

Again they were silent. For five minutes, ten minutes, a quarter of an hour the only sound was the water of the Thames and the occasional dip of the oars as the boat held its place on the river.

The cloaked man sat upright at last. "How far out are we?"

"Far enough to be rid o' this." And without another word, the fish-eyed man heaved the bundle into the blackness below. A small patch of bubbles rose suddenly, white against the dark of the water as if to mark the place, but it soon dispersed.

"Good," said the cloaked man, clearly thankful to be relieved of his charge. "Then let's continue this discussion elsewhere." He shuddered. "I don't like the river at night."

"Nor do I, Mistah Vick," the fish-eyed fellow chuckled, pulling hard back in the direction of the shore. "No more do I."

The boat and its occupants disappeared into the blackness. Behind them, the last white bubbles erupted on the surface of the water and danced about, drifting on the tide.

CHAPTER II
ON THE LONDON ROAD

T he raven circled twice into the highest reaches of Bellminster
Cathedral, its form a black mark upon the prismatic stream
of light flowing through the stained glass windows. It was
morning, just that time of day when the first rays catch the dew
still upon the glass, and suddenly the air swims in a sea of blues
and greens, reds and ambers hung in ethereal suspension, bold,
pure, honest color. The raven folded its darkling feathers as if in
defiance of such splendor and dropped like a millstone to earth.
But at the last moment, it spread its wings wide to alight gently on
Tuckworth's knee. The dean of Bellminster Cathedral eyed the bird
calmly, as though there were nothing so unusual in its presence
there, or in his being seated in his usual pew in the empty nave,
his usual spot for reflection and solitude.

Ridiculous creature, you're dead, he thought, with that uncanny
clarity that he brought even to his most outlandish dreams. When
did your wing mend?

The raven cast a black, lifeless eye at Tuckworth and opened its
beak. "Go home, old man," it squawked.

Tuckworth reached out a hand and suddenly the pew shook him
like a puppeteer dandling a marionette, and then the bird was gone
and the color was gone, and Tuckworth again found himself trav-

eling south inside the shade-drawn shadows of the London coach, being jostled in his unforgiving seat.

How he hated travel.

Some stone or hole in the hard, dry road had bounced the coach as it raced along, startling Tuckworth back to his senses. The bird was dead, of course. He had known as much, even in the dream. It had been murdered months ago by a madman. (Was it proper to say a bird was "murdered"?) Why did he still dream of the creature? He'd never felt any great affection toward it, had cared for it only because no one else in the world seemed to want to. (Wasn't *killed* a likelier word?) A bird with a twisted wing was a pathetic sight, after all. Still, why did he miss it so?

Tuckworth pulled a red kerchief from the pocket of his black coat, removed his spectacles, and mopped the rivulets of sweat from his cherubic face and from around his sad, glistening eyes. The stagnant air of the coach with its shades pulled down against the dust, the mildewed odor of the straw littering the floor, the constant banging and knocking of the road combined to make him feel, not quite ill, but far from well. He hoped for a stop soon where he might step out and have a pint.

Tuckworth knew why he dreamed of Bellminster Cathedral. It had been his home for three decades, had seen his years pass by lazily, his marriage to Eleanor ripen, his Lucy grow from child to woman, his life settle into a comfortable round of habit and regularity. Then it had stood by silently while his wife wasted from the cancer. Its cold walls watched her agony, heard her screams, and witnessed his one unforgivable act of love, the dreadful night he ended her suffering when God would not. And the cathedral finally sat idle as Tuckworth's faith shriveled inside him like a dried flower pressed hard by pain and loss, God now as dead to him as that black bird.

He was vicar then, only lately under the authority of Reverend Mortimer, Bellminster's young and ambitious rector. Now Tuckworth was dean of the cathedral, under the authority of no one but the bishop, who lived a casual life in London, rarely bothering himself with his see. But dean was a ludicrous post. The cathedral was nothing more than an ugly hole in the sky, destroyed by the same madman who had murdered the bird. Perhaps that was it, the reason bird and cathedral were so closely associated in his memory.

He looked across the close confinement of the coach to where Mortimer was trying to read a religious tract in the half-light, looking properly austere and evangelical in his clerical black, stained even darker under the arms and about the collar. Tuckworth noted the droplet of sweat forming slowly on the end of the rector's long nose. Mortimer would never lift a hand to wipe it away, or admit that the air in the coach was anything but the freshest. They had shared words before embarking from the Granby Arms to leave Bellminster behind in the dust. Tuckworth had wanted to sit on top of the coach with the more common throng, where the breeze might relieve the heat of the stifling day. Besides, it was cheaper to ride on top. But Mortimer would hear none of it.

"Scandalous, for a man of the cloth to expose himself to the public highway in that manner," the younger man had pronounced under his breath. "To arrive with the filth of the road upon you when there are perfectly respectable accommodations within."

"Oh, good heavens," Tuckworth said, exasperated at such posturing. "The day is hot for everyone, and I don't see how it's a scandal to be comfortable."

"Need I remind you, Mr. Tuckworth, that we are not *everyone,* and you are no longer a poor vicar? We are men of God, and so must find our comfort in Him."

Tuckworth was confounded if he knew what that had to do with the weather, and he might have climbed to the top regardless. In fact, he was prepared to do so, but Mortimer held the coach door open for him, forcing him either to step inside or to cut his traveling companion before the entire coach yard of people, including Lord Granby. Tuckworth sighed and got in.

Only one other passenger now shared the space with them, a beefy man who had joined the coach at Morley, just beyond the dark reaches of the Estwold. He was not much company, however, a seasoned traveler who had no trouble sleeping in the coach. Left to his own dreary thoughts, Tuckworth opened the shade, just a crack, and looked out the window at the passing green of the British landscape, a green that was slowly turning to dull yellow under the searing heat of the sun. A cold, wet winter followed by a hot, dry spring. Hard times ahead, he thought. Where had he heard that? Hard times ahead.

"Hard times, Tuckworth," Lord Granby had told him as they walked to the Granby Arms that morning. "The mill in danger of closing. Farms failing. Hard times ahead for everyone, and that includes our little church." His lordship had taken to calling Bellminster Cathedral "our little church" now that it was nothing more than a burned-out hovel, its naked walls reaching vainly to heaven.

Tuckworth shook his head. "I can't say that I feel right traveling all the way to London so I might squeeze out some contribution for the Cathedral Fund," he admitted. "If times are so hard, a cathedral seems like a great empty waste."

Granby, tall yet stooped, aged yet active and alert to everything, glanced sideways at the dean. "Now," he said, half smiling, "if I thought you meant that, I'd be disappointed in you."

Tuckworth didn't mean it. Granby knew him well enough to know that. The dean loved Bellminster Cathedral, or came as close to loving it as he deemed right in loving a heap of stone. Perhaps he merely felt guilty because he wanted so much to restore it, in spite of the hard times. He wanted to see it again as it once had been, its two towers rising over the rooftops of Bellminster on the hill overlooking the Medwin Ford, its single spire slender and sharp against the sky so that it could be seen from the wooded cover of the Estwold, distant evidence of men and community. He wanted to see it done, and he wanted to be the one to do it. Yet, in a world filled with suffering and pain, poverty and encroaching hunger, it seemed a frivolous thing to want.

"Hamlin Price has a great deal of money," Granby went on, striding slowly across the Cathedral Square, "and he has no right notion what to do with it all. No family, no dependents. Doesn't play at politics, doesn't live in society. Just doles it out to a handful of causes. Now, it took some little bit of doing to wrangle this invitation, and I expect you to pluck up and do the thing proper."

Tuckworth sighed. He didn't see why the thing couldn't be managed through the post. But, then again, he did. They were talking about thousands of pounds, after all, and no man would spend so much so blindly. Still, he hated dealing with money almost as much as he hated travel. "At my time of life, I never thought to be a mendicant friar," he muttered.

"That's right," Granby replied pleasantly, oblivious to Tuckworth's complaints.

The coach gave another quick shudder and lurch, and the dean went tumbling across the seat into the slumbering man. "Cucumbers!" the man cried for no reason, and apparently without waking, for he followed this exclamation with a prodigious snore.

Tuckworth righted himself, and he caught Mortimer shooting him a remonstrating glance. With no hope for conversation from that quarter, Tuckworth turned his attention once again to the passing scenery. He opened the shade another few inches. The sky was iron gray with the heat of summer, and the parched fields looked stark and barren. Soon, he knew, the earth would be as hard as the stone walls that quilted together these fields and valleys.

He shifted in his seat and felt something hard dig into his hip. Reaching into his pocket, he pulled out the last of the oatcakes Mrs. Cutler had forced on him as he was walking out the door that morning to meet Lord Granby.

"Not like to find fit food on the road," she had growled, thrusting three of the blistering-hot cakes into his hands. "I don't trust them country inns, with their filthy kitchens and their wormy cornmeal." The picture of her unsmiling face brought warm feelings of Bellminster back to Tuckworth's mind. Good woman, he thought, though hard, as hard and relentless as her oatcakes. He had eaten two of them right off, before they had even made Morley, and now he began nibbling at the third and last.

Finishing this repast, Tuckworth let his arm hang limply outside the coach, scooping his palm to bale the breeze. Some idea about a quilt rose at the back of his mind. The quilted traveling bag, of course. Bought by Lucy just for this journey, and given to him that morning as he was setting out his shirts and sundries. Silly expense, but she handled all the household finances now, and even managed the Cathedral Fund. She told him it could easily be afforded.

"We can't have you going up to London on such important business with that shameful old satchel of yours," she chided as only a loving child can chide a doting father.

"I don't see why everyone is making such a fuss over this trip," he complained, and saw at once that his idle words had hurt her, only just. He held up the bag to inspect it, with its red and green squares, its crisp metal clasp and leather fixtures. "Well, at least having this will make the whole business seem worthwhile," and she smiled at the effort he made to soothe her feelings.

Lucy brushed a stray wisp of raven-copper curl from her forehead and took over the task of arranging his articles neatly and placing them in the new bag. He stood back and watched her as she worked, listened while she hummed a tune, a sad little air. No one else would have spied the marks of anxiety about her, the restlessness of her movements, the constant fluttering of her hands about her hair, her nervous laughter when a shirtfront refused to lie flat or a collar was discovered to be hopelessly creased. To another set of eyes these would have seemed mere steps in a domestic dance, but to Tuckworth they spoke unmistakably of her true concern.

He placed a hand on her shoulder and she turned a pained smile toward him. "I'll look up Raphael as soon as I'm able," he assured her, and his gentleness gave rein to the tears she had fought to suppress. She clung to her father's chest, buried her head against his neck and wept freely, wept from the uncertain pain she suffered, and from the gratitude of knowing that she was understood so well by one she loved so much.

Raphael Amaldi. The young artist who had spent months painting Bellminster Cathedral from every angle, in every light, had become friend and companion to both father and daughter (though something infinitely more dear to her). Now he was gone to London to seek his fortune, had been absent for four months, with no telling when he would return. His letters, though regular, had turned formal and awkward. They had lost their warmth, and Lucy noticed. She found herself at that dreadful stage when her heart, if not actively breaking, had turned very brittle.

The coach shivered as though it would come apart, and Tuckworth pulled his hand inside to steady himself. He found his fingers coated in dust, and when he clapped his palms together to clean them the cloud he raised filled the air with grit before settling slowly to the floor. Mortimer coughed petulantly, darted an annoyed look at the dean, and then returned to his reading.

Tuckworth lay back in his seat. How long before they reached London? he wondered. Hours, certainly. He took his watch from his waistcoat pocket and looked at it. Twelve minutes past noon. He sat up. But that couldn't be right. They'd left Bellminster just past nine o'clock, gotten to Morley by eleven, and that was hours ago. He held the watch to his ear, heard nothing, tapped it, looked at it again, and shook it. Dust must have gotten into the works, he thought, and he thrust the timepiece deep into his pocket before throwing himself back in his seat again, feeling totally vexed at last. He huffed a bit, at no one and nothing in particular.

How he hated travel.

CHAPTER III
CONTROL AND COMMAND

Tuckworth descended from the coach into chaos, London assailing his every sense, a jangling, peeling, stinking, blinding, shrieking, glittering, braying spectacle. The dean clapped his cupped palm to his nose, failing to block the stench seeping through the city. Street offal and burning metal—smoke and spice—oil and sweat—cabbage and death created a pungent tapestry, single threads of odor adding to a greater, viler, more noxious whole.

About him rumbled a tumultuous din. He picked up snippets of coherence, a single voice raised high or a strain of music or the fearful whinnying of some horse being cruelly whipped, but no sooner did one sound emerge than the sea of noise whelmed over all again in a vast, unnatural roar. He looked about the coach yard and out the gate into the public thoroughfare but could discover no calamity that might give rise to such turmoil, no riot or house afire. On one nearby corner performed a barrel-organ grinder upon whose hat perched a large parrot, taunting the crowd with its mad antics, attracting a rapt audience, until the flow of traffic formed a teeming eddy that surged and shot back against itself and brought all to a swirling, roiling standstill. At another juncture stood a sandwich-board man, black as any African, ringing a bell and hawking his news at the top of his voice, but Tuckworth could neither hear his appeal nor read his sign. In the street he saw only moving currents of humanity, streaming around corners, rushing down alleyways, walking and running, stumbling and thronging, twisting and spinning, every class, every clan, poor and powerful, ragged and regal, the meek jostled, the slow abused, some racing to gain advantage, some fighting to pause against the tide of activity, and moving about like flotsam through it all, children, meager and dirty, scurrying everywhere, carried away on the tide of London life.

Dark was settling over the town, though it was a premature dusk, one manufactured more by the closeness of the bodies and the buildings and the yellow haze in the air than by any natural dimming of earth's light. Tuckworth began to reach for his watch, but remembered it had stopped, and his hand hung halfway in and halfway out of his waistcoat. He was frozen in a mass of people buzzing around the coach in confusion, pushing and shoving merely to assert their right to a square foot of ground.

The coachman tossed Tuckworth's bag down to a porter, who dropped it carelessly in the filth at the dean's feet. Before Tuckworth could bend over to rescue it, however, two thin young arms appeared from nowhere to take it for him, and a dirty face materialized, smiling a near-toothless grin.

"Port yer bag?" the child demanded. For one brief second Tuckworth's eyes met the boy's, and he saw there the hunger and the suffering, the scheming for relief, the rapacious life of the street urchin in whose soul was buried deep a dream of childhood. For a passing instant he recognized the one human thing in this factory of mayhem, and his heart went to the lad.

With sudden violence, the handle of an umbrella shot down from above and caught the young boy's wrists with a resounding *crack*, causing him to cry out and drop the bag into the dust before scuttling away.

Mortimer pointed the umbrella at the back of his retreating victim. "None of your tricks, scalawag, or I'll have the magistrate on you!" Then, turning to Tuckworth, he nodded down at the bag. "Keep that close until we're safely out of this."

Tuckworth looked in dismay at the rector, then reached down calmly and retrieved the bag, brushing its red and green squares with the hem of his coat. "Was it necessary to assault the boy?" he asked.

Mortimer glanced at the dean, and there was no mistaking his superior air. "We are no longer in Bellminster, Mr. Tuckworth. That imp was the very devil and would have stripped you of all you own."

Tuckworth sighed. Of course, the rector was probably correct. In all likelihood, if Mortimer had not intervened, and violently, Tuckworth would have lost everything. But his heart still ached for the boy in spite of that, and maybe more so now that he suspected the child's villainy, and the need that drove him to it.

Night was tumbling down fast, and Mortimer led the way through the coach yard to the street, using his umbrella to clear a path. The rector had made all the arrangements for their stay in London, being a man with more worldly experience than the dean possessed, a fact that he had pointed out to Tuckworth and Lord Granby when he imposed himself upon this venture. "I think I might assist the dean in navigating the waters of Babylon," he had announced in the study of the vicarage, much to Tuckworth's irritation. "I am familiar with a respectable address where we can be put up for some days or a week, as we require. Convenient place in a polite neighborhood. Besides, I have some pressing business of my own to transact in the City. That's what they call London proper. You know," he added smugly, "the oldest part—the City."

So here I am, Tuckworth thought as Mortimer led him to a nearby cabstand, an old man in London for the first time on serious business, being herded about like a child. Or an imbecile. Mortimer motioned toward a dirty cabriolet, and Tuckworth climbed in behind the rector, clutching his bag to his chest.

The two men maintained a marked silence as they passed

through the city on their trek to Westminster. Staring out the window, Tuckworth was amazed at the breadth of what he saw, the miles of storefronts and houses, the endless streets with their corkscrew turns and labyrinthine ways, the unabating flood of humanity. A miracle of the technical arts, this city, a great mirror held up to man's secret heart, to show what he dreamed, what he might be, and what he was. Yet the dean could not decide whether the prospect warmed or chilled him.

Dark had fully descended and the flickering lamplights swathed the street in sickly yellow when they arrived at a shabby-looking address. Mortimer left Tuckworth to pay the driver while he strode to the door and rang the bell. The dean followed in his wake, still clutching his bag. The door was opened after a few awkward moments, and both men entered into a gloomy foyer, lit by nothing more than a taper held in the palsied grip of an old woman.

"Mrs. Terlanne," Mortimer stated, flatly. "Reverend Jonathan Mortimer. Dean Tuckworth."

"Gen'lemen," she croaked.

"We'll want a meal, but first our rooms. And some hot water."

The old woman nodded and tottered off to arrange their food with the cook. Tuckworth glanced about at the dusky walls lined with dark family portraits and noted the cobwebs that hung about the frames like lace, signs of memories no longer kept alive. The old woman returned with a steaming kettle and showed them up a narrow staircase to their accommodations, a windowless sitting room with two adjoining chambers. Mortimer took the kettle and disappeared into his bedroom without a word. Tuckworth, however, paused a moment to observe their hostess. She was dressed in simple black and seemed to share the same impoverished state as the house. A widow, the dean noted, desperate for the odd shilling she could make from lodgers. Her features were lined and careworn, her hair almost gone and settled haphazardly in ugly cords about her mottled scalp. She kept her eyes turned down to Tuckworth's waistcoat and appeared the fearful image of servitude.

"Mrs. Terlanne," he ventured.

She made a noncommittal sound and nodded.

"It's a pleasure to meet you."

The woman only turned and left Tuckworth alone in the sitting room, still clutching his bag in front of him.

The next morning, Mortimer having left early on his own affairs, Tuckworth faced London alone, an adventure that stirred something brave and eager within him. Over breakfast, he tried to gather clear directions from Mrs. Terlanne of the way to Caldecott Lane, Hamlin Price's address near St. James's Park, but his simple request threw her into a state of dire consternation.

"It hardly matters," he tried to reassure her, and, "I'll have no trouble finding the place," and, "You know, I rather welcome the chance to discover what London is." But, notwithstanding such assurances, he left her still muttering apologies as he walked out the door.

The streets of Westminster were removed from the city's bustle and chaos by the gentle curve of the Thames, and while there was no doubt that Tuckworth was still in London, the crowds that passed him in the streets seemed less harried, less frantic, and more purposeful than the mob that had engulfed him yesterday. Did the difference lie in his surroundings, he wondered, or in the absence of Mortimer's strident nature? Certainly the day seemed brighter, though still threatening a hot and sultry afternoon. The sky was blue and a few hazy clouds glided wantonly overhead to promise the mercy of a breeze. Even the smell of the town seemed less acrid. Tuckworth filled his lungs with it, settled his thoughts, and set out to find his way.

Two and a half hours later, he found it. Though a mere forty-minute walk from Mrs. Terlanne's, Tuckworth had been forced along several false starts, dead ends, wrong turns, and blind alleys by the aid of a few benighted Samaritans and the amusement of a few playful devils. Still, he didn't regret the poor assistance he had received, and actually felt more relaxed after this ambling stroll about Westminster. Now he stood before number 18, a tall though nondescript house along a row of similar houses, each discreetly settled behind its small patch of earth, surrounded by its own iron railing, each one the image of its brothers, without so much as a flower in the window or a sprig upon the door to tell them apart. It hardly seemed the place to find a wealthy philanthropist, he considered, as he climbed the flight of steps to the door and rang.

The door was opened by a short man with a high forehead and closely cropped, peppery hair. He seemed neither butler nor valet, dressed neatly but not in the habit of a manservant. Still, there was something formal in his manner, a stiffness that implied service. He bowed very slightly and stood waiting to be addressed.

"I'm Dean Tuckworth of Bellminster Cathedral." The man remained silent, and for the first time in Tuckworth's life he wished that he had a card to give out. "I believe Lord Granby of Bellminster wrote to expect me here today," he added. "Is Mr. Price at home?"

The man took a step backward, and Tuckworth accepted this as his invitation to venture within. The house he entered was neat and bright, pleasing to look at, with chairs and tables placed conveniently around the rooms, sumptuous oriental rugs on the floors, attractive paintings in gilded frames on the walls. It was also distressingly chill and apparently deserted. The sharp sound of Tuckworth's heels upon the exposed woodwork resounded like gunshots and echoed in the upper stories. The house smelled of lye and sawdust, with no flowery hint of life or sweet scent of baking to convey a sense of homely warmth.

The short man followed Tuckworth in and motioned him to a chair. "I'll ask if he'll see you," he murmured and left through a side door.

Tuckworth waited, standing hat in hand, feeling like an intruder. Soon, however, the short man returned and motioned for him to pass in.

The dean found himself in a large, book-lined study at the end of which, behind a polished mahogany desk of ornate French design, beside a large window with green baize curtains tightly drawn, sat a balding, fresh scrubbed, busy-looking man. His face was florid and hearty, pinched by a too-tight collar, perhaps, and framed by slick skids of brown hair combed forward from his temples, but handsome nonetheless. Though neither young nor old, he seemed an image of still-youthful vigor, impatient and active, broad and bluff. He held a pen in one hand and clutched some papers in the other, and he struck Tuckworth as a man who felt it was better to look busy than actually to be so.

The dean walked slowly across the room. Without raising his eyes from the papers, Mr. Hamlin Price motioned with his pen toward a plush wing chair. Tuckworth sat.

"Post these letters."

For a moment, Tuckworth thought Price was addressing him. But the short man appeared suddenly and took a pile of correspondence from a corner of the desk.

"And don't disturb us for"—he glanced at a clock on a nearby bookcase that registered a quarter to eleven—"ten minutes' time." The short man bowed slightly and retreated through a side door. "Wick!" The short man reemerged. Price sat silent for half an instant, and then said, "That other business. What time did you say?"

Wick leaned in as he answered, "Noon, sir. Or thereabout."

Price paused, looked at the clock again, then said, "Come to me later." The short man nodded and left.

"Now, what is it you want?" He looked about his desk for something he failed to find. "What's your name? Tucker?"

"Tuckworth," the dean corrected gently. "I'm from Bellminster. It's in the Midlands."

"Yes, yes," Price said, producing a crumpled letter from a toppling pile of correspondence. "Your Lord Granby wrote all about it. Your church burned down and you want a new one." He looked sharply at Tuckworth, with a bland smile that seemed neither warm nor inviting, merely conventional.

"It's not a church. It's a cathedral."

"I can't afford to build you a cathedral," Price replied, chuckling as though a man of Tuckworth's age should know better. "There are other needs than yours in the world, Dean Tuckworth."

"I never expected that you could," Tuckworth said, hoping to hide his irritation. "But we're looking for any aid we can find. Just to get started."

"I daresay. I daresay you are," and Price chuckled again. "Lots of people looking for aid to start some such thing. Hard times for all, eh?"

"I understand you, Mr. Price," Tuckworth replied, feeling somehow chastened and guilty, "but rebuilding Bellminster Cathedral is an important undertaking."

"Why?"

"Well, it's historically significant, for one thing. The Gothic architecture is an almost complete record of a past age, and one worth preserving. Our tympanum alone is a masterpiece of the stonecutter's art. And the beauty of the clerestory—"

Price brushed these reasons aside with his hand. "Come now, it's an old building. Plenty of those falling down and no one comes to me." And the man smiled as before, an indulgent, thoughtless smile.

Tuckworth paused, not certain how to proceed. He had to admit to himself that his argument, so carefully plotted out beforehand by Granby and Mortimer, sounded rather facile and empty at the moment. He shifted in his chair, failing to get comfortable, and was suddenly disappointed with himself, with his attitude, his heartless appeal to history and art. "It's not just the building, you know," he said, thinking aloud. "It's the town, the people. It's Bellminster. It's an old town, Mr. Price. Not so little as you might expect, but little enough, and it feels like it's getting smaller all the time. We built a new mill a few years ago, and everyone thought that would revive things. I suppose it did, for a time. We even started renovating the old cathedral, making her bright and new again. But then the mill owner died last year, the same week the cathedral burned down, and they haven't found a buyer yet. Half the workers have been let go and the town feels to be slowly wasting. It's not right that Bellminster should die so." Something caught in Tuckworth's throat, and he let out a stifled gurgle. "Excuse me," he managed, and took a deep breath. "We need to see the cathedral rise again, Mr. Price. We need, not the building, but the idea of it, the thought of its coming back, just the way it used to be." Was he making any sense? What he said now seemed to be more honest, more real, yet it still failed miserably to express his true feelings. Why was he so desperate to see the cathedral restored? "I wish I could make you know what a good little town it is, or was. And how it could be that way again. Rebuilding the cathedral would put more than a hundred men to work, men who want to work, who want to work almost more than they want the food their work will buy."

Price sat back in his chair and laced his fingers across his heart. "What is the cost for your cathedral?"

"Not so much as it might have been," Tuckworth answered readily. "The walls are still sturdy, though the spire has collapsed and the roof is completely gone."

"And the cost?"

"Perhaps a hundred thousand pounds."

"Perhaps?"

"Perhaps less. But of course, we're not looking for anyone to cover the entire cost."

"Your Lord Granby," Price went on, "how much has he given to the Cathedral Fund?"

Tuckworth coughed. "Five hundred pounds."

"Five hundred?"

"Times are hard for everyone in Bellminster."

Price nodded. "What about God?"

"Excuse me?"

"Don't you want to tell me that God deserves a house as glorious as man can build? Isn't that the usual way in these things?"

Tuckworth paused again. He avoided talking of God whenever possible, to hide his festering unbelief. He was always fearful of being found out. "Of course—" he went on finally, but Price didn't allow him to finish.

"I tell you what. You come back here tonight. I entertain regularly, men and women with good causes, and tonight I'm having a little supper party. Form your thoughts, Dean Tuckworth. Command your resources. That's the way to do business." Price grinned a close-lipped grin, the kind given to children by people who don't like children. "Control and command. Get your thoughts together and you come back, let's say about eight, and we'll see what we can do. Good?" And with that, Hamlin Price returned to his papers, the man Wick materialized at Tuckworth's elbow, and the dean of Bellminster Cathedral found himself dismissed, once more standing outside looking down upon Caldecott Lane.

Tuckworth shuddered in spite of himself, trying to shake off the taint of humiliation that was slowly enveloping him like a cloud. The throng surged below, heartless, mindless. Tuckworth glanced up at the sky. The day was still bright, still blue, yet it appeared bleaker to him for all that. The sky seemed empty and vast, and he felt dizzy staring up into it. He looked back down at last, and plunged into the torrent of the passing crowd.

CHAPTER IV
LOVE'S LABORS

The Great Cross of Bellminster Cathedral lay upended where it had fallen from the spire, tilted toward the cloudless sky, its crushed top piercing the heart of the nave, its base raised to the heavens on a mound of rubble, its arms outstretched and cracked in vain supplication. On either side, the walls of the cathedral rose strong and gray and grim, their mullions empty of lead or glass, pillars and piers rising like limbless trees or scattered about like logs tinted green and yellow with dried moss, nature so quickly reclaiming her own. A fine dust hovered in the air, a brown-white cloud of stone, the cathedral itself taking flight in the merciless sunlight. But nothing else stirred about the place except the shadows, and their progress along the floor was as slow as time.

Suddenly, the cross shimmered in the haze, the sunlight glancing off it in subtle animation, and a rumbling rose from the ground as a puff of dusty air expelled a handful of men from beneath the floor.

A moment later, three figures appeared from a door hidden inside a chapel on the side of the open nave. Two were old and one was young. Two were women and one was a man. Lucy Tuckworth, the dean's daughter, burst through first with an air of responsibility quite foreign to her, frantic and stoic at once, like someone trying on an ill-fitting dress and daring the world to admit it didn't become her. She was held in that delicate place between girl and woman, her sky-blue frock and wild, black hair making her appear even more youthful, more springlike than she meant to seem. Behind her shot out briskly Mrs. Cutler, the housekeeper, dressed in black and looking hard and chill and stern. Trailing behind was the stooped, white, towering figure of Lord Granby.

"What's gone wrong now?" Lucy shouted above the dying echo of the rumble.

A man stepped forward, covered in dust and holding a large hammer. "Sorry, Miss Tuckworth," he said, shaking his head, "but that floor is doomed one way or t'other, and I'd as soon not be under it when it goes."

"Then shore it up," she demanded.

"It's like trying to shore up sand, miss," the fellow complained. "I'm sorry, but that's what it is. Like shorin' up sand. Each post we wedge up in there brings more dust down on our heads. A man can't hammer soft at such work, you know, and the harder we pound, the more of it comes loose."

The other men nodded their heads silently behind him, looking resolute, though guilty in their resolution.

"Well, you must think of something else to try tomorrow," Lucy acquiesced.

The man shook his head. "No, miss. Now, I'm sorry for't, and if we was all bein' paid for the work it'd be different. Man don't mind riskin' his neck in that crypt for a decent wage. But no, miss, we'll not do it for free no longer."

"Oh," Mrs. Cutler exclaimed, stepping forward with her hands clutched tightly before her. "Is that the size of your courage, Abraham Semple? Afraid to venture in among the dead in honest labor for the church?"

"Now, it ain't that and you know it," Semple defended himself with a wag of his chin. "It's that there cross. Really, miss," he said, turning in appeal to Lucy, "you might as well give the thing up. It'll have to be broke up anyway and carted off in bits. Take too much money to raise the thing proper."

Lucy shook her head. "No," she insisted, sounding strangely girlish in her obstinacy. "The dean has hopes to raise that cross before—" but she was given no chance to continue. Another rumble shook the floor of the cathedral, and another cloud of dust, thicker and more ominous than the first, exploded from below. A solitary figure materialized through the cloud this time, the burly shape of Adam Black, the man-child who, with his sister Mary, acted as sexton of Bellminster Cathedral.

Adam came up to Lucy breathing heavily, with a look on his fistlike face that spoke more surely than any words he might utter through his grief. There was no hope for it, that was clear, and he felt he had failed her. The floor would fall, the crypt be buried. If Adam knew it, who would have built a new cathedral with his own beefy hands, then Lucy must concede the fact herself. And in that knowledge she shared the pain that Adam suffered, the hurt of failing the one you love in what he most desires. She had no need to dismiss the others. She only put her arm around Adam's broad shoulders and led him into the vicarage, followed silently by Granby and Mrs. Cutler.

"Please find Mary for me," Lucy asked the housekeeper when she and Adam were seated inside. "It's all right, Adam," she went on, trying to soothe his child's soul. "We'll get your sister here, and then, I tell you what, we'll have a picnic out in the garden. Won't that be lovely after all that hard labor?"

The man's face tried to light up for her, a wan smile gracing his graceless features. Her smile in return was no more convincing. The only comfort they could find was in the honest longing each had to hide such pain from the other.

"That's right, stout fellow," Granby echoed cheerily, patting Adam on the back and raising a dust cloud in the study. "Forget all about it. What's to be, will be, eh? Can't keep the rain from falling."

For all his good intentions, however, Granby's words sounded hollow and meaningless. And later, when he had a chance to speak to Lucy privately in the study while the others were in the garden fighting to appear carefree, his words were even less hopeful.

"It's not the floor you should be worried about," he told her, with old age's prerogative to see disaster everywhere. "It's those walls. If the floor collapses into the crypt, who knows what damage might be done. It could send the whole thing right over onto the vicarage."

"Then we'll buttress the walls."

"Who will? You and Mary and Adam?"

Lucy thought, We'd find the men and the means to do it if you'd only open your pocketbook another inch. But she was silent.

"No, Lucy," Granby advised her. "Best to just move out for a time and hope to fate. I'm certain God won't let His house fall on yours." And he underscored his opinion with a firm nod and a smile, more polite than reassuring, before going off on his own affairs.

Lucy sat alone in the study, her father's sanctuary from the world. Only lately had he begun to trust her to sit with him there, to share his life amid its comfortable clutter, going over the books of the household and the Cathedral Fund with him. He had no head for numbers.

The thought of him now, as she sat in that place so very much his, made her feel his absence all the more. It was only a day since he had left, but the cathedral floor had begun its sudden collapse into the crypt almost before the coach was out of sight, taking him away from her for the first time in her life. The world since then had limped along as she tried to save this last buried piece of the cathedral's past glory. He had wanted to preserve the crypt, she knew. But the plan to raise the Great Cross again over Bellminster, that had been hers. Since she was a child it had peered down into her bedroom window, darkly lit in the moonlight, slender and orange at dawn, pink and glowing at dusk. It was her companion, her special piece of heaven, and she wanted to see it there again, in its old place. But it appeared her dream was just that, a nighttime hope that the day would dash asunder.

She had felt alone in her struggle, pleading and scheming, begging and shaming anyone who might help in a vain effort to shore up the floor from below. But no, she was not alone. Mrs. Cutler and Mary and Adam, they had stayed by her side when no one else would. A strange little family.

And there was another member to it, their family, one not there whose absence she always felt. Even more bitterly than her father's? She was ashamed to admit it. She had been certain her pain would ease as the days lengthened, his presence growing faint and dim in her heart. But it was like a sore that would not heal. It ached now more than ever, and she hung her head in her hands, desperate to stop the flow of tears she knew she could not hold back, not for long. Not forever.

She leaned forward in her chair, and her radiant black hair cascaded over her sorrow, enveloping her, so that she wept as though she were hiding from herself.

Lucy's fear, her helplessness and solitude, were mirrored at that moment in her father, stranded on the desert coast of a London street corner. Eight o'clock, he thought. He was on reprieve until eight o'clock. Already Tuckworth was beginning to think like a condemned man. Eight o'clock, and the heart of the day to waste in London until then. From Price's home on Caldecott Lane he had set out in the direction of Mrs. Terlanne's, partly from having nowhere else to go, partly because that was the prevailing direction of the traffic. The crowd buffeted him about as though he were riding in a tumbrel on his way to death. Yet he soon learned the knack of buffeting the crowd back again, a certain weaving gait, with the body plunged forward and the shoulders rolling this way and that. It was a London walk, and Tuckworth prided himself on how naturally it came to him.

Why should he return to his lodgings? he considered as he ambled along. Wasn't he a grown man in the most exciting city in the land, or in the world if it came to that? Wasn't this a great opportunity to expand the vista of his life, to test his resources, to see whether he might not have been something else, someone else, had he not been placed in the provincial daydream that was Bellminster? Was he a meek country parson, as Mortimer was always hinting, or a man of the world?

He stopped and instantly was made a victim of the surging throng, bumped and abused by every man, woman, and child whose way he blocked. He dodged and ducked about a bit, like a prizefighter in the ring, and then was pushed by some unseen traveler off the sidewalk and into the path of an omnibus. This he avoided with a deft leap farther out into the street, where he came up against a noisome glorywagon collecting its load of filth, spun away from that to butt into a man on horseback who aimed a kick at his ear, jerked backward away from the offending boot, collided with the rear of a pony cart, and just managed to bounce up onto the sidewalk again.

The sound of laughter cut through the city's roar, and Tuckworth saw a dirty, barefoot boy in rags leaning against a wall, holding a broom in one hand and his side with the other. The dean looked down to see his shoes and trousers splattered with the dust of the street. The lad came over, still laughing, and put his broom to work on Tuckworth's trousers, smearing the dirt about into new and fantastic shapes.

"Yer oughter be on stage," the lad crowed as he worked. "I been ter Drury Lane and din't see nothin' what compares. Yer really oughter go on stage. Yer really oughter. Folks'll pay for art like that."

Art, Tuckworth thought, and knew at once what he must do. He thanked the boy and handed him a penny, which the lad tossed into his mouth, the safest purse he had, and grinned.

"Where's the nearest cabstand?" Tuckworth asked.

The boy shrugged his shoulders, then put a hand to his mouth and whistled a piercing note. Instantly three cabbies rose from their boxes as they drove by and shouted, "Here, sir!" "Cab, sir!" "Service, m'lord!"

Tuckworth thanked the boy and hopped into an old hackney coach. "Horedale Alley in the Temple," he announced to the driver, feeling more like a native Londoner than ever, and away he rode.

Raphael, he thought as he watched the mass of humanity streaming past at a comfortable distance. I promised Lucy. She'd skin me to know I didn't stop to see him at once.

The sun was rising higher in the sky now, and the day was growing markedly, miserably humid. The moisture seemed to leech out of the street, to rise straight up into the nostrils with all the loamy scent of London about it. Indeed, it was a palpable humidity, for soon a haze developed, whether from the sky or the earth or from just around the corner, but very real and very alarming, a yellow, unhealthy cloud that seemed to drift at the height of a man's chest. Tuckworth sank back in his seat as he watched it materialize suddenly, a gauzy net draping the city, and he became distinctly aware of every breath that entered his lungs.

He arrived at his destination, still breathing, and paid the driver before looking about. Temple Bar was in the City, a darker, more ancient part of London than Westminster, with all the feel of youthful profligacy mixed with aged squalor. He found number 37, a tall, old, but not unwelcoming pile, and knocked. A young girl opened the door with a maid's crimped hat settled awkwardly on a heap of mousy brown hair. "Yeh?" she asked.

"Does a Mr. Amaldi live here?"

She shook her head and the hat wiggled alarmingly. "Nah. No eye-ties."

"No," Tuckworth corrected her, "he's not Italian. He's British, a painter."

"Ow." She nodded, her face lighting in comprehension as she

opened the door. "Painter! Up top back i' the garret. Pardon," she corrected with feigned gentility. "The stoodio," and she said the word with a mocking lilt that struck Tuckworth's heart cold for the dignity of his friend.

Tuckworth climbed the creaking steps up four flights and arrived at the top of the house with a dewy sweat clinging to his lip and brow. He pulled out his red kerchief, removed his spectacles, and wiped himself as he approached the door. Before he could knock, however, a shrill shriek broke from the room beyond, and the sounds of a struggle shook the entire floor. With no other invitation than this, Tuckworth burst into the room.

He put on his spectacles again and blinked. The space before him was small and dusty and spare, but bright, with a slanted roof out of which a large hole had been punched and a window laid over. Various rags and garments hung about, some from hooks and some from wires strung here and there to make, as it seemed, separate chambers. In the foreground stood a thin, pale, earnest-looking young woman, in a black frock with a white apron, who appeared to be on the verge of some tearful eruption. Running about her knees were three children, two girls and a boy, none older than five, all fat, all pink, all vicious. Standing at the far back beneath the window, with his head just peeking over a curtain, yellow hair hanging lankly about an open collar, stood Raphael.

"Can't you keep the children still for one minute?" he was pleading with the woman.

"Raphael!" exclaimed Tuckworth.

Raphael looked at, or rather through, the dean for a moment, rather like a man without fear staring at a ghost. Then a series of emotions played quickly across his face: recognition, joy, delight, recognition again, horror, consternation, panic, and, finally, resolution. "Vicar," he said, a bit too calmly.

"What is all this, Raphael?" the dean asked, looking about.

"You're in London."

"Yes," and Tuckworth might have smiled in spite of himself to see his young friend trying so desperately to maintain his self-respect—might have smiled, had he not offered up a thought for Lucy. "But really, my boy, what's going on here?" During this exchange, the rest of the scene proceeded without any alteration whatever, the children shrieking, the woman holding back her tears, all oblivious to the little man in clerical black who had just intruded so violently upon them.

Raphael looked quickly at the woman. "I'll be right back," he said, and added as a final, exasperated appeal, "Please do something with these children."

Raphael came from behind the curtain and, taking Tuckworth by the arm, escorted him out of the garret to the landing.

"You should have written to me that you were coming," he said, trying not to sound pettish. "I'd have met you somewhere more agreeable."

"I'm sorry," Tuckworth replied. "In all the planning, I forgot." And the two men stood there for a moment, a clumsy silence sitting like a block between them. "Raphael," the dean said at last, "that scene in there—"

"Supper, this evening," Raphael interrupted, forcing a smile. "Let's meet for supper."

"I'm engaged tonight."

"Then tomorrow. Dinner, about three. No, wait," he added, looking back toward his door. "I've got to . . . well, breakfast then. Ten o'clock. There's a coffeehouse at the corner. You can't miss it." At that instant, the sound of uncontrolled sobbing announced the commencement of the lady's tearful eruption. The two men shared a quick glance, the one guilty, ashamed, the other confused and disturbed, yet compassionate. "See you tomorrow, then, vicar. I should say 'dean,' I suppose." And Raphael disappeared.

Tuckworth descended the staircase, distinctly troubled by this mystery. He reconstructed for himself the scene that he had witnessed in the garret, the details, the sense of the room. Turmoil of domesticity? Perhaps. But how could Raphael have produced a family so quickly, in just a few short months? Marriage to a young widow? No, that didn't seem right. Not Raphael. What else, then? The room was mean and poor, yet the children were well fed. They even seemed to be dressed in more than modest finery. The woman looked plain enough in her simple frock, though. Might a mother not spend on her young ones what she withheld from herself? Still, such a disparity of luxury and want.

Suddenly, a picture appeared before Tuckworth. A nurse, not a mother. A servant bringing her charges to a poor garret. Why? To visit. Her lover? No! A painter, of course! Raphael was taking commissions to paint portraits!

Tuckworth got to the bottom of the stairs and let go a relieved sigh. The mystery cleared instantly, and Tuckworth felt the sudden weight that had oppressed him lift just as suddenly. The dear lad, he thought, ashamed to be supporting himself that way. Poor Raphael, after all his wonderful landscapes done in Bellminster. He must feel humiliated.

The dean let himself back out into the alley, only to find that the yellow mist had gone brown and now clouded the entire City, from street to steeple. Well, there was time enough tomorrow to help Raphael. For now, Tuckworth was feeling strangely tired again, and empty, and old. As though to confirm to him that time was indeed wearing away, the chimes of the City called out the hour, just gone two.

Six more hours. Time enough to do anything, Tuckworth told himself. He shook his head and found an empty cab at the corner. Giving the address to the driver, the dean made his way back to Westminster, back to Mrs. Terlanne's.

CHAPTER V
THE SINGULAR GENTLEMAN

S un warmed cloudless sky and verdant fields, lanes and byways,
rooftops and windows, swathing Bellminster in life's embrace.
The stone and plaster of the Old Town, the brick of the mill
with its rows of laborers' houses, the sprawling confusion of the
Granby Arms, the checkerboard irregularity of Cathedral Square,
the exposed timbers of the vicarage seemed to settle into deeper
hues of pink and white and mossy brown. Shadows, stunted and
dwarfish since midday, seeped away from the setting sun, climbing
walls and twining amid the ivy. A light breeze ruffled the air, tossing
the green and silver leaves about, twirling them like shimmering
toys until the trees sparkled in the orange-yellow of the approaching dusk. Yet no man or woman stirred in the streets. No child
played. No dog slumbered in the shade. No cat lolled around the
corner of a house to purr itself into sight. Only the black bird circled slowly in the sky above the steeple of Bellminster Cathedral.

Tuckworth woke. He blinked, yawned, reached for his watch,
and remembered it was broken. He remembered the bird, and the
cathedral, and home. He looked at the tray of dishes on the table
nearby and recalled the modest dinner he had nibbled in his room.
Then he remembered his appointment and bolted from the chair,

thrust his hat upon his head, raced down the stairs, and shot through the door.

By the time the hackney carriage had tumbled him out into the swirling mists of Caldecott Lane, the chimes of Westminster Abbey were tolling half past eight. Tuckworth paid the driver and hurried up the steps, where he just saved himself from colliding with a very singular gentleman at the moment the door was being opened.

It was opened, not by the short man who had opened it earlier that day, but by a thick, square, youthful-looking fellow dressed in elegant livery, with powdered hair and a red coat, crisp buckled breeches, and immaculate stockings. With an ingratiating bow, he ushered both men into a sparkling world of candlelight and silver. The entire house appeared to have undergone a fairy-tale transformation. Where before all was neat (if chilling) respectability, now lavish expense shone from every corner. Tuckworth handed the servant his hat and both he and his accidental companion were led upstairs into the drawing room, where a score or more of modest ladies and gentlemen stood gawking about them at the magnificence of gold and porcelain, plate and damask and silk. Clearly they were all as new to Price's hospitality as Tuckworth was, for they looked distinctly ill at ease, like children at a funeral. Indeed, for such an extravagant display of finery, the guests seemed more than usually plain and appeared to consist chiefly of clergymen, missionaries, and spinster women bent on good works. In the middle of them all stood Hamlin Price, positively regal in a very formal suit of black.

"What a cheery assembly," the singular gentleman at Tuckworth's elbow proclaimed, just loud enough for the dean to overhear. Tuckworth turned now to take his first close look at this man. He was slim, though not overly tall. Youthful, though not young. His face was smooth, too pretty to be handsome, perhaps, with only the faintest lines about the eyes and mouth, traces of past merriment, and the hair on his high, commanding forehead was wispy and pale, so that the streaks of gray mixed easily with the blond.

"I say, Price!" the fellow called out, waving.

Price looked over, startled, and immediately his brow darkened. He came striding up to them both and exclaimed under his breath in a voice infused with hostile intent, "What are you doing here?" Then, noticing Tuckworth for the first time, he asked with some unpleasantness, "Do you know each other?"

"Not yet," the other man said, turning to Tuckworth with an open smile. "But I daresay we shall know each other hereafter. Leigh Hunt, sir," and he bowed.

"Dean Tuckworth of Bellminster," replied Tuckworth, extending his hand in his simple, country manner. Hunt took the hand warmly, and Tuckworth found that he liked this singular gentleman.

"You'll have to excuse me, Price," Hunt went on, turning back to their host, "but I must have misplaced my invitation. Or wasn't I invited? It's so hard these days to keep up with the suppers one isn't invited to."

Price, unsure how to deal with this intrusion, appeared irked and shaken at once, and Tuckworth wondered who Leigh Hunt might be to occasion such alarm. But before Price could arrive at a course of action, another elegantly bewigged man entered and struck a small Chinese gong. "Ladies and gen'lemen," he said, trying to sound sonorous in his high-pitched voice, "dinner's served."

Price's role as the generous host determined his course. "Let's all go down," he announced, taking an elderly woman's arm and tossing a stiff and angry glare at Hunt. The company trooped down the stairs hurriedly in anticipation of the finest meal any of them was likely to enjoy in the next twelve months (or for many years to come, in the case of the missionaries).

They filed into the dining room and stood for a moment in rapt awe before settling nervously about. The table was set with gold-trimmed china, polished silver, sparkling crystal, an army of candelabra, and the food! Fat mountains of peas with onions rising in lush splendor against the snowy tablecloth! Plump loaves wrapped in scarlet cloths, like worldly friars, glowing in abundant pride from silver baskets! Hams and roasts and brown, crisp capons dripping their succulence amid golden potatoes and languid greens! Fish shimmering in seas of sauce, staring with glassy eyes as the guests seated themselves about this resplendent board!

Hunt's unexpected appearance had thrown off the numbers, so he was forced to find a place for himself, taking his cutlery and plate from a sideboard and squeezing in next to Tuckworth. "Will you join me?" he asked as he reached for a nearby decanter and poured a ruby stream into Tuckworth's glass. But a stentorian cough from the top of the table kept him from filling his own.

"Dean Tuckworth," Price called down to them. "We might have a grace before indulging our appetites."

For an instant Tuckworth was afraid that he would be called upon to serve that holy office, but a very old minister on Price's right hand was given the honor, and soon the dean was free to relax in the relative obscurity of the middle of the table.

"You say Bellminster is your country?" Hunt inquired, leaning over between bites of roast.

"Yes."

"Do I recall something about a great cathedral burning to the ground there?"

Tuckworth took a long sip of wine. "Not quite to the ground," he answered. "The roof is gone and the steeple collapsed. The walls are still standing, though."

"Well, I'm very glad to know it," Hunt said. "I love a good cathedral, and I've always heard that yours in Bellminster is a very good cathedral indeed." And he smiled a smile that was somewhere between true sincerity and the desire to please.

Tuckworth thanked him for the kind words.

"As for myself," Hunt continued, very happy to carry the brunt of the conversation, "I am a writer. An editor when it pays, a journalist when it doesn't pay, a poet when nobody pays."

"Is it hard work, Mr. Hunt?"

"Easiest work imaginable. Writing is easy, just scribble, scribble, scribble. Inducing others to read is impossible, though."

Tuckworth grinned. "What sorts of things do you write that no one reads?"

"Scandalous things. Politics, you know, and social critique. I'm always in trouble with the government, no matter who the government is at the time." He leaned over and whispered, rather proudly, "They put me in prison once."

The dean was genuinely shocked. "Who did?"

Hunt looked thoughtful for a moment before replying, "I'm dashed if I can recall. Whigs and Tories seem to be offended by my stuff equally."

"It wasn't for long, I hope."

"Almost two years. If they hadn't let my family come live with me, and given me access to all my library and fed me tolerably well, I don't know how I might have survived another hour." And Hunt actually winked at Tuckworth, so that the dean was forced to stifle a laugh.

Tuckworth could not help but notice that the rest of the table was maintaining a prodigious silence throughout Hunt's discourse, and their two voices carried from one end to the other alarmingly well. In fact, all the other guests were so intent upon their plates, and so little inclined to converse, that soon even Hunt's loquacity waned, and the meal was finished to the music of silver scraping across china and wine (and water) pouring into crystal.

In truth, as the dinner progressed, Tuckworth was under the very distinct impression that most of the guests were frightened, or at the very least intimidated. What sort of supper party was this, he wondered, where every show of extravagance only succeeded in casting a pall over the evening? Strange sort of entertainment, as though it were designed for discomfort.

But, of course, it was not an entertainment at all, a fact that became readily apparent once the meal was completed. Instead of the men and women separating, for cigars on the one hand and cards on the other, they all returned as a group to the drawing room. All except Price, that is. He retired to his study, where he met with his guests, one by one, to discuss their needs.

"Tyrannical system," Hunt clucked to Tuckworth, sipping a brandy. He was the only member of the assemblage either clucking or sipping, and Tuckworth was grateful for his company. About them, the guests milled in an aimless, agitated fashion, and the sense of sheepish fear seemed even more marked in Price's absence.

Tuckworth was probing with the tip of his tongue at a morsel of fat lodged in his teeth, pausing as he sucked at the offending scrap to ask, "So this is in the nature of an audience?"

"More like an audition. Although, I must say, Price has outdone himself with this lot," and Hunt motioned about the room at the dour faces, each trying desperately not to look at him. "Most times there's usually a little friendly backstabbing going on, you know? A sort of sideshow that's wonderfully amusing. But the old boy seems to have gone in for waxwork figures these days. Too scared to breathe."

"Yes," Tuckworth whispered. "I'd noticed."

Just then, a bewigged servant entered quietly and drew Tuckworth's attention with a gentle cough.

"Well, your innings," Hunt proclaimed, and Tuckworth was led away, back downstairs, back into the long study where he had met Hamlin Price that morning. There the great man sat as before, papers strewn about, curtains drawn, the light of a single green-shaded lamp burning at his side.

"Have a seat, Dean Tuckworth," Price offered, and Tuckworth did so. Price folded his hands on the desk and looked keenly across at the dean. What was there in the man's eyes that Tuckworth found disconcerting? A sort of anxious desire to be at ease? A nervous authority? "I'm sure you'll be pleased to know that I've decided to give a little something to your Cathedral Fund," Price began.

"Thank you."

There was a pause.

"You know," Price continued, "not everyone here tonight will be so fortunate."

"I see."

"I am prepared to give the Bellminster Cathedral Fund five hundred pounds," Price stated, and paused once more.

Tuckworth only sat, willing to wait out the silence.

"Did you hear me?"

"Yes," Tuckworth acknowledged. "Five hundred pounds."

"The same as was given by Lord Granby."

"Yes, it is."

"Well, what do you think?"

"I'm grateful."

"Is that the sum you were hoping for, five hundred?"

"I really had no idea what I should hope for." Tuckworth leaned back, certain that he should be displaying the most abject gratitude and feeling disinclined to do so.

Price was flustered at this, more flustered than seemed right, and Tuckworth considered that perhaps a degree of negotiating was expected. There might be more money to be had, he thought, but the very notion of such bargaining left him feeling cold and hollow within, and he determined only to sit.

"Well," Price said finally, and opened a large ledger in front of him. "I'll write you out an order on my bank, then." He reached across the table to dip his pen in the inkwell. He dipped several times, rather anxiously, but to no apparent purpose. Tuckworth could hear the nib clinking in the bottom of the well. Price looked at the dean. "Out of ink," he announced.

"So it would appear."

Price opened the various drawers in his desk one at a time and rummaged about uselessly. Closing the drawers again, he stood up and said, "I'll only be a moment," and left through a door that was close-by.

In the solitude of the silent, empty room, Tuckworth slumped in his chair and allowed a wave of suppressed indignation to sweep over him. Five hundred? The inconvenience, the humiliation, the disruption to his life, for five hundred? This they called *charity*? It was no more or less than Granby had given. But Granby had offered the money freely, openly, and even if it was a paltry sum, just one-half of one percent of the whole, it was still given with compassion and sympathy. But this? It was handed out like a circus performer rewards a trained dog.

Tuckworth huffed, his pride smarting at the thought, and reached into his pocket to remove his ivory toothpick, deftly pulling it from its case with one hand and digging away at the scrap of fat that remained stuck in his teeth. As he poked and probed, his temper receded, lost in the vacuum of the room. He looked about. Not unpleasant, but strangely impersonal, this study, with bookcases neat and dustless, tables here and there with bric-a-brac in ideal display upon them. Nothing out of place. Nothing out of order. Hardly a room where a person lived. Only the desk appeared to share in its owner's life, and the disordered papers scattered across it seemed more like stage dressing than healthy clutter.

Yes, he considered, that's what my life has become; and the dean was startled by the sudden truth of his observation. Stage dressing. This journey, this audience with Price, the supper party, like a turn upon the stage. All just play-acting and drama. And now five hundred pounds as payment for a mediocre performance. I'm not one to be sent about the country begging, so why do I put myself through it? he wondered. Why do any of them put themselves through it? And his thoughts turned to those others above him in the drawing room, those scared, simple people eager to fawn before Price for the bits of coin he might let drop upon them. He pricked the toothpick under his gum and, with a painful flick, disgorged the scrap with which he had been struggling.

Satisfied, the dean replaced his toothpick, leaned back in his chair, and his thoughts returned to this performance, this charitable melodrama. Should he have tried to squeeze a little more out of the fellow? he wondered. Certainly it had been expected. Indeed, a great deal seemed to have been expected, a great deal of servile scraping, of hand wringing and theatrics. So much seemed to be required that Tuckworth could not offer, would not offer. After all, it wasn't Price who had limited his donation to five hundred pounds. That was Tuckworth's own work, his pride getting in the way of the job he had been sent to perform. Mortimer certainly would have managed better, would have gotten more out of the man, praised Price's spirit of munificence, his Christian kindness, would have bowed before his pocketbook—and been that much closer to building a cathedral. No, Tuckworth realized, this position, this deanship, was not for him. When he had taken it, he had a cathedral to care for. Now he had nothing but five hundred pounds. A resolution began to form within him, a stern and painful resolution. When I return to Bellminster . . . Tuckworth thought.

But the thought had no chance to form, for an explosion thundered through the cold halls of Hamlin Price's home, the dull blast of a shotgun reverberating off the walls and ripping the quiet from around Tuckworth's world.

CHAPTER VI
"WHO IS HE?"

I n the upper story of the house on Caldecott Lane, in a small, stifling garret room just under the eaves, in the flickering of a lantern and a pair of candles, six men squeezed closely together around a seventh, who was dead.

The room was dull and austere, a monk's lonely cell with an iron bed, a chest of drawers, a plain armoire standing in one corner, and a single table beside which sat a hard chair with a black coat draped over its back. The dead man was lying, half reclined, against a neatly papered wall whose pattern of recurring gillyflowers seemed decidedly out of place. He might have been looking across the small space out the open window, except that he had no face. What had once been his face was a pulpy red and black and white mass.

"The shotgun must have been placed right up against his brow, then," a stout, tall, imposing character in a loose overcoat was saying, apparently to the corpse. "Pointed down here, like this. You can see bits of bone buried in the wainscoting."

"Odd."

"What?" the stout man said, and turned upon Dean Tuckworth.

"I'm only saying that it's an odd place for a man to be shot, that's all, lying against the wall like that. I mean, he looks as though he were placed there, doesn't he?"

The stout man glared at the dean and his drooping mustache bristled. "Don't know why a fellow can't expect to get killed lying against the wall."

Tuckworth coughed. "No, I suppose not." He was trying desperately not to look at the grisly sight at his feet, at least not at the faceless head. Still, he wouldn't appear squeamish if he could help it, so his eyes wandered nervously about the floor, and he removed his spectacles every so often to give them a needless wiping.

The inspector noted Tuckworth's nervousness, reached over to the coat on the back of the chair, and tossed it clumsily over the face.

"You found him then, right?" he asked the dean.

Leigh Hunt inched forward. "Mr. Tuckworth and I found him together, inspector."

"Like this?"

"Like this."

"How'd you know where to look?"

"We didn't. In fact, we searched around quite a bit. I think we actually passed this door twice before peering in."

"Yes," Tuckworth confirmed. "There was no other sound to guide us. After the gunshot, that is."

The Bow Street inspector acknowledged this statement with a grunt. Then he turned his attention to the two blue-suited bobbies holding their top hats in front of them. "And you two come up later, eh?"

"Aye," one of them, the elder, answered for both. "Great row from them others downstairs called us in. Discovered 'im just as you see."

"And you found the shotgun down in the bushes below," the inspector added, crossing to the window and looking down.

"That's right. That's all we found."

The Bow Street man scanned the moonlit world outside the tiny room. "Might have scampered across the rooftops. Easy leap from one to the other."

"That's how we seen it," the bobby announced.

The inspector drew in his head and stared the bobbies up and down with what Tuckworth took to be a contemptuous sneer. Between Bow Street and Scotland Yard there was little room for affection, or so it appeared. "The guests?" the inspector asked curtly.

"All too scared to 'ave seen nothin'. We asked a few questions, but it didn't do no good. Got names and addresses, then sent 'em all home to their beds. I never knew such a nervous lot."

"What about the servants?"

"All hired for the evening. No regular servants on the premises."

"None?"

"No, inspector," Price explained, fixing his eyes steadily on the corpse. "I sacked my cook just today."

"Today? Why's that?"

"I learned the woman's morals were not fitted for a life of service, inspector. I will not have that in my household." The inspector nodded. "Wick has been my only other servant. This is his room. I keep a simple house."

"You Mr. Price?"

The man nodded. "Wick was my secretary for almost ten years," he said. "I want to find who did this, inspector, and I want justice for it. I don't care what it costs. I'll pay all expenses."

The bobby coughed needlessly and chimed in with, "Scotland Yard won't require—"

"I want Bow Street on this," Price snapped.

The bobby looked at his partner with damaged pride and fell silent.

The inspector appeared gratified, however. Tuckworth noticed that the man had been asking his questions with the authority of one who knows already what he wants to know, and is annoyed at anything that might appear suddenly outside that comfortable course. His mind, it seemed, was simply traveling a path along which it was already familiar, The Surprised Burglar or The Spurned Lover or perhaps even The Return of the Vengeful Past, but all easy, well-worn roads to follow. And Price's confidence, to say nothing of his money, would make the inspector's way even easier. "You come in with these other two gents, Mr. Price?"

"I got here just after Hunt and Dean Tuckworth."

"Where were you before then?"

"Looking for the cause of the gunshot, like the others. But I was at the back of the house."

The inspector nodded, then motioned toward the body. "You say his name was Wick?"

"Yes. Malcolm Wick."

"Excuse me," Tuckworth interjected, "but how do you know this is your secretary?"

The inspector glared over his broad shoulder at the dean, but said nothing and turned back to Price, giving him leave to answer.

"Those are Wick's clothes," Price said, pointing to the corpse. "They're not very remarkable, I know, but that's how he always dressed. And there's the ring on his right hand. Look at it." He pointed to a simple silver band set with a small bluish stone on the little finger of the dead man's right hand.

"Ah," hummed the inspector, thoughtfully.

"Yes," Tuckworth went on, his eyes seemingly turned to the floor, "those might be his clothes, but I don't think this is your man."

They all looked away from the corpse and stared at the dean for a moment, before the inspector exploded in exasperation. "What the bloody hell—" he began.

"His fingernails," Tuckworth said calmly. "Note his fingernails."

They all turned back and looked down.

"He's got dirty fingernails," stated the inspector dryly.

"Not just dirty," Tuckworth went on. "Cracked and broken. And his knuckles are gnarled. This man, whoever he was, was no secretary. And, if I might ask you, Mr. Price, did your man Wick usually wear this ring on his little finger?"

"Now that you mention it," Price answered, "I don't recall that he did. He wore it on his index finger."

One of the bobbies, the younger one, knelt down to the dead right hand, pulled off the ring, and tried it on the other finger. It would not go past the first knuckle.

"It don't seem to be 'is ring at all," the man said, looking up.

"No," Tuckworth went on, "and the buttons on his shirt are wrong. There's a buttonhole left over at the collar. In fact, those clothes seem to be at least a size too small for this man."

The inspector turned on Price. "You certain this is your servant?"

Price reached out and took the ring from the young bobby. "This is his ring. Look here inside," and he held it out to the others. " 'MW' engraved under the stone."

"Malcolm Wick," murmured the inspector, as though this was a great point indeed. He took the ring and peered deeply into it, his mind laboring along its iron course, trying hard not to be derailed by this curious detail.

Tuckworth very quietly heaved a sigh. He had been through this sort of thing before, question and answer, although he hadn't seen it handled as clumsily as it was by this blunt official. It was an elegant game when done correctly, and one that the dean was ashamed to admit he enjoyed. He was engaged in it now in his own mind, silently, stealthily, question and answer.

Price leaned toward the inspector and asked in a hushed voice, "What can it mean, do you suppose?"

But it was Tuckworth who answered. "Whoever murdered this man obviously wants us to assume that Malcolm Wick is the victim."

"Obviously," the inspector repeated, somewhat too coarsely. "And that can only mean Malcolm Wick is the murderer."

Price looked about at the others. "I can't believe it," he said, though sounding to Tuckworth rather as if he might believe it.

"Oh, I grant you he's a cunning character," the inspector confided, looking more relaxed now that he'd solved the mystery to his satisfaction. "Must have killed this here fellow, put his own clothes on him while the rest of you was fumbling about searching for the body, scampered out the window to the roof where he dropped his shotgun, then leaped across and so away. Thought to send us barking after his own murderer," he chuckled, appearing very pleased with himself, as though he had just presented them all with a neat and convenient package, wrapped in brown paper and twine. It was simple. It was tidy. And to Tuckworth's mind, it was entirely wrong.

"Are we to understand that the murderer took the time to dress a lifeless corpse while we were hunting him?" he asked, failing to sound as simple and naive as he had meant to sound.

The inspector once again glared and was silent.

"I have to agree with Dean Tuckworth," Price offered. "I simply can't imagine Wick doing anything as devilish as this. Switching clothes with this fellow and then murdering him? It's preposterous."

"That's it!" the inspector crowed. "Wick forced this chap to put the clothes on first, then shot him."

"Yes," Tuckworth continued, "that's all very possible, but who *is* this chap? Shouldn't we concern ourselves with discovering the victim's name before we settle on his murderer? We can't even say the reason this crime was committed."

"*We* ain't going to settle on nothing!" the inspector boomed, his patience spent at last. "Because *you* ain't no official part of this!"

"Inspector," Price interceded, stepping forward, "perhaps we can retire to my study to complete this investigation. Unless there's more to be discovered here, I think the heat is causing all our nerves to chafe a bit."

The inspector huffed, clearly annoyed with Tuckworth's incessant questions, but at last he was convinced to move the investigation elsewhere. They descended the stairs (all except the bobbies, who were left to attend to the victim), and as they descended, Tuckworth turned a critical eye upon himself. Why was he so sure the inspector was mistaken? Doubting the man's farfetched solution was one thing, but the dean felt certain it was, for all its complexity, too simple. What did they really know, and know for a fact, about this crime? That it was a rushed and sloppy job, yet apparently planned ahead of time, both passionate and premeditated. Were the clothes already on the dead man when he was killed, as the inspector suggested? Tuckworth had to admit that would make more sense. Yet if the murderer wanted to hide his victim's identity, why choose someone so obviously different from himself? Even the inspector would have noticed that the dead man wasn't Malcolm Wick before long. Which meant that the murderer couldn't have been free to choose his victim. He must have been forced to kill this man and no other.

Even these surmises seemed misapplied, however, as though they all pointed somewhere Tuckworth didn't know to look. This blatant charade was ingenious, after a fashion, but what kind of mind would dream such a plan and then get it so completely wrong from the start? Why such an elaborate scheme with so many clear mistakes, so much planning that seemed in the end haphazard? All manner of strange facts swirled about just beyond Tuckworth's understanding, and yet this bull-headed inspector had already arrived at his conclusion.

Tuckworth had known such men before, these Bow Street officials, more interested in closing a case than in solving it. Still, could the man be correct? None of the facts disproved his theory, it was true, but none of them made it inevitable, either. Who was this man lying dead up in the garret room? That's what Tuckworth wanted to know above all. Who was he, and why had this been done?

They filed into the study and the dean sat down in the first chair beside the door, left alone in a pale circle of dim lamplight like a castaway, while Hunt, Price, and the inspector walked the length of the room to gather about the desk. The inspector took his place behind it and pulled out a notepad and pencil.

"Now, let's go back over this," he announced officiously, and turned to Hunt. "Your name?"

"Leigh Hunt, inspector. L-E-I-G-H."

"-I-G-H Hunt," the inspector repeated methodically and started scribbling away, while Tuckworth removed his spectacles once more, rubbed his eyes, and returned to the beginning, examining his memory to learn what he knew. He had heard a gunshot. That he knew. He had rushed up the stairs to find Hunt on the landing. That he knew as well. Together they had gone from room to room. The guests, being frightened, and the servants, being hired, had waited below. He and Hunt had found the body finally, lying there, face gone, opposite the open window. Time enough for anything to happen in the interim, yet hardly a space of time that the murderer could have counted on. Could he?

"Mr. Tuckworth!"

The dean tore himself from his thoughts to look up at the inspector. "Yes?"

"Might I trouble you to step over here and answer a few questions for me?" the man asked wearily.

Tuckworth replaced his spectacles and came forward. "Of course, inspector."

"Where were you when you heard the gunshot?"

"Sitting in that chair there," he said, pointing.

"You were alone."

"That's right."

Price leaned forward. "I had only just left the room a moment before, inspector. Out the rear door here into the back of the house."

"Some minutes before, I think," Tuckworth corrected.

"Oh, not more than two or three."

Tuckworth paused to recollect. "I'd have said closer to ten, actually."

"Ten minutes?" the inspector asked, making a note of the fact. "How do you know? Did you mark the time?"

Tuckworth reached instinctively for his watch, then stopped. He looked about, but realized to his surprise that there was no clock in the room. "No," he answered finally. "No, I didn't mark the time. My watch is broken, and—"

The inspector grunted, and set about to scratch out Tuckworth's statement. "Damn!" he blurted suddenly. The tip of his pencil had snapped off, and he had no other. He looked about the cluttered desktop for something with which to continue his note taking, and his eye lit on the pen. He took it and dipped it in the empty inkwell. "Dry," he stated, examining the nib.

"There's ink in the left-hand drawer," Price offered.

The inspector opened the drawer, removed the bottle, and filled the well. And as he did so, Tuckworth and Price shared a look, an involuntary and instantaneous glance, the one of shock and amazement, the other of fear.

It was only a moment, half a moment, and yet the look was unmistakable. Fear in Price's eyes, fear unleashed from the tight reins against which it had been straining. Fear, rabid and hungry. The next instant, and Price looked away. But Tuckworth had seen the fear, and at once he understood with a certainty what it meant.

It wasn't just the ink. Any man might have overlooked a bottle of ink in a dark drawer. It was the fear itself. Price had been caught, had recognized his peril at once, and by instinct he had turned to

Tuckworth, the only man who knew that there was not supposed to be ink in the left-hand drawer, that it was ink that had sent Price out of the room at the time the murder was committed.

A moment later, however, and Tuckworth's certainty began to fade. Memory was forced to take its place, and memory transformed fact into suspicion and clouded suspicion with doubt. Tuckworth tried to reconstruct Price's face, his eyes, to capture again that look of fear. Or was it fear? Maybe only surprise or embarrassment. Perhaps it was just an honest mistake, he considered. Any man might overlook a bottle of ink. Doubt, Tuckworth's perpetual companion, threw his thoughts into a whirlwind of supposition and tangled images. And all he was left with at last was the certainty that he had been certain, if only for an instant.

CHAPTER VII
THE FACELESS ONES

T he dean of Bellminster Cathedral stood on the doorstep of 18 Caldecott Lane staring up into a spangled night. The fog, which had made the day little more than a faint notion, had by now dissolved into air, leaving behind an otherworldly clarity. The stars twinkled gaily from their cold distance, and Tuckworth considered how separate and disinterested the heavens seemed. With a pinpoint purity they looked down upon the night, certain and irrevocable, just as they had for aeons past, ever mindful, never faltering. At least that's how they seemed from the doorstep of 18 Caldecott Lane.

He descended to the street, where the day's roaring stream of humanity had dwindled to a trickle, but before he had the chance to move another foot, the door behind him opened and he heard the cheery voice of Leigh Hunt calling down to him.

"Dean Tuckworth!" The dean wondered how anyone could appear so lightly moved by the evening's dread events, but Hunt had displayed an easy, almost carefree attitude throughout the investigation. "Would you care to share a cab?" the man asked as he came near, waving at a passing hackney.

"I believe I'll walk," Tuckworth said, moving away down the pavement.

"Excellent suggestion," declared Hunt, dismissing the disgruntled cabbie and weaving his arm through Tuckworth's to stroll as freely as though they were old friends. "Exercise is just the thing after that wretched confinement. Standing and waiting about all night. Answering an endless string of senseless questions. I don't think I've ever witnessed a more ham-fisted interrogation in my life."

Tuckworth might have been taken aback at this unwonted familiarity, except that he felt an unaccustomed need for company just then. His mind was too full of forebodings and suspicions, and he welcomed Hunt's casual manner as a release from the gravid sense of responsibility growing within him. "Investigations are rarely graceful things," he commented, trying to sound easy and wise. "One generally has to cover the same ground repeatedly before uncovering something worth knowing."

"Yes," Hunt observed, "but not you. You rather pounced upon the truth about Wick."

"I only saw what was there for all of us to see."

"But that's what's so interesting. It's all there, yet not everyone sees it. I certainly didn't. For example, what else did you see tonight that you found . . . well, odd, let's say?"

"That's the word I used to describe the body, the way it was situated against the wall." Tuckworth thought a bit and shuddered, recalling the grisly scene.

"And it *was* odd, wasn't it? Almost as if the man were already unconscious, you know."

"More likely he was already dead. Did you not notice the lack of blood against the wainscoting where the bone was embedded?"

"There you are! No, I did not notice it, nor I daresay did the inspector."

The two men walked on a way in silence. It felt wrong to be speaking about such things in the open air like this, about murder and violence and bloodshed. Still, Tuckworth thought, this was

London. Perhaps these things didn't matter so much here.

"Shall I tell you something else I noticed?" Tuckworth asked.

"By all means."

"I noticed how angry Price was when you arrived."

"But there you disappoint me," Hunt chirped. "It hardly takes unusual powers of observation to have noticed that."

"Yes, but why should he be so angry?"

"Now that's a question I'd like an answer to myself," Hunt confided. "Let me tell you the rather curious history of my dealings with Hamlin Price. You've seen tonight how he handles his charitable giving, rather like a munificent deity doling out benisons. Miserable business. Well, one evening the man sent for me. Quite out of the blue. I received a card with a quick appeal scribbled on the back. I'd never met the fellow. Had hardly even heard of him, he's such a private little godling. But his message seemed almost urgent, so I dropped what I was working on—which I don't mind telling you was nothing important to begin with—and I toddled right off.

"He wanted to give me money. Just like that. No audition, no dinner. No sense of gravity and duty. Just a fistful of banknotes. He'd read a piece I'd written on the execrable way children are abused in this most civilized nation, how they are abandoned, cast off, forced into slavish labor, deformed from what they should be, broken and beaten worse than one would drive an ass. You've not been in London long," Hunt said, turning to look upon the dean, "and yet you must have seen it, the ravenous way this city devours its young, like Saturn tearing at his children. Well, Price had read my little tract, and he had somehow determined that I was the very man to help him distribute his largesse. From that day to this, and it's been many years now, I have been the willing tool of Hamlin Price's charity to those societies that help the young and orphaned. His gifts are generous, one might say extravagant, and carefully anonymous. But now, here's what's so remarkable. In all that time I have never been treated any differently than you witnessed tonight. The man seems to despise me, which would be maddening if I had any much higher opinion of myself."

They walked on in silence for a time, and Tuckworth considered his new companion. What he considered was that he had been wrong, completely wrong in his assessment of Leigh Hunt. All evening he had observed the man casually, for Hunt appeared to be a very casual sort of man. He seemed all glib repartee with very little substance, merely the image of a gentleman, although a very pleasant and engaging image. Now, however, Tuckworth felt that he had heard the real man beneath, the one kept in shadow, wary perhaps of too much light, too much notice. As he spoke of children, of their ill usage and suffering, there had been a passionate ring to his voice, a fervency that could not be feigned, could not be pretense. The two men had walked along arm in arm, and Tuckworth had felt Hunt's muscles tense in anger and frustration at such injustice. He had seen the determined gleam of his eyes, the rigid set of his jaw. For the briefest instant he had seen below the surface of the man, and he had found something akin to a crusader. Yes, the dean considered, there was a good deal more to Leigh Hunt than one might realize.

"So," Hunt said at last, sounding once more the casual gentleman, "what conclusions have you drawn from our little set-to this evening?"

Tuckworth shook his head. "I'm not so quick to leap to my conclusions as our friend from Bow Street."

"True, it would take a veritable Hermes among snails to outstrip that fellow. But come now. Surely there are some little notions darting about in your mind. Someone as observant as you must certainly be able to put his observations together and venture a guess."

"That's all it would be," Tuckworth said. "A guess. And I'm not going to malign anyone by divulging suspicions based on nothing more than guesswork."

"I knew it!" exclaimed Hunt, giving the dean's arm a squeeze. "You suspect him!"

"I never—"

"Don't deny it. We both know we mean the same man, though we've neither said his name."

Tuckworth stopped where he was and pulled away from Hunt, looking about nervously at the passing faces, all of which seemed happy to ignore this outburst. "I will not be lured into this business as if it were some parlor game," he insisted.

"Now, please, don't be cross with me," Hunt begged, once more drawing his arm through Tuckworth's and leading him along. "I'm a journalist, you know, and so I have some interest in this affair. Sensational stuff, a murder in a rich man's home, with so many proper and upright witnesses who saw nothing."

"Is that all this is to you, Hunt?" the dean muttered, angry with himself and angry with his companion. "Some gross opportunity for gain? Need I remind you that a man has been murdered tonight, a life snuffed out with all the cold efficiency of someone extinguishing a candle?"

"You're right," Hunt confessed, shaking his head. "I daresay this city does it to you. Makes you senseless and heartless. One might easily live in Arctic reaches and know as much warmth as one finds in London. But please don't suppose that my sole interest in this is gain. Believe me, dear fellow, I've seen little enough of that commodity in my lifetime. But this feels to me like an injustice aborning. I *am* thinking of that poor chap back there, his face blown to atoms. I'm thinking he has no one to avenge him, no one, it appears, even to acknowledge him. I'm thinking that the inspector is a great fool and I'm thinking there's far more at work here than he's willing to look into. And I'm thinking you know it every bit as well as I do."

Tuckworth frowned, partly from irritation at being drawn into something that was none of his concern, but mostly because he felt, deep within himself, that Hunt was correct. The dean did rebel at this injustice against a faceless, unknown man, against an uncaring universe that might allow so outrageous an act and no one to stop it. It wasn't right. God or no God, it wasn't right.

"Come," Hunt offered, "we'll change the subject. How are you liking the city so far?"

"I like it well enough," Tuckworth replied, still feeling cross and dodging the truth.

"Well enough?" Hunt echoed in mock amazement. "Then you haven't had a chance to know it properly. London must be either loved or loathed. There is no 'well enough.' Allow me to show it to you tomorrow. A private tour."

Tuckworth shook his head. "I'm afraid I'm engaged tomorrow morning with an old friend and I hope to spend all day with him."

"How delightful for you! Somewhere here in Westminster, no doubt."

"In the Temple."

"You shock me, Dean Tuckworth. Temple Bar? Now there's a promising locality for adventure."

It struck Tuckworth that this sudden turn in the conversation was a ruse, purposely made by Hunt to sound petty and ridiculous, and that their true topic lay still between them, unfinished. "You mustn't misunderstand me, Hunt," Tuckworth began. "I sympathize with your desire to follow this thing through. I sympathize more than you know. But it isn't my business. It isn't my city or my affair. I don't know that man back there in the garret, and until this morning I didn't know Hamlin Price or you."

Hunt paused in their walk and sighed. "Perhaps that's why I feel so strongly about this business myself," he answered, more thoughtfully than might have seemed possible a moment before. "There is something about that faceless man back there, a kinship, a brotherhood I feel for him. He's simply one of all the faceless souls who inhabit this city." Hunt looked about him and drew Tuckworth's gaze to the world that continued to flow past them. "Do you see them, Mr. Tuckworth? The ones who can't see each other, who can't even see themselves? They trod these streets blind and deaf to everything. Yet underfoot a world exists they never dreamed of. I've seen it, a world of filth and pain, a world where children are just the worst, not the only victims. That faceless man speaks to me of this world I know, and I want to do something for him. Or at least, to do something more than that inspector will do."

They turned and walked on again, and as they walked Tuckworth saw the world Hunt spoke of. They were everywhere, the mean and dirty refuse of that world, huddled in every dark corner, seeping through every alley and lane. And moving about within that dark world a darker yet, a world of filthy, lice-eaten children scrounging for scraps in the street, kicked and reviled by weak and powerful alike, for they were merely children, less even than the lowest whom society acknowledged. He had seen their faces wherever he had turned in London. He had noted them, but not known them. Now, through Hunt's eyes, he made their dire acquaintance.

They walked the rest of their way in silence, until together they arrived at Mrs. Terlanne's. Tuckworth stopped before going in and turned to confront Leigh Hunt with a steady, troubled gaze.

"I know this business you want to be about, Hunt," Tuckworth confided to his companion before parting. "I might not look it, but I've known the business of question and answer, slowly mining a truth that other men would kill to keep hidden, placing the innocent and the guilty alike in peril. It's a very dangerous game, Hunt. A dangerous game."

Leigh Hunt looked deeply into Dean Tuckworth's eyes in return. "You mistake me if you think I believe it to be a game at all," he said.

CHAPTER VIII
A BREAKFAST PARTY

T
he next morning dawned clear, which is to say the solid bank of clouds overhead kept to the sky and did not descend to smother the city's traffic in an obscure miasma. But its lowering presence promised scant relief from the heat, which was already oppressive by nine o'clock, and the roar of the city seemed to gather strength from the sky's weight, like the echoing tumult of a large crowd in a close ballroom. Tuckworth, looking out the window of his bedchamber, felt a pressing down in the air that hung heavy about his chest and darkened his heart. He took his hat, with its short, round crown and broad brim, and having given a letter to Mrs. Terlanne to be posted with the day's mail (a quick and meaningless narrative for Lucy, a mere act of duty that withheld more than it revealed), and being relieved once again to have missed Mortimer, the dean struck out for his appointment with Raphael.

He arrived some twenty minutes before his time in Horedale Alley, and being loath to disturb his young friend after their last awkward meeting, he decided to take a seat in the coffeehouse and wait there. The room was expansive but ill lit for such a dreary day, with a few oil lamps guttering against the paneled walls to such dim effect that they seemed to cast more shadow than light about the place. Yet there was a sense of merry camaraderie among the company that no amount of shadow could dispel, and the dean felt quite comfortable and at home there. Tuckworth ordered breakfast from a rather stiff and proper waiter, a man who knew his business well, and soon the dean was sitting behind a rasher of bacon, a plate of sausages, toasted bread with jam and cheese, and a steaming pot of coffee. The meat was still sizzling when Raphael appeared and sat down with a woefully inadequate smile.

"Dean Tuckworth," he said too gaily, "how are you?"

It took Tuckworth only a moment to see Raphael's story: the pale and sunken cheeks still red from where he had shaved too closely with a bad razor; the frayed white threads bristling about a dirty, limp collar; the flecks of paint on his coat that had yet to be washed off; the hungry dart of his eyes as he scanned the meal before him. Even his sweeping blond locks looked impoverished.

"My boy," Tuckworth said, and caught himself before he sounded pitying, "please, help yourself to the sausages. And anything else that suits you. Travel always dulls my appetite."

Raphael did not need to be invited twice, but served himself with a relish, the first honest act he had performed in Tuckworth's presence since they had renewed their acquaintance the day before.

"So, how are you progressing in the city?" the dean asked, hoping that a full mouth would be less likely to lie.

"Well," Raphael mumbled through the toast and jam.

Tuckworth remained silent.

"Not well," Raphael confessed, looking as sheepish as he could while forking a sausage into his mouth. "Nothing but these damn portraits all the time, for these damn merchants and their brats," and he at once excused himself for his language. "That's what this city does to a person, though," he went on. "It coarsens you, everything about you. Your language, your dress, your work, everything becomes base and ugly."

"Then why don't you come back to Bellminster?"

"Bellminster." Raphael laughed weakly, with a wan and longing look in his eyes. "What use is an artist in Bellminster? How could I make a living there, doing what I do? How could I support—" He stopped and glanced sideways at the dean. "Well, even myself. How could I support myself doing nothing but landscapes and studies of the cathedral?"

"No," Tuckworth admitted. "I suppose that doesn't pay very handsomely in Bellminster. Especially now that the cathedral is in such a state. But what about your earlier works? Couldn't you sell those and build a reputation?"

Raphael put down his fork for a minute, taking a momentary pause in his exertions to pour a cup of coffee. "It's not so easy as you think, getting a viewing with anyone. I can't just set my paintings up along the street and hawk them like a common costermonger."

"Don't you have any old relations at the Royal Academy, then? Someone who might provide you with an opportunity? I'm sure that's all you'd need, the chance to be seen."

Raphael shook his head. "No," he stated proudly, and he looked all the more pathetic for this empty show of pride. "My work isn't ready yet."

"A man's work is never ready, Raphael," Tuckworth tried to advise his young friend. "It's simply shown or it's not shown. But it's never ready."

"Oh, you don't know anything about it," the younger man snapped. A moment later and he was shocked at his own presumption. But he didn't apologize. He only sat looking glum and ashamed and proud all at the same time. And in truth, Tuckworth required no apology, there was something so sad in Raphael's anger.

"Well, what a remarkable coincidence this is!"

Tuckworth looked up into the beaming face of Leigh Hunt.

"I set off on my morning walk—I take a walk every morning, if the mood is upon me, sometimes toward one place and sometimes another—and I set off today and find myself in the Temple. So just on a hunch, mind you, I poke my head in here and there about the coffeehouses and whom should I find but my good friend the dean of Bellminster!"

Tuckworth was not happy to see Hunt. He had succeeded in forgetting the events of the previous night, caught up in the dearer claims made by Raphael's turmoil, but now the two problems collided within him.

"Raphael," Tuckworth said, perhaps a bit tersely, "this is Mr. Leigh Hunt. Hunt, Raphael Amaldi."

"But not Leigh Hunt the critic?" Raphael exclaimed, half rising in his chair and looking in confused amazement at the dean.

"What an execrable term, *critic,*" Hunt said, seating himself. "I'm merely a poor scribbler, Mr. Amaldi."

"But your reviews! Byron, Shelley, Keats—"

"Departed friends," murmured Hunt, glancing down.

"You helped establish them with your reviews."

Hunt shook his head. "If anything, they helped to establish me. But I'm interrupting a most interesting conversation. May I?" And he reached out and helped himself to the toasted bread and cheese. "Pray, what is this work that is never ready?"

Tuckworth explained Raphael's history briefly, his early promise, its slow fruition in Bellminster, his decision to return to London to try his chance at fame. The rest was too apparent to be mentioned.

"But why fame?" asked Hunt with a smile.

"Excuse me?" Raphael uttered in surprise.

"Why fame?"

"Why?" Raphael repeated. "How can *you* ask that, of all people? Isn't notice the reason we practice art? Isn't fame, the desire to be thought of, and thought well of, to leave a mark upon the world, isn't that what spurs us on? You've helped enough young poets to fame to know what it is."

"My young poets are now dead, Mr. Amaldi."

"Yes, but their fame lives on."

"Perhaps for a time, you're right," he acknowledged sadly. "But in the end it's all dust. 'I met a traveler from an antique land,' you know. Shelley, he understood."

Raphael shook his head violently as he sipped his coffee, almost spilling it on the table. "No," he said, swallowing. "Their fame will live on. Like Titian and Caravaggio and Leonardo and Michelangelo. They worked and suffered and painted, and their genius defies time."

"You left out Raphael," Hunt added, grinning.

The young painter coughed in gentle embarrassment.

"Well, I suppose you're right," Hunt said, suddenly ending the discussion. "Here's to the hope that we may none of us die," and he poured himself a cup of coffee. Tuckworth eyed him with a thoughtful air, this seemingly insubstantial man who had so easily charged Raphael with spirit again. "Now, my dear Dean Tuckworth," Hunt continued. "What have you considered about our little affair last night?"

"Nothing, Hunt. Nothing whatever. I haven't given it a thought."

"What affair is this?" inquired Raphael, and Hunt went over the details of the murder, and the dean's reluctance to pursue the business further.

"But you must," Raphael insisted, turning to Tuckworth.

"Must I?" Tuckworth shot back. Hunt's persistence and Raphael's mercurial moods were wearing his nerves thin.

"Of course you must. It's only right to try to stop an injustice."

"And what's more unjust than accusing a man of so heinous a crime when there isn't the least basis for the accusation," Tuckworth replied. "*There's* injustice for you."

"Is there no basis?" Hunt asked innocently.

Tuckworth thought to himself. What was there? A look, a feeling, a misplaced ink pot, a furtive glance. Weighed against an accusation of murder, such facts seemed almost nonexistent.

"No," he said at last. "I can see no just basis for such a claim."

"Not yet. And you're absolutely correct, of course," Hunt acquiesced. "That's why I'm so anxious for you to consider this awful affair. You proved to me last night that you possess a genuine gift for observation."

"He does," Raphael said, more proudly than Tuckworth was comfortable hearing.

"And you aren't afraid to ask the most difficult questions. And to follow your reasoning wherever it leads. In short, my dear dean, you are a natural skeptic. Where most men draw conclusions from thin air and then nail all the facts together to fit themselves, you only take at face value what appears before your face. I gave you every opportunity last night to invent, to imagine, to suppose what might be the truth of what occurred. And you refused even to make idle conversation about it. Your powers of observation were beyond the inspector's, beyond mine, yet you stayed your imagination from running off with your reason. You will forgive me for asserting that your entire behavior was remarkable. And I don't mind warning you, I think I was not the only person there last night who noted your performance. I believe our munificent friend also marked your talents."

The idea of this warning struck Tuckworth as needlessly melodramatic, and it soured him even more to this business. "I have no authority to get involved in this at all," he said. "I'm only a simple country parson come to London on business, and I'm not about to interfere with an official investigation. I've had enough of that sort of thing in my life, and I don't cherish the thought of repeating the experience."

Hunt leaned back in his chair and smiled. "But you won't be interfering in any official investigation," he said. "There is no investigation."

"What?"

From the pocket of his coat, Hunt produced a single-sheet newspaper, folded neatly to a story on the murder. The details were presented clearly, succinctly, dryly. The man Wick had committed a daring crime and escaped, possibly in disguise. Bow Street had concluded its report and now it was up to Scotland Yard to apprehend the villain. The citizens of London could rest easy, knowing that justice would soon be brought to bear against this monster in human form.

"But what of an inquest?" demanded the dean.

"Already concluded. The magistrate was satisfied with the inspector's testimony. I understand the body has been summarily disposed of in some potter's field."

Tuckworth handed the paper back thoughtfully. "So it's over," he murmured.

"It would appear, from an official standpoint, to be quite over," Hunt concluded.

"And Price?"

"Nothing of the man whatever," replied Hunt, referring again to the newspaper. " 'In the home of a well-admired philanthropist.' That's all it has to say about our good host. Doubtless his name is withheld from motives of the truest delicacy." But Hunt was not smiling as he said this, and the words had an edge to them that seemed uncommon for this lighthearted man.

Tuckworth sat in silence for a time, while his two companions waited expectantly.

"It's just . . . ," he started, and allowed his thought to trail off. Then, looking back and forth between Raphael and Hunt, he tried again. "I must return home. I really can't get myself involved in something like this."

"But—" objected Raphael.

"Of course," Hunt interrupted. "Of course, you must return to your lovely country. Bellminster, I'm sure, is more delightful than London at this time of year. Or any time of year, if it comes to that," he added, laughing. "Only you must allow me to give you a dinner. Nothing fancy, naturally. Just myself and two or three friends whose acquaintance I'm sure you'll enjoy."

"But I can't stay another day," Tuckworth demurred, nearly lying.

"Then I won't ask you to. This evening suits me very well. Come, it seems a shame to allow a new friendship to wither from want of memories. Polite memories, I should say. We'll have memories enough of last night to carry us through the years."

Tuckworth tried twice more to avoid the invitation, but all his efforts were useless. Hunt possessed the knack of always agreeing with everything his companion said, and yet always overcoming every objection with his simplicity. In the end, Tuckworth gave up and committed himself to a dinner. He even managed to do so gratefully, for all his misgivings. He welcomed the opportunity to take some pleasant memories of London away with him, as Hunt had surmised.

The trio parted ways, Hunt first, announcing, "I have such planning to do! A dinner party for just a few select guests is so much more exhausting than a lavish affair. It's easier not to care about fifty than it is to care about three."

He was followed by Raphael, who would not be delayed for a minute. Indeed, once his mind had returned to his own situation, he grew even more despondent and morose than before. "I can't waste my day," he insisted, sounding pathetically self-important. "I have two potential subjects coming this afternoon and a sitting this evening." And he shuddered as though he could picture already the three children rampaging around their wailing nurse.

Tuckworth was left alone with the tally to be paid, which he did with a heavy heart. He seemed to have done very little good since arriving in London, he considered, and somehow his determination to return to Bellminster with his five hundred pounds (or at least the promise of his five hundred, since the gift itself had been interrupted) felt unmistakably like a retreat.

But why shouldn't he be free to retreat? As he walked through the streets of the Temple, heading through alien landscapes in a direction he took to be more or less toward Westminster, he wondered what there was in all of this for him to regret. Nothing. Nothing whatever, he felt sure. He had made the journey for a reason, and that reason being satisfied (or nominally so), that goal having been obtained, he was returning home. It should be the most pleasant thought in the world, to be going back to Bellminster, to Lucy and Mrs. Cutler, Adam and Mary and the cathedral. Yes, even to that burned-out hulk of a cathedral.

Yet he took no pleasure in the thought. The more he recalled those endearing connections to which he should be running with relief and joy, the more he felt that he was running away in shame. But from what?

He looked about him as he strolled, glanced idly at the passing faces, which hardly seemed faces at all, so closed up and inaccessible they appeared, not the open, honest faces he was used to seeing in Bellminster. Not that his home was some pastoral refuge. Far from it; the petty maneuverings within a small town could rival the machinations of Gibbon's Rome. Few knew that better than Tuckworth. Men were no more honest there than they were here or anywhere else, he thought. They were neither worse sinners nor greater saints. They were just men, after all. Still, there was that about Bellminster, a forthright simplicity, even to its darker secrets, a glow of home and hearth that no amount of worldliness could dim. Maybe this glow lived only in his memories of the place, this sense of warmth and good-fellowship. But if it was there at all, it was there because Bellminster had planted it there when he was young, and it had flourished since.

Hours later, and Tuckworth arrived finally at the door of Mrs. Terlanne's. He failed to consider that he had not once asked for directions, that he had found the place by some miracle of memory, following the almost unseen path he had taken before in the cabriolet. Such little accomplishments would have seemed slight indeed now that he was planning to leave.

He entered and was met at once by his hostess, who handed him a note from her trembling hand.

"As brung it not two hour hence," the old woman said, apologizing. Tuckworth broke the wax seal and unfolded the paper to read a single line, and a name:

I must see you at once. Price.

CHAPTER IX
AN OFFER FOR THE DEAN

Tuckworth stood outside the door on Caldecott Lane carefully dabbing the sweat from his brow with his red kerchief. He didn't want any look of haste about him, any reflection of the excited thoughts darting through his brain, the suspicions and hopes and fears, the stratagems and doubts. All calm assurance, all confidence and ease, this was the face he wished to present to Hamlin Price when they should meet again.

But five minutes later, as he stood upon the doorstep debating whether to ring a fourth time, he felt cold prickles of sweat beading anew upon his forehead. He wiped these quickly away just as the door gave a sharp click and creaked softly open to reveal Hamlin Price standing before him with a subtle smile of welcome.

"Dean Tuckworth, I'm sorry you had to wait," the man said kindly as he ushered the dean in. "I have no servants about the place now, as you know. I'm sure I should hire someone immediately, but it's a matter of inviting an unknown man under my roof. You understand, a question of allowing a stranger so close, after the unpleasantness of last night. Whom to trust, that's the trouble. I relied on poor Wick for everything." The man shuddered. "Just the thought of it unsettles me."

"Don't say a word about it," Tuckworth replied, noting at the same time that Price was going to some lengths to explain himself. There was about the man an earnestness in his tone and actions, as though he desperately desired to be understood, like a hopeful lad involved in a difficult courtship. Was it mere nervousness after the events of the past several hours, the change his life had taken, or something else?

"If you'll come this way," Price said, leading Tuckworth, not back to the study where they had met before, but into the more homely surroundings of the parlor. It was a tidy little room, decorated in such ideal perfection that, much like the rest of the house, it seemed to bear no mark of being lived in at all. "I hope that I have good news for you," Price went on as the two men sat opposite each other in twin chairs that were even more excessively comfortable than they looked. "I suppose I should offer you some tea," he added, looking about rather helplessly.

"Don't trouble yourself," insisted Tuckworth, and Price seemed to relax a bit at the words, as though they were a command. Indeed, his entire demeanor was mildly submissive, and he presented a very different aspect from that which Tuckworth had seen in him before, so that the dean felt a wave of sympathy go out to Price, in spite of himself. For a moment both men sat in silence. "Your message had a ring of urgency to it," the dean offered.

"Yes, of course. It's just that I feel I must first apologize for last night."

"There's no reason for you to apologize, is there," Tuckworth affirmed. "You had nothing to do with it."

"No, no. Of course not. Only, well, it was so awkward, and I must, um . . . apologize."

"Very well," Tuckworth acknowledged with a smile, feeling magnanimous and openhearted. "I accept your apology." The two sat in expectant silence once more. "Is that all you wanted with me?"

"No," Price replied, coming to himself. "Of course not. I have rather good news for you, as I said. At least, I hope it's good news.

I've rethought my donation to your fine cause. The Cathedral Fund, you know."

"Very kind of you, I'm sure."

Price cleared his throat dramatically. "I am prepared to grant you five thousand pounds toward the rebuilding of Bellminster Cathedral."

The world spun about very sharply, and Tuckworth almost leaped forward in his chair at the shock. "Five *thousand*?" he repeated, as though he were speaking to a man of less than perfect sanity. "*Five* thousand?" he tried again, more quietly, as if the insane man might be himself.

"Yes," Price answered, breathing a sigh and seeming more relaxed, almost happy knowing that he had shaken the dean's studied calm with his offer. "I'd hoped to surprise you."

"But why?"

"Why the change?" Price looked at the floor between his feet. "Perhaps it's the horrid events of the past day. Perhaps I feel a closer call to heaven. But your cathedral suddenly appeals to me. I want to make something like that, something of stone and mortar that might outlast generations after me. I have no family, you know, no children. I don't need to tell you that a time comes when a man looks to eternity." He glanced up suddenly, with a shrewd, searching gaze. "I don't want to go out like that miserable man last night, wretched, forgotten soul. No one will ever know who he is."

Was Tuckworth mistaken, or was there a sudden pointedness in that last statement. "No man can ever be truly forgotten," the dean observed. "I imagine that poor fellow had friends who will miss him, a family to wonder what became of him, why he never returned home. They might look to see him years from now, hoping beyond hope. The least they should get from this is the certain knowledge that he's dead."

"Yes, they should. But they will be disappointed," Price stated flatly.

"That would be a great shame, if it were true."

"I feel certain it's true."

Tuckworth stared at Price, stared deeply into him, and he was shocked to come up against a wall, hard and unrelenting. No, not so much a wall as the picture of a man upon a wall, the image of a harried soul hung there for the world to notice and nod at in sympathy, while something else lurked behind. Was Price letting Tuckworth see this, allowing him to peek at the image and the wall behind it? Was this offer a subdued threat? The dean had played chess against such men before, men of supreme control who let you catch sight into their plans, but only far enough to learn that those plans existed, taunting you with their opaque minds. Was Price such a man? Yet there could be no doubt that he was anxious, too. That much of his character was no wall. His hand fidgeted slightly, and he blinked hard once or twice. Perhaps this wall might be tested.

"Five thousand pounds," Tuckworth began. "It will doubtless get us started on our way with the cathedral, but—"

"But it's only a beginning, I know," Price interrupted him. "Five thousand now. Next year I might do as much again."

"Might?"

"Of course, it's up to you."

"What can I do?" Tuckworth asked guardedly.

"Do nothing."

The dean paused. "And exactly how is my inactivity a guarantee of future munificence?"

"Oh, you needn't be inactive," Price said, leaning back in his chair and looking very assured now, very confident. "You need only be silent."

Tuckworth *was* silent, if only for a moment. "And by my silence," he said at last, "I ensure another five thousand next year?"

Price laced his fingers together across his waistcoat and grinned an indulgent grin. "Let me explain. I have a desire to remain anonymous in this business. I don't like my name bandied about too freely, you understand. Fame and renown hold no allure for me, and so I place this one stipulation on my bequest." He hesitated an instant before stating, very distinctly, "No mention of my name must ever be attached to this business."

"To the cathedral," Tuckworth clarified.

"Naturally, the cathedral," and Price almost purred as he spoke the words.

Tuckworth sat as still as he could and said nothing. He only looked at Price, and tried to capture in his memory every thread of their conversation thus far, every nuance of the man's posture, every telltale mark that might betray his attitude. For a time, the two men only looked at each other, a lightning tension sparking between them. Then, Tuckworth leaned back in imitation of Price. "Your offer is generous, Mr. Price," he noted. "Might I have time to consider it?"

Price smiled more broadly still, and even chuckled, though quietly. "You want to consider an offer of five thousand pounds, Dean Tuckworth? You astonish me."

"But it will take time to arrange the transfer of such funds."

Price shook his head and produced a folded note from his coat pocket. "I believe this is all that's needed. Instructions to make the necessary funds available. You can present it to my bankers this afternoon and return to Bellminster to manage things at your end. You'll be returning at once, won't you."

This was no question, Tuckworth realized, but a command, and it occurred to him that he had been led to this moment, led as a sheep is to its shearing. He took the note. Odd, he considered, staring at it, how thin and weightless it seemed, to hold so many thousands of pounds of gold. What a miracle, to take something so massive and turn it into a slip of nothing. He looked up again and suddenly Price was transformed once more into the nervous, apologetic man.

"I hope you don't mind if I hurry you off. My life is such a tumble now," he confided, motioning Tuckworth toward the outer door. "I regret that we won't be seeing each other again, but really," and he laughed a weak and ugly laugh, "following last night, you'll probably want to wipe every memory of me clear from your mind. Just keep my little secret—my name, you know—and my bankers will attend to everything else for years and years to come. Farewell."

"Good day, Mr. Price," was all Tuckworth replied. "And I thank you for this," he added as he waved the check cavalierly in the air before folding it up small and stuffing it deep inside his waistcoat pocket. The door closed behind him with a sharp and dismissive click, and Tuckworth walked calmly, cautiously down the steps of the house, out into Caldecott Lane, and around the corner. Only then did he stop and draw a very long, very hot and moist breath from the fetid London air, passing a hand through his thinning hair. His nerves were still jangled from what had just transpired, and the dean reached up with a fingertip barely trembling to touch his forehead. Dry, he thought, not without a hint of pride.

Yes, pride. He paused and looked within himself, his pulsing heart, his filling lungs, the sense of exultant triumph now that he had . . . a what? A hint? A purpose to go on? What triumph was there for him in this? Yet triumph there was, though he must not waste another moment enjoying it. He knew what he had to do now, and he was eager to get started. Tuckworth shot his hand into the air to hail a cab. Just as he was getting in, however, he paused, and stepped back down to the pavement.

The dean appeared to think for a moment, then waved off the grumbling cabbie and looked about at the activity surrounding him, the flow of London's blood. Glancing up the street, he saw the opening to an alley that skirted along the back of Caldecott Lane. Quickly, Tuckworth maneuvered through the crowd to this narrow passage and was soon lost to the bustle of Westminster.

CHAPTER X
WHAT WE KNOW

No, no, no, no, no!" and Tuckworth slapped his thigh more emphatically with each utterance.

"But if the ink pot was empty," Hunt insisted, "then Price must have emptied it."

"Did you see him empty the ink pot?"

"No, but—"

"And neither did I, so we cannot accept it as a fact. The ink pot was dry, that's all."

The two men were sitting in Hunt's parlor on Milk Lane, facing each other in soft, worn, secondhand easy chairs before a dark and ashy hearth. A tray with tea and cakes rested, ignored, on a small table between them, and through the open parlor door a beefy young girl kept an eye on the discussion, still suspicious that the dean was in fact a bill collector come to spirit her master away to the Marshalsea for debt. The house, as much as Tuckworth had seen before telling his news to Hunt and settling into the parlor, was awash with the clutter of a very active, very careless domestic life. From below came the clang and clatter of pots being tossed about in the cellar kitchen. The upper stories might have been used as a parade ground, so much running and crashing and childish screaming could be heard. Behind the parlor a modest dining room gave the appearance of a general workroom, with papers, pens, and blotters lying about, and through the closed doors of the study across the foyer a pair of voices shared a muffled, though heated, disagreement. ("A pair of friends," Hunt had explained cryptically, "talking shop.") A moment later and the beefy young girl, evidently satisfied that the dean was innocent of subterfuge, left the two men to their debate.

"We can't allow imagination to cloud our reasoning," Tuckworth went on, "or we'd be no better than that Bow Street inspector, trying to paste all the facts together to fit some design we already have in mind."

Hunt leaned back deep in his chair in frustrated acceptance. "I do see your point," he admitted, "but I'm not the sort of man to stifle the whims of imagining. Unless we're willing to indulge in just an ounce of fancy, I don't see how we're expected to tie Price to the murder."

"I'm not interested in tying Price to anything just yet. To my mind there is only one mystery before us, and that's the identity of the dead man. Beyond that there's nothing."

"At the moment."

"At the moment," the dean conceded, and the two men seemed to draw a sort of truce along that line. "Now, if we could return to listing only those facts of which we're certain."

"Very good," Hunt replied, his equanimity miraculously restored, and he took a slip of paper from the table and ticked off the items listed on it. "No one in the house had ever been there before that day, excepting Price and myself."

"And you were not expected."

"No. The servants had been hired for the occasion and a new cook was only just hired a few hours before the party. The guests seem to have been selected for timidity—"

Tuckworth raised an admonishing hand. "We can't say for certain how they were selected. We know only that they were too intimidated by circumstances to provide assistance."

"Very well," Hunt acknowledged. "We *don't* know for certain that Price counted on their timidity. But you admit they were a remarkably meek lot."

"Looking to inherit the earth, they must be."

Hunt grinned, in spite of himself. "We know that Price's ink pot was dry, and he left you alone for some minutes in a room that conveniently had no clock."

"Yes," Tuckworth murmured softly, "though something tells me there was a clock in that room before." The dean was silent for a moment, then shook his head. "It's no use. I can't remember. Besides, Price couldn't have known that my watch was broken, and there was no reason for him to suppose that I would note the time of his exit."

"Still, if we could prove he removed the clock—"

"We could show definitively that he had a broken clock. Go on."

Hunt huffed in vexation and continued. "We know we heard a gunshot. I came out to the landing to see you running up the staircase, and together we went up to investigate. We found the body after several minutes—"

"Almost a quarter of an hour."

Hunt looked wryly at Tuckworth. "Do we *know* as much?"

The dean grinned. "Several minutes," he allowed.

"And Price came up behind us shortly after we arrived on the scene."

"He said he'd been searching at the back of the house all that time," Tuckworth mentioned, and for a moment he appeared lost in a reverie. "Tell me something, Hunt. Those children playing upstairs, are they yours?"

"Various nieces and nephews and the odd grandchild."

"Where are they just now?"

Hunt looked vaguely at the ceiling for a moment. "I should say they're on the second floor, in the hallway. There or in the garret under the eaves."

"In any case, you can pinpoint the noises to within a few rooms?"

"Yes," Hunt answered, a light slowly dawning within him, "and all the rooms being in the same general area, I could narrow my search very effectively in just a few moments."

"Yet Price—"

"Was nowhere near the garret when we started searching through the rooms!"

"Tell me," Tuckworth pursued, "did you hear Price come running up behind us?"

Hunt thought for a moment. "No!" he said at last. "No, I did not! He was just there!"

The dean held up a cautionary finger. "Careful now. Is it that you didn't hear him, or you don't remember having heard him?"

Hunt sighed. "I don't remember having heard him."

The dean leaned forward and poured himself a cup of tea. "You see," he declared, raising the cup to his lips, "we have nothing to go on but speculation and supposition."

"What about the reappearance of your ink pot?" Hunt insisted again. "And the look of guilt Price gave you?"

"So the man overlooked an ink pot. Is that fit evidence for an accusation of murder? And as for the look, I have no way of proving that it meant anything, that it even occurred."

"But it did occur."

Tuckworth paused, placing down the teacup again. "Yes," he conceded. "Yes, it did. He looked at me with the startled fear of discovery, and looked away just as quickly."

"Which explains how he knew you suspected him, and why he is trying to purchase your cooperative silence."

The dean nodded. "He must know I suspect him, and he must be equally certain that I can prove nothing."

"All right," Hunt acknowledged reluctantly. "So here we are. Immersed in supposition. Yet some very telling supposition it is."

"I don't deny that," Tuckworth said, settling back in his chair. "But none of it relates to the mystery at hand. Who is the dead man? Discover that, and perhaps we can start turning supposition into something resembling fact."

Hunt reached for a tea cake. "But we know nothing about him, what he looked like or why he was there."

Tuckworth leaned forward again. "We know his height, generally speaking. He was a head taller than Wick, who was short. Say he was just six feet. A tallish man. His hands tell us he was a laborer, or at least used to hard work, probably outdoors. That should tell us something about his dress. I don't imagine many such men came regularly to Price's house."

"Do we know he came there regularly?"

"In all likelihood he did. One rarely murders complete strangers. And we also know that someone else in that house might have seen him."

Hunt sat up straight with excitement. "Who?"

"The cook."

"But the cook had never been there before that day," Hunt objected, referring to his list of facts.

"Not *that* cook."

"The one who was sacked? But how do we know she saw him?"

"Why else would Price have sacked her, except to get her beyond the reach of inquiry?"

"So our next step is to find this woman and see what she knows."

"Her name is Dolly Merton," Tuckworth announced, a bit proudly.

Hunt faded back in his chair. "Now how the deuce did you get that out of Price?"

"I didn't. I asked the servants at number 16, just next door. I paid a visit there after leaving Price. One of the maids told me that Miss Merton is an older woman who lives with her daughter and son-in-law near Notting Hill. I have the address."

"So she didn't lodge with Price?"

"No, and you can add that item to your list of interesting facts. Price and Wick lived in complete solitude in that house. It appears he didn't even trust having a cook nearby."

Hunt smiled. "Didn't he? That sounds like supposition to me."

Tuckworth was about to defend himself against this highly warrantable charge when the door across the foyer burst open and, to the dean's amazement, Raphael bolted out holding up a large painting of Bellminster at dawn, the cathedral rising like burnished gold over the town and surrounding fields. "Well, the light's murky in there," he was arguing. "Look at it outdoors," and he turned and marched out the front of the house.

Raphael was followed by an aged gentleman, stooped and slender and elegantly attired, who tottered behind with the help of a gold-handled cane. "You can't expect someone to hang the thing out-of-doors just to get the advantage of the light," the man croaked hotly before stepping outside.

The dean looked at Hunt.

"My two artistic friends," he replied to the question etched upon Tuckworth's brow. The front door opened again, and Raphael reentered with his pursuer close at heel.

"Raphael!"

"Dean Tuckworth," the lad responded, not in the least surprised, "tell him that this is the very image of the cathedral. He insists it's not a fair representation."

"I didn't say the depiction wasn't fair," the old gentleman insisted angrily. "I commented that the image was more idealized than real. You're painting yourself into the picture, young man."

"And where else should I be but in the picture? My eye sees, my mind interprets, and my hand executes."

"The trick is to leave the mind out of it."

"That's your trick, not mine. I'm part of the scene so I must be part of the painting."

Hunt stood up and interposed himself between the two combatants. "Gentlemen, there is nothing I love to witness more than an energetic debate on a significant topic, but if I might interrupt long enough to introduce Dean Tuckworth of Bellminster to John Constable, one of our foremost artists."

"Mr. Constable," Tuckworth said, extending his hand.

Constable gave Tuckworth a darting glance as one who is not accustomed to making so many new acquaintances in one day, but he took the offered hand and the dean noticed that his grip was firm and steady. "I take it you were this young rascal's patron in Bellminster?" Constable inquired with that directness that only age makes tolerable.

"I encouraged Raphael as best I could, but I was no patron."

"Yes, well," the old man added, "it seems to me a little encouragement is the only patronage he needs."

"I hope you don't mind that I included Constable in our party," Hunt remarked. "He's such an old friend. And as for my new friend Amaldi, I was extremely curious to see Bellminster Cathedral, and you mentioned at breakfast that he had made several studies of it, studies that you recommended yourself."

"I see," Tuckworth said. "So you asked Raphael to bring along one of his paintings—"

"Five," Raphael corrected.

"Five of his paintings," the dean continued, "where Mr. Constable here might have a look at them."

"Now, you make it all sound so diabolical," Hunt responded. "I only like introducing people, that's all. I'm a sort of platonic matchmaker."

"Platonic busybody," observed Constable. "Still, the boy has talent, no question. But discipline, my lad, discipline."

"What of passion, then?" Raphael demanded. "What of feeling?"

"Oh, bother feeling. Feeling will always be there, but it must be controlled."

"Yes, but too much control—"

"Now," interrupted Hunt once more, "see how well the two of you get on? Fast friends in no time."

Tuckworth could only shake his head in disbelief. Raphael looked like his old self again, with the same energy and vitality, the same impetuous temper and eager honesty. It was good to see him happy again, though sad to lose him so completely to London. "So," the dean commented, "I expect you'll have an easier time in the city now with two such friends as you've made here."

"But I'm returning to Bellminster," Raphael announced casually.

"What?"

"Yes," the young painter said, smiling. "I brought along some of my portraits as well, and Mr. Constable convinced me that I'm no portrait painter."

Constable rapped his cane emphatically on the floor. "That's not what I said! I detest being misrepresented. My advice is to get out of this cursed city and make good paintings. A landscape is merely God's portrait, after all, and He sits more steadily than any shopkeeper's brood. Now, Hunt," the old sage went on, turning his attention to their host, "you promised me a dinner if I met your young friend, and a dinner I expect. I'm old, and these artistic debates tire me."

"You're a spry chick, old Constable," Hunt declared, and reached for his coat. "Gentlemen, I think we might try the fish at the Hawthorn Bush this evening. I hear it's reasonably fresh. And, Constable, if you could lend me a fiver, it would be too kind of you."

"I daresay it would be," the old man answered.

Tuckworth paused in momentary confusion. "I thought we were to dine here."

Constable erupted in a wheezing cough. "Nonsense!" he managed finally. "Hunt hasn't entertained a soul on his own resources in years. The man's a sponge, but an engaging sponge."

The two painters went to retrieve their coats, leaving Tuckworth and Hunt alone in the parlor. "I must thank you," the dean said, and the depth of his gratitude shone unmistakably from his eyes.

"But really, you mustn't thank me," Hunt replied. "My motives were entirely selfish. I fully expected Constable to deflate the boy's ambition and send him packing in discouragement back to Bellminster."

"You don't know Raphael."

"Evidently not. Though I'd hoped that if I might assist you with your problem, you would be more inclined to help me with mine. But, you see, all my machinations were needless at last. You found sufficient cause for your suspicions in Price's transparent offer, and Amaldi, as it turns out, really was squandering his talents in London. So I don't see what thanks could be required."

"Then you've done more good than you can know, and without meaning to. Sometimes I think that all the best things in life are happy accidents."

"And not the hand of a providential God?"

Tuckworth glanced at Hunt, a furtive glance. The question startled him, and at first he didn't realize that it was only an offhand comment. Yet now Hunt was peering into the dean's face with a questioning look, startled as well, and searching. Tuckworth turned away quickly, awkwardly. Before either man had the chance to say a word, however, they were joined by the others, still arguing about art, and together the four went out into the gathering dusk.

Hours later, when all the world was dark and dismal, and puffs of fog hung thickly about the street corners near Caldecott Lane, a muffled cry, a startled whimper, might have been heard above the distant thunder that rolled upon the charged firmament. Soon, a flickering glow peeked about the billowing edges of heavy curtains high up in the air, announcing the presence of a wakeful mind stirring at number 18.

Hamlin Price sat up in the plush comfort of his mattress, the sheets made damp and sodden by the humid air blowing in from the windows, and by the sweating fears that had assailed his dreams. He had felt again the hands, tiny hands, inhuman hands, some dirty and sharp like claws, some plump and pink, reaching out and plucking at him, tugging at his skin, his flesh. Not in violence. Violence would not have been half so dreadful. But clutching in appeal, begging to be known, grasping and pulling at his mind, his soul.

He had waked with a start, flailing at the sheets, the dark echo of his cries dying in the night. He sat up, eyes wide, knees tucked in sharply, clutching the bedclothes. Minutes passed, and nothing happened. Eventually the fear settled more deeply into him, into the lowest part of his soul, where it sat like a toad at the bottom of a dark pond, waiting, feeding off his safety, his sanity, devouring his security from within.

He leaped from the bed suddenly, scrambled to the far wall of his chamber, clawing for a doorknob he knew must be there, couldn't have been moved, not by human hands. Where was it? His fingers brushed, then clutched it, and he stumbled through to another room, his secret room.

The bedchamber was left to the shadows, left to the unseen things that hovered at the ceiling, flitted in the corners, the things with tiny, tiny hands. The only sound was the whimpering sobs of Hamlin Price, crashing like waves against the nothing of silence.

CHAPTER XI
THE COOK AND HER LOVER

he next morning dawned with a thunderclap, the heat of recent days cracking the sky at last so that an Eastern monsoon seemed to have wandered a wayward path from India, striking vengeance at the heart of a heartless empire. Tuckworth sat on the edge of his bed, the nightshirt clinging maddeningly to his puffy frame. Nights were worst, he considered, and this past night the worst in a long while. Up and down every hour. That infernal fish, no doubt.

Tuckworth rose again and paced a bit as another flash lit the world beyond the window and a clap shook the room like the gates of eternity slamming shut. Even the weather felt less like weather in London than it did in Bellminster, perhaps because a city storm was nothing but mockery and show, theatrics put on display for the wonderment of man. Weather meant something in the country, to crops and to animals, to a man's future. But in London? Rain was wet and cold, the sun was hot, and the wind blew hats off men's heads. That's all the weather amounted to in London.

What was he still doing there? Caught up in other men's lives, meddling in things he had no just cause to meddle in. But surely it was worth the doing, to find out the truth in this business. Truth is almost the only thing that matters, the dean knew, matters deeply and always. Truth and love. Strange, too, how these were the two things you never quite felt certain of, not completely. Your whole life you searched and searched after them, like hunting shadows, but could never get your hands on them firmly enough. Always fear and doubt snuck in like an oily film. Certainty? No, even with Eleanor, amid a mountain of certainty an ounce of doubt slunk in at times, ungovernable times. Even with her there had been impatience, anger, feelings of regret, and a longing for what might have been, that other life left behind.

A thought of Eleanor, and the same pain welled up inside him, duller now. Not so sharp, not nearly. It was a familiar pain at last, but pain still. He raised his hand over his eyes and through his fingers saw the flash of light that preceded the thunder. A far echoing crash, and the pain subsided.

Tuckworth lowered his hand and strode to the window. The darkness outside cast his dark image back at him. He'd done it because he loved her, because he couldn't see her suffer so hopelessly, so totally. She'd begged him, in the end, for the release that God withheld. What of that? he thought harshly. Murder was murder. Yes, but if death can be a blessing, and it *can* be a blessing, can murder be love? He shook his head, confounded by the darkness.

The wind blew rattling shards of water against the thick panes of his window as Tuckworth looked out at a colorless world. Colorless, but not lightless. Even here, in the middle of the tempest, dawn was making itself known, causing his image in the window to fade and grow pale, lighting the clouds from above and beyond, etching the lines of the rooftops, revealing an alien landscape, a vastness of chimneys and steeples. It was all so removed from Bellminster, from his life. Why did he stay here to bother about other men's affairs, like a worried old hen busy about nothing?

An answering clap shook him from his lonely thoughts. He looked about the room for candle and matches, to get himself ready for the task ahead, the game of question and answer. Now that he had taken it up, he would not be able to put it down again until it was truly finished.

By the time Tuckworth had dressed and breakfasted on tea and buttered toast, the rain had passed and the heat was settling in again. As his cab pulled up before Hunt's address, the mud of the streets began to stiffen to a clay, and once the two men were deposited in Notting Hill (for, eager though Raphael was to join them, he had arrangements to make), the sun had forced its way through the clouds and the ground was baking to a deep and crusty hardness. The lanes around them, with their heavy odor of sawdust and offal, sweat and plaster, showed ample evidence of a district in transition, caught in that ebb and flow of fortune that left deserted, eyeless buildings confronting blocks of modern flats, and smart junior clerks sharing the pavement with the destitute and the decrepit. Tuckworth could not tell in which direction fate was moving here, only that it moved.

They approached a featureless pile of brick and descended from the street to a door just below in a sort of dank well. The morning's rain lay puddled below them, and Hunt had to lean over from the last step to rap on the door.

A sound of wet scuffling, and the door opened just enough for a face to come forward into the half-light. The face was a woman's, weary yet attractive, with hair gathered roughly in back and stray, auburn wisps framing cheeks that were dull and pale, though still retaining some of the plumpness of youth. She looked at the two faces before her, this woman, with tired eyes that could not raise even a glint of curiosity.

"We'd like to speak to Mrs. Merton," Hunt said quite easily, as though he were a duke addressing a duchess. "It's a matter of some importance."

The woman eyed them each for a moment before opening the door to let them in. The room was poorly lit, but it gained something from the darkness, a shadowy hint of comfort, though a sharp eye could detect the threadbare curtains, the rude chairs and plain table, the scanty furnishings. Still, there was a freshness in the air and a neatness about the place, not least because of the rug hanging from a line in front of the hearth and the mop and bucket leaning against a wall. It was a room that might once have owned ambitions of something better. The same could be said about the woman, her simple frock looking oddly full and appealing on her, in a down-trodden way.

"What is it you want? They forget to ask somethin'?" the woman demanded in a voice marked by resignation, her back to Hunt and Tuckworth as she crossed the floor and sat at the table.

"Excuse me?" the dean replied.

"Them others put enough questions before. They forget somethin' and send you two about it?"

"Are you Mrs. Merton?" Tuckworth inquired, frankly surprised. From the young maid's description he had been expecting someone older. "Dolly Merton, who used to cook for Hamlin Price?"

She looked from one to the other sharply. "You ain't bobbies or Bow Street men," she stated, suddenly curious.

"No, my dear," Hunt explained, making himself comfortable at the table across from her. "My name is Leigh Hunt. This is Mr. Tuckworth. We are only interested friends looking into this matter." He motioned for Tuckworth to join them.

"Yes, we were present two nights ago, when it happened," the dean said as he sat down, and he saw at once that something seemed to drop away from Dolly Merton, like a curtain being pushed aside, just barely.

"What's yer interest?"

Tuckworth leaned forward toward her. "We only want to find out the truth. For ourselves, our peace of mind. I assume the authorities told you about it. Still, there are some things in this business that seem . . . well, not right, and we were hoping you could shed some light on them for us."

She shrugged, trying to look unconcerned and failing. "Why don't you ask down to Scotland Yard?"

"Because, my dear," put in Hunt, "the authorities seem convinced that Mr. Wick had a hand in this, and we feel he did not."

She started ever so slightly and eyed them even more closely for a moment. Then she laced her hands in front of her on the table and began. "They come askin' after Wick yesterday, what I know about him, where I thought he's run off to. I told 'em he don't have no one he can run to, no one 'cept me. And he *didn't* run to me, so I don't know where he is." Tuckworth glanced at Hunt, who seemed content to let the dean run the interrogation, and whose attention was cast upon Mrs. Merton with a tenderness that was truly touching to witness. "They was here 'most four hours, askin' the same questions over and over. What're his habits? Who're his friends? Where's he go when he ain't workin'?" She paused, and looked down at her folded hands. "What are we to each other?"

She spoke readily, with no coaxing, her eyes on the table in front of her, her words steady and soft, like one who had been forced to give her story in fits and starts and was now eager to tell it whole. "They never asked what sorta feller he is. They seemed settled on that already."

"And what sort of fellow is he?" asked Tuckworth.

Dolly Merton sat up erect, her back straight, and for a moment she looked achingly lovely. "Malcolm Wick is a gen'leman," she said. With a rough, red hand she smoothed a transient lock behind her ear, while from the back of the flat came the sound of a baby cooing itself awake.

The two men exchanged a quick glance at this, a glance that Dolly Merton understood too well. "Nah," she explained. "The babe's my daughter's."

"Tell me," Tuckworth asked, trying to be delicate, "what is your relationship to Mr. Wick?"

She shrugged again, proudly. "Yeah, it's what you think. And then, it ain't. There been no promises, nor nothin' underhand neither. He's a kind man, and a gentle man. A woman needs that, gettin' on in years. We was just a bit o' comfort to each other in a hard world."

Tuckworth let the subject drop. "And what was Wick's relationship to Mr. Price?"

Dolly Merton sniffed. "Wick's a proud one, but a man's got to make do, and Mr. Price pays good money. More'n a body can make doin' the same thing anywhere else."

"Did Wick like his employment?"

"Nah, he didn't. Nor did he like his employer. Wick was smarter than to be another man's secretary. He'd even spent time at university, so he said. But I told you, a man's got to make do."

"What didn't he like about it?"

She considered for a long moment. "He never spoke outright," she confided at last. "But some of Wick's duties, they rubbed him wrong. Some things he had to do made him wretched at times. He'd never say what they might be, but I could tell when he'd been doin' of 'em. When he was with me, I could tell if he'd been about his master's business, as he called it."

"He was a faithful secretary, then."

Mrs. Merton looked at Tuckworth, then rose and began to wander about the room, her hands idly straightening the odd articles that lay about. "Wick's the most faithful man I ever knew, nor ever am like to know. He always kept Mr. Price's accounts to the farthing. If he got off by so much as a ha'penny in that book of his, he'd fuss and fume until he could make it all come out right again." A gentle smile graced her lips and she shook her head fondly at the memory.

It was wrong to intrude on her sorrow, Tuckworth felt. His curiosity seemed hard and unfeeling next to her false bravery, yet he knew he must go on. Question and answer, that was the game. "This book you mention. It was an account book, I assume? A record of his master's business?"

"A brown leather notebook," she recalled, "all tied up with a leather strap. He kept it always about him, in his inside coat pocket or locked in a drawer by his bed." She stopped in her wandering for a moment, aware that she had divulged more about her knowledge of Malcolm Wick's personal habits than she cared to. That qualm passed, however, and she renewed her pacing. "He kept it stuffed with all kinda notes and papers. He made a record of all Mr. Price's business."

"Everything?"

She shook her head and smiled her wan, sad smile again. "Nothing escaped Wick," she said. "If it happened in that house, he had it writ there in that book."

Here was something, Tuckworth thought to himself. "Did you ever get a look in the book?"

"Me? Nah. Can't read. Malcolm tried once to teach me, but I weren't made for such things."

"I assume Mr. Price had access to this notebook."

She shrugged. "He might have done. I wouldn't know. I weren't part of Price's business."

"Did Mr. Wick ever tell you what that business was?"

"Price just makes money is all I know. Like a farmer growing corn. It come natural to him."

"What's your opinion of Hamlin Price?"

She sniffed. "I didn't have no opinion 'til yesterday. Now my opinion don't matter."

"How did he sack you?"

"About luncheon time Malcolm come and told me to be off home for an hour. So that's what I done. When I come back, Price meets me in the kitchen and sacks me like that," and she snapped her fingers.

"He let you go, even with his grand banquet that night?"

Dolly Merton laughed noiselessly. "I never cooked his fancy parties. He always hired in for that."

"He told the authorities that you . . ." The dean let his voice trail off, embarrassed to go on.

"Yeah," she answered scornfully. "I know what he told 'em."

"How did Wick behave the last time you saw him?"

She paused before answering, and cast her eyes down at the floor. "He didn't act no way in particular," she said, though sounding as though there were more to say.

"How did he act?"

She turned and confronted Tuckworth, her eyes watery with pain. "He took my hand as I left and he kissed it. He never done like that before, not in the kitchen, not anywhere but upstairs." And she turned away again.

Tuckworth fought the urge to glance at Hunt. He only proceeded with the game, question and answer. "Was there ever anyone unusual you saw at Mr. Price's, a laborer perhaps? He might have been a rough-looking character, with gnarled hands. Did you ever see someone like that?"

"You mean the one-eyed chap."

Tuckworth tensed at the words. "Yes, what of him?"

"Not much to tell. I didn't see him much. Had an eye, his left, that was all milky white from a scar what cut across it. Sometimes he'd come knockin' at the kitchen door, and I'd let him in. He usually showed up after I'd gone home, though." She shuddered. "Creepy-looking feller, with that dead eye. And always smilin'. I think Wick hated that part of his job most, dealin' with that one."

"Do you perhaps know his name, or where we might find him?"

She shook her head. "Never spoke more'n two words to him myself."

"One more question, and we'll be going," Tuckworth said, rising from the table. "The men from Scotland Yard, did you tell them about the one-eyed man?"

"Nah. They asked if Wick had any enemies, but I never thought of ol' One-Eye as such. He was a bad'un, right enough. Kinda face you expect to see swingin' from a rope at Tyburn Tree. But he was just more of Mr. Price's business is all."

The baby started crying in the back room, and Tuckworth made his way to the door. Hunt rose and stepped to Dolly Merton's side. She turned and looked at him and for an instant the woman seemed frozen, for the first time unsure and vulnerable. Gently, Hunt took her hand in both of his. "We'll find what happened, my dear," he told her softly, and her harshness melted away as she bowed her head to hide her sorrow, a sorrow that would not weep, would not mourn, not for the world to see. "Here is my card," Hunt went on, pressing it into her hand. "Should you require anything, you have only to send for me."

Back on the street, Tuckworth turned to Hunt as the two men walked along, weaving their way through the crowd. "That was kind of you," he commented.

"The woman is in love," Hunt replied. "Love should always be respected. There's little enough of it in the world."

Tuckworth sighed. "I'm afraid she has scant reason to be hopeful."

"You think Wick is dead?"

"I think it likely. The murderer would rest easier knowing that the authorities were out chasing a man they could never find."

They turned a corner by an abandoned storefront, and Hunt immediately grasped Tuckworth's arm and pulled him back against the building. He peered around the edge, back down the lane in front of Dolly Merton's door. "Did you notice him?" Hunt asked.

"The fellow in the long coat," Tuckworth answered, inwardly pleased with himself for having spotted the man as they came out.

Hunt continued to look. "The inspector from last night. Any child on the street could pick him out," he remarked with a hint of scorn, and the dean felt suddenly crestfallen.

"I'm not so certain it was that obvious," he observed defensively.

Hunt came away from the corner and continued down the street, his arm laced through Tuckworth's. "He's gone now. Probably off to report on us. Another black mark against poor Leigh Hunt."

"Really, I thought the fellow was quite inconspicuous."

"And so he was, good Tuckworth, so he was," Hunt crowed, his mercurial spirits having returned to him double charged. "Now, what is our next order of business?"

Tuckworth thought for a moment before responding. "In all honesty, I'd welcome a good suggestion. I want to learn more of this one-eyed man, that's certain. And I'd like a look at this leather notebook."

"Do you think the one-eyed chap was our poor friend from Price's garret the other night?"

Tuckworth nodded. "It's certainly possible."

"And does that possibility suggest our next move?"

"I'm afraid not. So," Tuckworth admitted with a suffering glance at Hunt, "I believe we must supplement certainty with a little imaginative speculation."

"Excellent!"

"Just a little, to nudge us on our way," the dean insisted. "I believe, and I want you to correct me if I'm mistaken, but I believe we can infer that this one-eyed man was operating outside the law."

"I would wholeheartedly correct you if I could follow your reasoning."

"It's not reasoning, just an educated guess. Mrs. Merton called him a 'bad'un' and she might have had cause. He always paid his visits after the normal hour for respectable business. His appearance was distasteful to Wick, who it seems was a fairly upright sort."

"Although a woman in love is not always the finest judge of character."

"True. But add to that the fact of the murder, not passionate and heated, but deliberate. It strikes me that such a murder is one of the last crimes to which a man will bring himself, that a very many other crimes must pave the way. It seems likely to me that whoever killed our man in the garret was involved with him in some prior criminal activity."

Hunt nodded. "A very sound and educated guess indeed."

"Therefore," Tuckworth concluded, "I'm afraid we'll have to apply to the authorities to discover the one-eyed man's identity."

"And why the authorities?"

"Because they have the most complete knowledge of London's criminals. If we're to discover the one-eyed man's name, and confirm that he's in fact the victim of this crime, then that's where we must go."

Hunt pulled Tuckworth to a halt and waved for a passing cab. "That is most certainly where we must not go," he stated flatly. "If you will allow me to play the role of Virgil, perhaps I can suggest a course for us to take that will leave us free of the plodding entanglements of Scotland Yard and Bow Street." He stepped into the waiting cab and turned back to leer wickedly at the dean. "Tell me, Dante, are you up for a stroll through Inferno?"

CHAPTER XII
THE DEVIL'S ACRE

*H*is name is Arthur, but whether that's surname or Christian, I can't say."

"How did you ever meet such a person?" the dean asked as the cab trundled jarringly along the crowded street.

"I believe I mentioned my months spent as a guest of the government. Well, we passed some little time in rather close proximity, Arthur and I. Near neighbors, you might say."

"In prison?"

"In Newgate. As vile and rotten a den as you could imagine. Arthur became my *valet de chambre,* after a fashion. Helped me through the rough times. And, as I was situated somewhat more kindly by my keepers, I helped Arthur to a bit of ease himself. Of course, he's an old man now. In constant pain."

"Have you seen him lately?"

"I have cause to pay my respects every year or so. We stay in touch. You know, Tuckworth, London is not altogether the heartless Leviathan it's made out to be. I'm sure it's no different from your Bellminster, at times. It's not one city, after all, but dozens. Westminster, Holborn, St. Pancras, Southwark, just a series of little villages, all sewn together like a Quaker's quilt. The well positioned like our Mr. Price might move about readily, but the mob are more settled. Notting Hill knows as little of Cheapside as you or I know of the Antipodes."

"Which would suggest that if our man operated in Westminster, operated criminally, I mean—"

"Then it's likely he was known in Westminster, and if he *was* known here, Arthur will know him."

The cab pulled to a stop and Tuckworth and Hunt disembarked in front of Westminster Palace, the home of Parliament and seat of empire. (And the dean once more was made to foot the fare; he was beginning to wonder if Hunt carried any coin with him at all.)

"Lords and Commons!" Hunt proclaimed with a magisterial sweep of his arm, as they stepped out before the lofty edifice, ancient and imposing. "Lords and Commons, Tuckworth. Would you say that phrase encompasses the breadth of British citizenry?"

"I'd say it's as good as any," the dean replied.

"Really, these guarded answers of yours are enough to spoil a man's eloquence," Hunt pettishly observed. "Now, as I was in the process of pointing out, this timeless palace, this Westminster, has stood for many and many an age as a symbol of all that is sturdy and true in British law. It is vast. It is strong. It is eternal and will stand, I have no doubt, until time itself has ceased to beat its Newtonian tattoo. And yet beneath this stony and imperturbable visage, in the very shadow of the civil authority, we are about to venture into a realm beyond law's reach."

Tuckworth shook his head. "I don't follow you."

"But you must, old boy, you must, or you're sure to get lost." Hunt laughed, taking the dean by the arm and leading him away. "Have you ever heard of the Devil's Acre?"

"I don't believe I have."

"Well," Hunt began, clearly delighting in this chance to expound, "the Devil's Acre is one of the rookeries, a species of nether-London, an underworld amid the overworld. Within the very sight of Parliament, that unflagging symbol of order, the Devil's Acre provides sanctuary to every thief, murderer, cutpurse, pickpocket, every harlot and confidence trickster, every forger and counterfeiter the dear old city spawns."

Tuckworth tried very hard to sound abashed, for the benefit of his friend. "Does the constabulary know of its existence?"

"Oh, Scotland Yard knows about the Devil's Acre right enough. I mean they know its limits, its boundaries. But what happens within? No, of that they are as ignorant as if it were located on the moon's dark face. It would take more men than the Yard can muster with Bow Street thrown in to clear that den of thieves."

This talk of dens and rookeries sounded suitably melodramatic, and the dean would have been lying to say that his nerves didn't feel a chill at Hunt's performance, but Tuckworth fought bravely to pass it off as just more of his companion's natural exuberance. Only as they continued on their way, weaving here and there up lane and alley, down mews and court, did he begin to feel any real trepidation. At every turning the world appeared to transform subtly, slightly, almost undetectably. Buildings that a moment before seemed new and majestic, the architecture of a worldly and world-drunk power, now grew smaller and meaner, less noble, more mundane. The people they passed, blindly intent upon their own lives, appeared to diminish in the social distance, to change from ministers and aides and assistant undersecretaries to clerks and shopkeepers. Slowly, even this semblance of middling commerce gave way to hints of distress. The clerks became laborers and costermongers, men of indeterminate occupation or no occupation at all, and women whose lives were forfeit to dreary necessity. About them, boarded windows and seedy squares, unkempt doorways and empty storefronts, scattered bottles and oyster shells strewn along the gutter spoke of impinging depression, the noose of poverty tightening itself inexorably about the throat of the slack-witted world. Another turn brought destitution and the hopeless human tragedy of men and women trapped within the prison of their lives. The smell of decay, acrid and human, rotten with death and sickness, ran like tainted rivulets in the air. Glassless windows gaped everywhere, the ravenous, jagged maws of dirty buildings that themselves were crumbling onto the pavement, looking less like blocks of flats than hovels nailed randomly together. And scuttling about this desperate landscape, the dirty, hungry, naked eyes of children.

They stopped before a blocked alleyway, little more than a crack in the city's facade with four or five feet of boards nailed up as a weak deterrent to the curious. Hunt reached out and pushed one of these boards so that it swung easily aside. With a meaningful glance at Tuckworth, he murmured, "Abandon all hope," and led the way within.

Once past this gate, Tuckworth felt the air about him collapse into a moist miasma. The closeness of the alley, the stench of the filth through which they shuffled, the muffled noises that slogged down this thick and stifling tunnel gave Tuckworth the sense that he was moving at the bottom of a very deep, very dank well. They trudged on for what seemed many yards before emerging into a close yet comparatively breezy courtyard. Men and women lounged or walked or slunk about the place, smoking or tippling or talking in subdued voices, no one bothering to look at these two interlopers from the outside world, yet everyone aware of them. Tuckworth glanced above to see clothes hanging from window to window overhead, like pennants in some gay medieval pageant, a Sienna holiday. They might have hung there to dry through all eternity, the dean thought, for all the sun that managed to find its way to them. Tuckworth and Hunt moved on, leaving the courtyard behind and coming out into a lightly peopled lane that stretched for a brief space beside a fetid creek, one of those infested, festering sewers that ties the Thames to London in bonds of wretchedness, bounded by stony banks and spanned here and there by plank bridges.

"Stay close to me and say nothing," Hunt cautioned. "We've not much farther to go."

Tuckworth had heard of people who could make themselves felt merely by the power of their unseen eyes, but he had never had any cause to believe such a thing possible until now. He had a certain and inexplicable sensation that his every movement was under intense scrutiny, and that the least gesture on his part that might be deemed threatening, that might give him away as a magistrate's man or officer of the law, might be the last gesture he would make.

They finally turned off the lane and stepped into a looming old building. Just past the outer door a staircase rose into the darkness. Up they went, slowly, so that their eyes might adjust. An odd quiet accompanied them on their way, as though the walls were listening, and once more Tuckworth was made to feel that someone, somewhere, was taking a very great interest in him.

They came at last to the top floor, some four stories up, and the dean paused to get his breath. "Now," Hunt said, panting gently himself, "you are in a place that I daresay is unlike any you have been before. I have to confess—and at the last moment, I'm afraid—that Arthur doesn't like the clergy, and he'll spot you as a clergyman dead on. It's a gift he has, to see clear through a man at once and know all his secrets. But trust me, you are quite safe as long as you're with me. Don't sit down and don't get comfortable. We'll be as quick about it as we can be. Oh, and for God's sake," Hunt admonished, taking Tuckworth by the wrists and forcing his hands into his trouser pockets, "keep your hands there and don't let them out if you can help it."

Tuckworth was beyond astonishment at this point and only nodded. Then the two men turned to the only door that presented itself and, with a cursory knock, Hunt strode boldly in while the dean followed.

The room they entered was simple and raggedly furnished. A few hard chairs with upturned boxes for tables, some smoky candles stuck in green and brown bottles, an old and doorless cupboard, thin curtains billowing over the windows, and a small grate for a stove were all the comforts to be seen. From an open door opposite, a croaking voice called to them out of the darkness.

"Now, 'oo is it come callin' so early, eh? Day ain't 'ardly broke."

"You know very well who's calling, old hobgoblin," Hunt answered. "Not a rat scurries through this place that you don't know about. And it's not early, either—not for honest employment!"

A cackling laugh followed, and there appeared in the doorway the wizened, gnomelike figure of an aged, crippled man, bent almost double and walking with a pair of sticks. He tottered into the room with an insidious leer, his hair thin and dingy, his skin pockmarked, his clothing dirty and stained.

"You're out'n your nat'ral element, Marster Leigh," Arthur observed, slowly making his way toward the nearest chair as his jaw worked vainly, gnawing his single tooth.

Hunt obliged him by nudging the chair closer, and the man settled down with a nod of thanks, a groan, and a wheezing cough, before leaning slowly, achingly back.

"And 'oo might this be?" the man asked, poking a stick in Tuckworth's direction. "You with the clergy now, marster?"

"May I present the reverend dean of Bellminster, Mr. Tuckworth. Tuckworth, this is His Royal Highness, King Arthur of Westminster."

The old man ignored the dean and glared at Hunt from the sides of his squinting eyes. Hunt could only shrug, and the King of Westminster suddenly rapped the floor three sharp raps with one of his sticks. At the sound, five others—three men, a woman, and a child—entered the room.

They entered, but not by either door. To Tuckworth's amazement, they seemed to melt into the room from the walls. Hidden traps, little more than flaps of wallpaper and wood hung over rat holes, opened from all about the place, disgorging a secret human treasure. They each appeared as impoverished and dirty as their ancient relative (for they gave the appearance of being a family, of sorts), yet they were merry, too, easy in their poverty and contented. After a few unintelligible gibes directed, it seemed, at Tuckworth, they were soon busy about their own mysterious affairs.

One of them, a mop-haired girl who tumbled out of a dark corner, walked furtively up to the dean, coming close to him and laying her unwashed face against his waistcoat. Moved by compassion, Tuckworth placed a hand gently on her head and smiled down at her, feeling once again the pang of remorse that any child must live like this. She smiled back in turn with a look of sugary sweetness, before backing slowly away and tossing the dean's purse into her grandfather's lap.

Tuckworth slapped his hand to his pocket to confirm the theft, and Hunt could only shake his head ruefully. Arthur weighed the purse in his hand, his fingers palpating it as though it were a living thing. He clearly appreciated its heft. "Well done, child," he croaked. "Artful, but not too thorny, I'd wager. Your friend's a fair mark, Marster Leigh, and must pay the forfeit."

Hunt sighed. "Please, go easy with him, Arthur," he pleaded. "His purse is all the money I have."

Arthur cackled, then opened the clasp slowly and took out three shillings. "This 'ere fer you, Bishop Folly," he said, stretching out his hand toward Tuckworth. "The congr'gation appeals to charity for the rest, but we can spare this much to see you 'ome." And he laughed his dreadful, hacking laugh. Tuckworth reached out and took the coins. "God left you at the door, old Bishop. 'E don't come about 'ere much, but if 'e ever shows 'is face, I'll tell 'im you was askin' arter 'im."

Arthur's laughter died in solitude, and the old monarch eyed the dean closely now, and suspiciously. "Can't say I trust a religious feller comin' up all this way to see me." He coughed and spat on the floor. "Ain't never 'ad no parsons up 'ere. It's not what I'm accustomed to, and a man don't like new things at my age."

"Then we won't keep you long," Hunt stated pleasantly. "We've come for information about someone." The old man coughed again, and the cough appeared to have some meaning to it. "We're not asking you to turn king's evidence," Hunt explained. "We simply want a name to go with a face."

"What face?"

"A man over average height, say six feet or thereabouts. Not dandyish, but he wouldn't be afraid to move in refined company. Always through the back door, you understand. And he had one milky eye with a scar cut through it."

" '*Ad*, you say?"

"Yes. He's dead. At least, we think he's dead."

"When?"

"Two nights past."

"Well," considered Arthur, "can't object to peachin' on a dead 'un. Girl!" The woman came over, skinny and sallow. "Quarles, Bernley, and Linker. Run to the pub and find out which might've been seen these two days past, and which ain't." She hurried out without a word. "Only three good eyes amongst 'em. Evil-lookin' chaps, which don't do 'em no good in this business. Nor no great 'arm, either. Sit! Sit down!" he commanded.

Hunt remained where he was, however, and Tuckworth stood by as well, following his friend's example.

Arthur shrugged. "As suits you. Can't say the furniture's none too soft," and he shifted, grunting, in his chair. "Now, ol' Bishop, what would you say if I told you I ain't never been to church in my long life, not even as a baby?" It was clear that the man was trying to goad Tuckworth. What's more, he seemed to be doing it out of pure malicious joy.

"I suspect religion comes differently to each," the dean muttered.

Arthur threw his head back in surprise, then threw it forward again aggressively. "That ain't no right answer!"

"I only mean that every person must find his own way to salvation or . . ." Tuckworth's voice trailed off.

"Or to the devil? Is that it?"

"Yes, I suppose."

Arthur shook his head angrily. "What kinda preachin' is that? Marster Leigh, I think you'd best run your deacon o' Bellwether back to church. 'E ain't learnt 'is lessons yet."

"Now, now," Hunt said pleasantly, "he's only nervous to be in such grand surroundings, amid such rare company."

Arthur spat again and leered long and searchingly, so that Tuckworth winced under his scrutiny. If only he could lie, the dean thought. If only he could tell the old man what he expected to hear. If only he could make himself sound like Mortimer, sanctified and pious. And yet he knew, as soon as he had spoken the words, devised some fitting sermon about the wages of sin and the glories of redemption, they would be seen for the lies they were. He had no faith to protect him in this place. He was open and defenseless against this old man's gaze. Only in stillness could he hope to escape, by confounding the man's prying nature with silence.

Suddenly, Arthur leaned back in his chair and cackled. "It's like you, Marster! So like you!" And he gasped at the appalling humor of the joke. "To come 'ere with a parson what ain't got no better opinion o' God than myself!"

Tuckworth's blood froze within him, and his heart skipped.

"Now really," Hunt admonished. "My friend here is a respected and reverend member of the clergy." And he glanced at Tuckworth to laugh away the old man's indiscretion.

But Tuckworth could not laugh. He could not speak. He had lived his life these years immersed in a web of half-truth and prevarication, but now, confronted openly with the secret he had kept encased in the bleak prison of his heart, he could not lie. He had never been able to lie.

"One 'ypocrite'll always spot another!" old Arthur crowed triumphantly. "Look at the poor fat feller sweatin' the truth out'n 'imself now!"

Tuckworth touched his hand to his forehead. He was awash in a clammy film. He kept his eyes turned down, chastened by this vile devil, this old sinner whose ages of deceit had given him a gift for truth. He's right, Tuckworth thought, I *am* a hypocrite. I'm as bad as any of these here. I'm worse.

"Now hush yourself, you miserable sprite," Hunt commanded in a voice as light and breezy as the dawn of a spring morning, "and stop insulting my friend, or I'll take my commerce elsewhere."

This joke tickled the old man as much as the other, and he laughed himself into a fit of coughing. By the time he had sufficiently recovered, the woman was back.

"I seen Linker down i' the pub," she reported. " 'E says Bernley's in Newgate, to swing o'Monday. Ain't no one seen Quarles these days past."

"No one?"

"Nah," she answered. "Jobbers says 'e was s'posed to meet 'im last night, but Quarles never showed."

Arthur mused for a moment in his chair, rocking slowly side to side.

"Is this Quarles our man, then?" Hunt pursued.

"As might be. Where was the deed done?"

Hunt gave Arthur a hurried account of the crime, being certain to leave out all names and keeping one eye on Tuckworth, who appeared lost in his thoughts.

Arthur listened attentively, nodding his head, a sour look on his face. "Aye," he muttered at last. "Always said Solomon Quarles wouldn't never come to no good. I do believe that's your feller."

Hunt reached out and gently shook Tuckworth, who appeared to wake from a light slumber.

"What? Quarles?" the dean asked.

"Solomon Quarles," Arthur said again, motioning for his little granddaughter. "Nothin' but a low-grade pimp."

"A pimp?" Tuckworth repeated. "He was bringing women, then? Is that what this is about?"

Arthur shook his head. "Not women, ol' Bishop. Not like you mean. Quarles' trade weren't with the ladies." He placed a withered hand on the child's head as she rested it against his knees. "Quarles dealt in the little ones. Just the young 'uns, as young as you'd like." The old man leaned away and spat. "Yep, as young as you'd like. That was what was writ on Quarles' shingle. 'Dainty flesh. As young as you'd like.' "

CHAPTER XIII
CHARITY

The purity of a pure blue sky, made bluer yet by the white of a few tufted clouds, hung over an English summer meadow. The sun had seared the grass to straw, yet cowslip and bluebell, gillyflower and dandelion, foxglove and daffodil and eglantine poked up in defiant patches here and there, adorning the meadow in provocation, tempting a host of butterflies to dance in the light of late afternoon. Nearing in the distance, a gentleman on horseback, out to ride before dusk, galloped through the field, tall and rigid in the saddle, mustache bristling, muscles tensing, guiding his mount effortlessly up a short rise and on through the tall, brittle grass, a veritable hussar charging bravely against phantom guns. His horse's iron-shod hooves rumbled like distant thunder against the packed earth as he passed, showering dry, brown clods in his wake while he rode out of sight. The two men watching him from the footpath turned away and continued their stroll.

"It's enough to make one forget how squalid the world can be," Hunt commented as he walked beside Tuckworth.

"It reminds me of Bellminster," the dean replied, dreamily.

"They offer the same sort of serenity, I would imagine. Your town and Hyde Park are both sanctuaries for the soul."

"The town? No, I meant the cathedral. The town can be more sordid than you know. As sordid as anyplace."

Hunt heaved a sigh of resignation. "I suppose every town of any size harbors its own Devil's Acre."

Every town and every man, thought Tuckworth, a little patch of villainy for each to cultivate. But as he had no open reply to make, they wandered on a bit farther in silence. They had come to Hyde Park directly after leaving Arthur and his clan, wandering there for hours. It was Hunt's usual practice after such an excursion into the underworld to "cleanse the spiritual palate," as he told the dean, with a stroll through Hyde Park. "Delicious juxtaposition," he had called it. "One of the unique charms of London."

Yet this unique charm felt unnatural now, hollow and false. The serenity of wood and meadow amid the brick and mortar reality of the city proved a desperate lie, a thin veneer to hide the corruption lying just beyond and beneath. It tainted their stroll. Their silence was not the peaceful quiet of calm reflection. It was charged with things unsaid, unsayable. Something had arisen between them so awful in its merciless veracity, its terrible, wretched truth, that no amount of politeness could dispel it. The trifle that was their few days' acquaintance lay exposed before them, and silence was their only recourse.

Or is it so? Tuckworth wondered, adrift on his own inner sea. Had this dark, awful crime silenced him, or was it something else, a sense of personal corruption, humiliation in the face of discovery? Was it their acquaintance that had been exposed, or was it merely his own self-absorption? Perhaps, with a man he had known better, the dean might not have managed so well. A growing panic had arisen within him in the face of old Arthur, a feeling that all was lost, that his deepest fear was to be realized, the black secret within him brought out into the light. And it *had* been realized, after all, but to what end? The awful truth he carried with him always,

wrapped within him, concealed and stuffed away in the hidden re-
cess of his soul, the fact of his faithlessness, had been pulled forcibly from him, wrested from its hiding place, and almost in the
same instant he was made to feel ashamed.

Ashamed, not at the fact of his atheism, discovered so intuitively
(one hypocrite to another, as Arthur had said), but at the weight
he himself had placed upon it, the importance it had held for him,
when there was such greater suffering in the world. What mattered
the shallow pitch and roll of his conscience when children, little
children, were being abused in the most abominable manner, were
being robbed of their innocence, raped and savaged, adrift in a
deluge of evil? In the end, the grand revelation of his unbelief had
gone almost unnoticed, rendered little more than a joke for Arthur
to gasp at, while this other, this horrible thing they now found
themselves embroiled in, hung about them still, silencing them,
stifling them, muffling their hearts in shame.

They walked like this, in private reverie, each pursuing his own
thoughts, until the light of day dimmed and they were forced to
start back to the streets of the city. "Unlike your peaceful country
nights, the London pastoral can be dangerous after dark," Hunt
observed. "Man is a nocturnal predator."

"Yes," the dean said as they passed beneath the trees, light and
shadow playing across their path. "Yes, he is."

Hunt looked at the dean, marking again the awful shade that had
fallen over his spirits. "Well," he commented idly, "I must say I'm
surprised at how simple this whole business has been."

"Simple?"

"Indeed. Once you set us on the right track, discovering Price's
secret was . . . well, it was *simple*," he said, substituting the word
for the more apt and dreadful simile that had died on his lips.

Child's play, Tuckworth thought. It was child's play.

They were silent again, made mute by a crime so much more

horrendous than the murder itself. Even Arthur had felt it, there among the degradation of his moral poverty. Even he had sensed the abominable nature of this crime.

"Of course," Hunt declared finally, "we have no true evidence."

"No, none," acknowledged Tuckworth, and he stopped and turned to his companion. "Never forget that, Hunt. The stakes are greater now, and we can't be careless. We're still dealing in speculation. We have nothing that can tie Price to this. We can't prove that Solomon Quarles is the victim. We can't prove that Wick is dead. We can't prove that Price is a pedophile. We are only free to talk of this between ourselves, no one else."

"Then what bloody good have we done?" and for the first time Hunt's voice registered the depth of his very genuine frustration.

"I don't know," Tuckworth replied as they resumed their walk. "You see, it's not so simple, after all." And once more they fell silent.

A few minutes later, Hunt wondered aloud, "How do you suppose Price managed to overpower both men at once? They were fit, able men. Either one would have been a daunting foe."

Tuckworth glanced sideways at his companion. "Now you're beginning to ask the right questions."

Hunt laughed halfheartedly. "I prefer the right answers."

"There are never any right answers, Hunt," Tuckworth told him. "The answers we've been getting are mere opinions, half-remembered notions, and faulty memories. What we need are facts, something we can show to others, to force them to see the truth."

"Such as?"

"I don't know. Something about the body, the gun, the room—"

"The inkwell?"

Tuckworth shot an annoyed look at his companion. "Wick's notebook, that's what I'd like to have a look at."

"Mrs. Merton said he always kept it on his person or locked beside his bed."

"Yes, and we have no way of getting to his bedroom and no idea where to find his body."

They walked on a bit longer. Slowly the noises of the city intruded on their stroll, and soon they were back on the hard pavement of the city streets. It was truly dusk now, a lowering, ugly evening with a thick brown haze settling over the world so that the lamplights were mere smudges on the air. On they walked, surrounded not by trees but by an equally hard and unyielding forest of humanity. They would have pursued the day's findings if they could, but their minds were spent, unable to form the least connection, to make the least imaginative leap, to tie together any sort of plan to take them that much farther on their way. Exhaustion thwarts even the best intentions, and their minds were left stumbling along. They only walked, moving in the direction of Westminster, toward Mrs. Terlanne's, toward a parting that seemed a failure, a retreat. Yet they had learned so much.

And what had they learned? Tuckworth thought. They had learned that this game was now in deadly earnest. They had learned that they were up against a villain whose worst crimes they had not so much as suspected a few hours ago, a man who was free to continue his atrocity unnoticed and unabated.

"I suppose this also explains why Price treats me so rudely," Hunt said suddenly.

"How's that?"

"I'm the vessel of his guilt, the chalice to receive his penance. He throws money at me to balance his depravity."

"Only after a fashion, I imagine. No man, even the vilest monster, ever sees his own evil in the mirror."

"Yet Price must be aware of his crime," Hunt insisted. "He must feel some guilt at his actions or he wouldn't always be sending money my way."

"Yes, the answer for him is always money, isn't it. To you and your charities. To me and my cathedral."

"You know, sometimes I think most of the good in this world is merely atonement for an equal quantity of sin."

Tuckworth paused just for an instant. "Is that why we do it, Hunt?"

"Do what?"

The dean spread his hands wide. "This investigation. Is that the reason we pursue this, to atone for something in ourselves?"

"Is our reason really so important?"

"Yes, to me it is."

Hunt smiled. "The ways of the human heart are more labyrinthine than my poor mind can follow," he replied. "My own soul is a particular maze. I know that I do it because it seems right to me. It seemed right at the outset and it seems even more so now. I daresay you do it for much the same reason."

"I wish I could be certain," the dean said. "You know, Hunt, what that old man said about me—"

"Arthur? He's usually right about people. It's a gift of his trade. He needs to size up a man quickly if he's to spot his mark. His victim, you understand. A pickpocket's got to know an easy mark from a sharp one. Still, I wouldn't place too much faith in what he says."

Faith, Tuckworth thought, and then leaped. "I have no faith," he confessed, and in that confession he felt that he had dropped a great stone into the world and made not a ripple.

"Nonsense," Hunt chided good-naturedly. "Every man has a faith. Some are merely more orthodox than others. Orthodoxy," he scoffed. "It's a chimera. I've known poets and artists and philosophers, along with knaves and cutpurses, *and* a few bishops, and no two of them ever believed the same thing. No, not even the most reverend archbishop you can name believes exactly the same as his flock. Orthodoxy is a will-o'-the-wisp."

"Yes, but I believe nothing," Tuckworth insisted, frantic to be understood by this man he hardly knew, yet fearful still, anxious that he not come apart completely, but only stretch at the seams a bit. "Do you know what that means for a man in my position, not to believe? To find it all a cold and empty nothing? Do you know what a wretch that makes me? I'm a hypocrite and a fraud, Hunt, no better than Arthur. A hypocrite and a fraud."

Hunt shook his head. "Well, that's as may be. I've never known a man who wasn't a hypocrite about something. But you do yourself an injustice. It's part of our nature to think better of ourselves than we are, or worse. Either way, we're hypocrites. But I'll tell you this," and Hunt stopped and looked into the dean's eyes with a heartfelt sincerity that Tuckworth had rarely noticed before. "Here is what I believe, and I believe it with all my soul. I believe that what a man believes is worthless, and what he believes that he believes is more worthless still. What a man says, to another or to himself, is mere wind. We are what we do, Tuckworth. Action is the only measure of a man. Believe that, if nothing else. We are what we do."

They walked on, and the dean placed his secret back into its dark, hidden place. He had taken it out, this once, and seen for himself its size, its shape. It was smaller than he had thought it was, and less terrible. But it still had the power to hurt. His thoughts went to Lucy, and he wondered where she was and what she was doing, his child. He would protect her from everything, even from himself, even from the truth if he could. And if he must sacrifice his honor to do it, make his life a lie? Well, he had done worse in his life for love. Much worse.

At the moment, Lucy was busy not thinking of her father. She was not thinking of Raphael, or the crypt, or the Great Cross of Bellminster. Lucy was praying in the empty nave of the roofless cathedral in the gloom of twilight, praying the way her father had taught her to pray, with an empty, thankful heart, with a mind clear of any desire or passion save divine love.

"Don't ask God for anything," her father had always instructed her as a child, when she wanted so desperately to pray for a pony cart or a new dress or ribbons for the May festival. "Simply let God know you're here, and that you love Him."

"But I want ribbons."

"Maybe," her mother would add, leaning down to lay a gentle kiss on the top of her head, "instead of praying for what you want, you should pray for what God wants."

"But how will that get me the ribbons?"

"Pray with a thankful heart, Lucy," her father had taught, "and God will give you better than you want. He'll give you what you need."

And so she had prayed, "I *need* ribbons," until she was old enough to understand. Yet even now it was hard, almost impossible to empty her soul of desire. This cathedral was His place, after all. Surely He wanted it restored. Surely He would not let it sit like this, empty and abandoned.

Presumptuous, she knew, to give her voice to the Almighty's will. She rose and returned inside to her father's study, where she might sit and think her problems through, try once more to find the solution that had escaped her. The floor must be shored up, and it must be done from below, from the crypt. But the weight of the Great Cross was threatening every hour to crash down into the netherworld beneath the cathedral. Where were the men to help her? They were there, waiting on the money. And where was the money? It was caught in the awful realm of Charity. That one word was enough to free men of their pennies while their pounds went into hiding. Charity.

A knock at the study door roused her, and Lucy rose and opened it. Mary Black and Adam were standing in the hallway.

"Yes, Mary?" she asked, trying to sound hopeful and eager, not discouraged at all.

"It's Adam, Miss Tuckworth," Mary said, turning an eye upon her elder brother, who was only a child himself, for all his strength and size. "He has something for you, miss."

"Have you, Adam?"

The man nodded his head.

Lucy led them out to the parlor, where they were accustomed to gather at the end of the day, a homelier setting than the dean's disheveled study, and they all sat down around the cold, dark fireplace. It was that awkward time of day when the lit lamp in the parlor and the dimming glow of the sky reached a sort of equilibrium, so that indoors and outdoors seemed like needless distinctions. From outside the open windows, the last human sounds of evening could be heard, stragglers crossing Cathedral Square going home, or going to the tavern at the Granby Arms.

"Now, Adam," Lucy said cheerily. "What do you have?"

"It's just this, Miss Lucy," and he bent forward and held out a thick fist before him.

Lucy reached out to Adam and took from him six copper coins, six pennies that he had saved from his wages. She looked quizzically at the treasure, knowing very well what having his own money meant to Adam. "What's this for?"

"For the church, Miss Lucy. It's for the church."

Lucy leaned back in her chair and took a deep breath to steady herself.

"It's what it says in the Bible," Adam went on, excited now to reveal his plan. "Mary read it out to me. If you give to God, He'll give you ten times back. Well, that'd be ten times them there, miss. That's . . ."

Mary leaned over and whispered, "Sixty, Adam."

"Right!" he beamed. "That's sixty coppers, which is a whole crown, Mary says. And then, when I give that to the church, God'll give us ten times more again, I figure. See, miss?"

"Yes, Adam, I see." And Lucy did not weep as she said it. No, she beamed back at Adam. She could not bring herself to dampen his frank enthusiasm, or to devalue with her tears the sacrifice he was making. "Tell me, Adam, do you know what the word *charity* means?"

Adam smiled broadly so that his fistlike face glowed with pride as he pointed to the coins in Lucy's hand. "That there is charity, miss."

"Yes." She nodded. "Yes, it is. And it's something else, too. Charity means love. It's a very old word, but that's what it means. Thank you." She reached out and grasped his massive hand in her own tiny one, and smiled at Adam and his sister. And in a strange way that she could not fully comprehend, her desire to appear satisfied and happy made her feel satisfied and happy. Somehow, the dark seemed less dismal as they sat there together, and the uncertainty of tomorrow felt less dreadful. True, she was no nearer an answer, but for the moment she could be resigned to her uncertainty and relax in something that was real and true. The simple joy of one managed to multiply itself by three, three honest hearts honestly pleased.

"Well, it's a marvelous plan you've devised, Adam," she admitted. "Nothing short of a miracle, I imagine, but I daresay it's worth a try. Come on." Lucy stood up. "Let's go into the study now and enter it into the cathedral's ledger. 'Sixpence, donated by Adam Black.' We'll see if it doesn't turn into a whole crown."

"And then ten crowns," Adam told her, turning to Mary with a smile at his success. Together the three left the parlor as though they were setting forth on a grand adventure, while outside, the quiet of night settled over the town and over the fields and meadows, a true pastoral night, a Bellminster night.

CHAPTER XIV
RAT IN THE CORNER

T uckworth could hear Mortimer's voice from halfway up the stairs. Even behind the closed door of their shared sitting room, the rector's declamatory style was unmistakable. The dean had known him to conduct a civilized discussion in moderate tones, it was true, known him to sustain an even, dignified, almost casual exchange. Yet, when the Pentecostal fire of oratory was upon him, when he delivered a sermon or engaged in debate, even if the topic was the price of turnips, he spoke with an evangelical flourish that confused sincerity with resonance and honest discourse with volume. Tuckworth knew that it was possible to speak a simple truth softly, but he rather doubted that it was very much done in the world, and certainly not by Mortimer.

"*Caritas* must be the watchword for these modern times!" Tuckworth heard him proclaim. Whenever the rector fell into Greek, one could be certain that the subject was something laudable. Mortimer rarely wasted his education while chastising the flock, at which times he stuck to plain Anglo-Saxon English. "Charity our precept, the salvation of our fellow man the goal. Faith, hope, and charity, to the abiding perfection of these does the apostle preeminently command us, but of these which is the greatest? *Caritas,* my friend, *caritas.*"

The dean reached the top of the stairs and opened the door with a disheartened air. "Good evening, Mortimer," he said, and found himself looking into the dark, darting eyes of Hamlin Price.

Price was sitting, clearly at his ease, in the one comfortable chair the room afforded. He smiled benignly, staring at Tuckworth with a superior confidence, his hands idly stroking a small terrier that lay curled in his lap, to all appearances a gentleman in command of the situation and delighting in the dean's evident and immediate shock.

"Mr. Tuckworth, at last," Mortimer said, sounding markedly reproachful as he crossed to the dean and dragged him forcibly into the room. "As you can see, your guest has arrived."

Tuckworth avoided repeating the word *guest* in his dismay and merely nodded. So this was part of the game, he thought, and realized that he was up against an aggressive player. Of course Price knew where Tuckworth had been that day, had probably heard from the inspector that he and Hunt had visited Dolly Merton, might even know about the Devil's Acre. In spite of his discomfiture, however, the dean managed to avoid too great a show of confusion. "You must forgive my lateness, Mr. Price," he ventured, accepting the terms of the game. "These London streets are a maze for a country parson like myself. I've been wandering lost for hours. I apologize."

"Nonsense," Price exclaimed magnanimously, scratching the dog's ears. "I'm sure I got the time wrong. But it's no matter now, since I have spent a delightful hour or two with your Mr. Mortimer. He's filled me in very handsomely on the state of affairs at Bellminster."

The rector bowed. "Any pleasure was mine to be had," he demurred, then turned to Tuckworth. "I only took this opportunity to provide Mr. Price with some details regarding the Cathedral Fund. I was startled to learn how ill-informed he was about the situation. The financial situation I refer to, naturally." This last was

spoken with more than a slight degree of archness to it, so that
Tuckworth might know he was being scolded, and that Price might
recognize Mortimer's superior opinion in these matters.

"Yes, well, I hope to clear up a few points with Mr. Price myself
this evening," Tuckworth acknowledged.

"And I look for you to cure me of my ignorance," Price added
with a smile. "There are so many things I wish to know. So many
questions. And as good as Mr. Mortimer has been, I feel certain that
only you can enlighten me, Dean Tuckworth."

Mortimer bowed again, as though the compliment were his to
enjoy. "Well, then," he said, "I'll leave the two of you to your much-
delayed business."

"Actually," Price responded, rising and placing the dog at his feet
and attaching its leash, "I was rather hoping I might take a turn
out-of-doors with the dean. I could stay here for hours still, you
understand, but not poor Reggie. He's displayed signs of impatience." Price looked at Tuckworth, a baleful look, an anxious and
expectant look, the look of a man who has marshaled his forces
across the chessboard and is eager to press the attack.

Tuckworth simply nodded, with a smile that he could only hope
appeared collected and calm.

"In that case," Mortimer said, "if I might beg Mr. Tuckworth's
attention in my chamber before you depart. I have a clerical matter
to discuss briefly with him. We'll be leaving London tomorrow," and
Mortimer glanced meaningfully at the dean, "so, of course, there
are some minor arrangements to be made. It won't take a moment."

Tuckworth accompanied Mortimer into his private room, leaving
Price and the dog alone.

The rector turned on him as soon as the door was closed and
hissed his angry reprimand in a thick whisper. "Praise God that I
happened to be here to receive him when he arrived."

"I can assure you, his presence here is as much a surprise to me
as it is to you."

"You invited him yourself! He told me so. I fear I must remind you of the importance of your mission here, Mr. Tuckworth. You are in London for the express purpose of subscribing Mr. Price to the Cathedral Fund, and any lapses of memory might do irreparable harm."

"I know why I'm in London, Mortimer."

"Do you, sir? Are you certain? You seem to have adopted a very cavalier manner in the business," Mortimer fretted. "Out at all hours. Idling your time with that painter. Yes, he was here briefly as well. I know what you're up to in that quarter. And now I learn from Mr. Price that you have barely shared one-quarter of an hour in conference together since you arrived. A quarter of an hour in three days, Mr. Tuckworth! That hardly sounds like diligence to me. We're leaving tomorrow, so you may take this as your final opportunity to do some good with the man."

"You may leave tomorrow, Mortimer. I still have business here."

The rector shook his head. "Mr. Price has informed me that he is leaving town tomorrow as well."

"He is?" Tuckworth replied in surprise. "Tomorrow?"

"So your presence won't be needed any further."

"The business I speak of is my own. It's personal business."

Mortimer appeared stunned for a moment, then spluttered, "What business can you have in London to keep you? It's certainly nothing to do with the cathedral. You've demonstrated your lax regard there. Need I remind you, sir, that any costs you may incur from this moment are your own and will not be reimbursed from the ecclesiastical coffers?"

"Then I'll use the Cathedral Fund."

Mortimer's eyes narrowed and a grim smile creased his thin lips. "What Cathedral Fund?" he asked, and the two clergymen stood nose to nose, the one young yet stern, the other aged and defiant.

"Mr. Mortimer," Tuckworth whispered, softly seething, "the manner with which I am pursuing this affair is my own. While it might not meet your modern standard, while it might not appear businesslike to you, I will ask you to recall that *I* am the dean of Bellminster Cathedral, and as such I will follow my own course. I'm too old to follow another man's, even yours." Tuckworth did not like losing his temper, but he was just beginning to realize how little he liked Mortimer.

The rector, for his part, remained calm now, though no less unforgiving. "Your course may suit you," he replied, "but you will find that modern business practices are better suited to modern times."

"That's as may be."

"Another characteristic of modern business, Mr. Tuckworth, is a certain volatility. Conditions change very rapidly, and often with no warning. You would do well to bear that in mind. For now, I suggest you reconsider your decision to remain in London, and do what you can with Mr. Price tonight. He has already waited upon your wayward course long enough."

Tuckworth hesitated for a moment, pausing to look into Mortimer's eyes. There was something there, something calculating and secret. The man was at work on some mischief, though Tuckworth could not say yet just what it was. Still, he realized that this was one mystery too many, and he turned away at last, leaving Mortimer to join Price.

"Imagine how surprised I was to learn that you were still in London," Price began as soon as they were in the street, lost amid the cloaked anonymity of the surging crowd.

"Somewhat less surprised than I was to find you speaking with Mortimer," Tuckworth observed.

Price chuckled nervously, and Tuckworth noted a change in his demeanor, an eager and awkward note that had crept into his voice, his manner. "What do you think of little Reggie?" he asked, apropos of nothing. "That house felt so lonely that I went out today and bought a little companion, a little someone to keep me company."

Bought a little companion, Tuckworth thought, and recoiled in-

wardly at the picture Price's words conjured within him, the re-
pulsive image they called to mind. He controlled his revulsion,
however, and commented that he thought Reggie a fine animal.

"He's a terrier, you see. Wizard at catching rats. Follows them
right into their holes and tears them to bits. That's what one looks
for in a terrier, or so I'm told. Tenacity. We share that, don't we,
Reggie?" he said to the dog, reaching down to scratch its ear. "A
tenacious spirit. Once we have our mind set on the rat, we don't
give up."

The dean struggled to maintain his composure. This infernal
chitchat was meant to unnerve him, he knew, but he would not be
unnerved. No, no matter how threadbare his patience might be
worn, he would maintain his composure. He would not lose his
temper as he had with Mortimer. Yet all the while they walked his
mind was racing, examining the problem from every side. What
could he learn from Price with just the right question? How might
he lay his own trap? What could he safely divulge to reap a harvest
of information with but a little judicious sowing? Or might he instead give himself away and make his already difficult path impossible? What did Price suspect the dean suspected, and could his
adversary learn enough to be able to close off his inquiries? His
little bark was in danger of being swamped in a rolling tide of doubt,
and he must set his course now, or perhaps lose the chance forever.
Yet all he asked was, "Did we venture out this evening to discuss
Reggie?"

Price paused, only a slight hesitation in his pace, and then
walked on. "You're a blunt man this evening, Mr. Tuckworth."

"I'm a weary man, Mr. Price."

"Yes, you should be weary. You've been busy." Price coughed and
hemmed for a moment. "Allow me to observe again that you're still
in London."

"You didn't tell Mortimer of your contribution to the Cathedral
Fund?" the dean pressed.

"Curiously enough, neither did you."

"No."

"I would have thought five thousand pounds was just the answer to that little tirade he threw at you."

Price must have been listening at the door. "If I didn't tell him about the money, it was for your sake."

"My sake?" And now it was Price's turn to maintain his composure.

"To preserve your anonymity. That was your one condition, wasn't it? I don't suppose that even Mortimer would fail to guess where five thousand pounds came from if I were to produce it now."

Price considered this for a long moment. "Yes," he said at last, "but that's only half the truth, isn't it?"

"What do you mean?"

"You didn't tell Mr. Mortimer, but neither did you wait upon my bankers to arrange the transfer. You're up to something else, Mr. Tuckworth. You're meddling in my business," Price stated, looking sharply at the dean, "and I don't like it."

"Excuse me, but how is this affair your business any longer? The authorities don't hold you under suspicion. You're free to leave whenever you like, to put all this behind you. I understand from Mortimer that you *are* leaving," the dean commented, hoping to learn something.

"You've been to see my cook," Price stated, his mind not wavering any longer from its fixed point.

"Mrs. Merton is no longer your cook."

"Nor is she of interest to you."

"I may visit whom I please in London, I think."

"You're trying to implicate me in this," and Price's voice cracked in his excitement, taking on a frantic edge. "You have no idea what you're letting yourself in for."

"I am trying to discover what happened at your house."

"Scotland Yard is conducting—"

"Scotland Yard is chasing a dead man!"

The two stood on the pavement glaring at each other under the sickly yellow glow of the lamplights, ignored by the crowd passing around them. Tuckworth knew he was playing a dangerous gambit, but he was tired of patience and caution. He was tired of the game. Sometimes, he knew, when your queen is captured and your king hopelessly exposed, the only recourse is to upset the board.

"Scotland Yard is after a dead man," he repeated hotly. "Malcolm Wick is dead, and that means someone else killed him and killed the other. There's a murderer free—"

"And what is that to you?" Price gasped. "How is that your business?"

"It's everything to me! It's my business because I was there, because I make it my business!"

Price eyed him narrowly. Then, with a swift jerk at Reggie's leash, he darted into a darkened alley. Tuckworth followed.

"What evidence have you?" Price demanded when they were alone in the shadows. "Tell me and we'll take it to the authorities together."

The dean said nothing.

Price chuckled pettishly. "No evidence? No proof? What did the cook tell you, after all? That Wick couldn't have killed that man, not good, noble Malcolm Wick?"

Tuckworth stood still.

"Come, Dean Tuckworth," and Price sounded his confident self again, magnanimous, condescending, and subtly cruel. "Come, sir. I'm prepared to forget all your foolishness today. Chalk it up to an overexcited old man lost in the city for the first time. But you must leave tomorrow with Mr. Mortimer. And you must keep my little secret. Or else bad things might happen."

"Like the bad thing that happened to Solomon Quarles?"

Tuckworth didn't know why he said it, even as he said it. All the day's tension seemed to well up in him at once, and he simply blurted it out. He didn't speak the name with any intent other than to strike out wildly at this arrogant, cocksure man. And yet, the effect was the same as if he had struck Price a blow across the cheek. Even in the shadows, Tuckworth could see the blood rush from Price's face. His mouth hung limp and stupid, and his eyes went white with fear.

The look stayed on his face for a moment, before it was supplanted by another, harder and darker, a look of hatred and frenzy. Suddenly, Tuckworth realized where he was, alone in a dark alley with a killer, and he cursed his own stupidity. His eyes shot to the street, where even now men and women were passing, oblivious to the nightmare enacting just a few yards away.

"Where . . . where did you learn that name?" Price hissed.

Tuckworth said nothing, but only stared defiantly at this murderer, crushing his own fear, smothering it.

Price stared back at Tuckworth, and suddenly, something else emerged through the wildness behind his eyes, something awful, something damned. "You don't understand anything!" he shouted, sounding plaintive and pathetic. "You don't understand! Stupid, stupid fool!"

Tuckworth was silent still, afraid to utter a word, to provoke this madness.

Price looked down, glancing away from Tuckworth almost shamefully, down at his feet where the dog was sitting in timid affection. The dean looked out to the street and considered bolting, but Price glanced up again, sharply, wildly, his eyes watery with frantic emotion.

"Be careful, Mr. Tuckworth," he warned, his voice cold yet tremulous, ferocious and frightened at once. "You're a tenacious man yourself. I see that. But have you never seen the rat turn on the terrier?" He reached down and took the dog in his arms. "Have you never seen a cornered rat rear up and attack its attacker?" He looked at Reggie, stared full into his panting face, and appeared to steel himself. Then, with a sharp twist, he snapped the dog's neck.

The animal gave a muffled yelp, a convulsed spasm, then went limp. Tuckworth stepped back from Price and looked, horrified, into the man's eyes. To his amazement, he found there a horror to match his own. Price stood for a moment, apparently dumbfounded by his own actions. Then, throwing the ragged corpse down at Tuckworth's feet, he turned and fled.

CHAPTER XV
TRAPPED

You're certain he's gone?" Tuckworth asked.

"He's gone," Hunt replied, with a glance at Raphael. "I set the most reliable young chap to keep an eye on affairs at Caldecott Lane. This afternoon he reported seeing a private coach arrive and drive off again."

"With Price?"

"Indeed, with Price. He had bags and baggage to last him for weeks, mountains of stuff. When last I received word an hour ago, the house was still and dark."

The three men sat in Hunt's study around the flickering flame of a smoky lamp. It was twenty-four hours since Price had thrown the dog at Tuckworth's feet, a day since the dean had raced to Hunt to tell him everything, since they had planned their next move and recruited Raphael to assist them, an office the young man was too eager to accept. They should none of them be eager to adopt this course, the dean thought. It was daring, even reckless, but desperate, too, and desperation was never a harbinger of success. Yet it was the only course of action he could see before them. He took another sip of sherry.

"Watch that," Hunt advised. "We'll need cool heads tonight."

"And cold nerves," Tuckworth answered, draining the glass and pushing it away. The plan was simple, almost predestined. With Price gone and his house empty, they must make their way in and search for Wick's lost notebook, the notebook that Dolly Merton said was stuffed with papers, into which Wick recorded every expenditure and article of his business, every appointment and meeting, the notebook that might provide them with the proof they sought. Or at least it would very likely point them to their next step, Hunt had argued.

No, thought Tuckworth as they sat in silence waiting for midnight. At the very least, it would provide sufficient grounds to send them all to prison.

They had adopted midnight as their time of departure at Hunt's urging, and Raphael had strongly seconded the suggestion, but as the moment approached, the dean wished they had chosen some less melodramatic hour. He glanced back and forth between his two companions—Hunt fiddling with the dark lantern and lock picks procured from unnamed sources, Raphael eager and happy, delighted to be engaged in any activity that did not involve shopkeepers' children and their nursemaids—and the dean considered how this entire investigation was simply a game to them both, a diversion with a worthy end, a commendable pastime, but still something outside themselves. Yet they would not feel quite so easy had they seen Price as he had seen him, a man crazed and murderous, almost mad, had they seen how deliberately he had killed that dog and tossed its limp body to the street.

Tuckworth glanced at the sherry bottle but left it alone. He had seen something else in Price, he recalled, something that haunted him now. Not remorse or guilt exactly, nothing so penitential, but something that spoke of conscience. Was it the note of hopelessness in his voice? The glint of fear in his eye? No, but there was something else, something anxious and heartfelt, a reaching out to fulfill a lost desire. Tuckworth struggled with his memory to bring it back, this moment he wished to examine, but he could not get his mind to grip it firmly enough, and it dissolved into forgetfulness.

At last, a distant clock chimed the dying of the old day, the birth of the new, and Raphael rose. "It's midnight," he informed the other two, who remained seated.

Hunt looked at Tuckworth. "You needn't come along," he observed. "You're under no compulsion. We two are enough to search an empty house."

"No," Tuckworth replied. "If it's to be done, I should be a part of it. We *are* all agreed it should be done?"

"Of course," Raphael answered energetically.

Hunt nodded. "You mentioned yourself that without some real evidence, we have nothing but supposition."

The dean took a deep breath. "All right," he said at last. "Let's go."

They stepped out into the night and were soon swallowed by the damp, steaming fog. Even at this late hour, traffic trickled through the streets and passersby floated in and out of the mist without warning, furtive shades of humanity. The street lamps cast a yellow pall about their own iron forms, making them appear stalwart but immobile, frozen guardians of the light, helpless to offer any but illusory aid. The dean glanced up to the sky, but the stars were invisible behind the blanket of cloud and mist. An evening such as this, Tuckworth thought, and a man might believe that light was an intruder in the heavens, that darkness was the natural state of all.

The three men had determined not to trust their fortunes to a carriage but to walk the few miles to Price's door. After only a quarter of the distance, however, the oppressive heat and the eerie night wore away their resolve, and they hailed the next cab they saw.

"We'll have him drop us beyond Caldecott Lane, and then walk back," Hunt schemed, and Raphael nodded. The dean only looked out the window, lost in his thoughts.

Silly to harbor reservations about this business, he reasoned coldly. They were no mere thieves, set to violate a man's privacy for their own gain, were they? They weren't like the old man in that filthy room, old Arthur, living off what others rightly earned. They pursued a higher cause. Didn't that make this right? Not a crime, really. Just a necessary intrusion brought about by circumstance.

Then why did he feel it was wrong? Not unjustified, not ill-advised, but wrong. In spite of all that might be accomplished for a good end, why did Tuckworth's stomach feel uneasy that he was about to break into another man's home, to force his way, to search in the darkness and perpetrate a theft? Yes, they were thieves. No other word fit them so well. Whether for their personal gain or some greater good, they were robbing Price. Robbing a murderer, true, stealing from a depraved molester of youth and innocence, but thieves notwithstanding. Thieves set to catch a killer. Tuckworth had always believed that, for a just end, just means were required. But at the moment he knew that such caviling was the empty wind of rhetoric. For a truly just end, who knew what might be required?

They traveled in silence, and were let off (with a bit of wrangling over the fare, which Tuckworth and Raphael had to dig out from the lint of their pockets) a half-dozen blocks past their destination. Then, once the cab had disappeared into the thick night, they turned and walked back. Before too very long, they stood at the opening of the alley, behind the houses of Caldecott Lane.

The invisible chimes of London, muffled in the void above, rang out the three-quarters of the hour. With the uneasy steps of lost souls, Hunt, Tuckworth, and Raphael disappeared down that spectral byway, surrounded by tall brick walls and iron bars so close on either side they might almost reach out with both hands and touch them. Ahead and behind all was suffocated in fog, and it took no great act of fancy to imagine that they were traveling down the hallway of some infernal asylum, being led on toward madness.

They had gone no more than a few dozen yards when Hunt leaned close to Tuckworth's ear and whispered, "You've been down here before. Which house is it?"

The dean stopped and peered about the fog at the ghostly shapes hidden within, each looking oddly like the next, a line of uniform shades. "I don't know," he answered, his voice confused and apologetic. "They're all so alike. It's number 18, I know that."

They stared at each other in dismay for just an instant before Raphael spoke up. "I'll go down the lane and count the houses," he whispered, and vanished back into the mist.

Hunt and Tuckworth waited impatiently in the alley, afraid to speak, afraid almost to move, yet certain that each held tight within his breast the same dread foreboding that this business had gotten off to a wretched beginning. We're perfect fools, Tuckworth thought to himself, and this must end badly.

After what felt like too many minutes, Raphael emerged from the fog. "Number 18 is that one," he whispered, and pointed to a dark stain on the milky night. They moved on until they came to their next obstacle, an ornate gate, wrought-iron rods made wet by the night, twisted and bent into elaborate designs. Hunt went forward first and gently raised the latch. It clicked agreeably, and he smiled and looked back at his two companions. He pushed, and the gate screamed on its hinges like a banshee crying out for the slain, its shriek echoing hideously off the surrounding walls, seeming to get louder before dying at last.

They all stood, breathless, for a moment. Then, slowly, terribly slowly and gently, Hunt opened the gate so that its screams became just a strangled moan. He squeezed through, followed by Tuckworth, who had to take a deep breath and push the gate open a bit more to let himself by, with Raphael sneaking in noiselessly behind.

The back garden of Price's home was small and close, neat yet somehow poor, and Tuckworth wondered why a man of such limitless resources lived so modestly. The three moved quickly across an open space before huddling at the shallow well that led down to the kitchen door. Hunt proceeded first again, kneeling at the bottom, and produced his lock picks from a hidden pocket inside his large overcoat. He handed the dark lantern to Tuckworth. Hidden from the other houses, the dean could open its metal shutters without fear and release a narrow stream of light that he directed upon the lock. Hunt was a practiced hand with the picks, and soon the door swung easily, and quietly, open.

Before they moved on, Tuckworth placed a hand on Hunt's shoulder and bent to his ear. "Should one of us stay here to stand guard?" he asked. "In case someone comes along?"

Hunt looked up at the dean, and in the light of the lantern Tuckworth could see the quizzical expression on his face. "What could any of us do if someone came along?"

The dean considered this point for a moment, then shrugged his shoulders, and all three snuck in together.

They were below the street, in the kitchen. Tuckworth searched about with the lantern, swinging its beam back and forth to reveal a scene of corruption and disarray. Pots and pans lay about in confusion, food stood rotting on the counters, a slow drip at the pump beat a weary tattoo, and a pungent, fetid odor permeated the room, causing Tuckworth's nostrils to wrinkle in disgust. Price must not have ventured down here since the night of the party, he realized, and thought about the terrible state things would be in a month from now. A nearby flight of stairs soon led them up to a pantry and so on into the dining room, where Price had entertained his collection of nervous missionaries and timid humanitarians on the evening of the murder. The table still lay as the hired servants had left it when they heard the gunshot, dishes piled high at one end like the ruined towers of Babylon, the tablecloth stained and strewn with scraps and crumbs.

Tuckworth pointed this out to Hunt, and whispered, "Don't you find that odd?"

"What odd?"

"That he should leave it like this, after three days. He hasn't lifted a finger."

Hunt shrugged. "I wouldn't expect him to, not a man like Price."

"But he hasn't had anyone in, either. Wouldn't he hire someone to clean this up?"

Hunt nodded slowly, but as neither man had an immediate explanation, they moved on, crossing out of the dining room to the stairs, and so up toward Wick's room. They trooped upward, a trio of mice in the empty house, keeping close to walls, pausing at open doors, creeping with the utmost caution through the abandoned hallways. Up they went, past the parlor, past the bedchambers, up again, nearing that room under the eaves, that lonely little space where Malcolm Wick had lived and Solomon Quarles had died.

They arrived at last and entered the darkened room, the light of the lantern leading the way. The room appeared the same, and for a moment the dean was afraid to cast his beam of light too freely about the place lest it fall upon the faceless corpse of Quarles. But that grisly figure had been removed long before, he knew, and the room stood empty. The window had been left open and a pool of water lay blackly glistening on the floor. Otherwise, nothing was changed. Even the peppery holes of the shotgun blast were still evident in the wall.

Hunt stepped forward and, taking a blanket from the foot of the iron bed, draped it over the open window.

"Now," he said, speaking low in spite of himself, "open that lantern full and let's have a look about."

Tuckworth threw the shutters wide, bathing the room in light. He set the lantern down on the nightstand beside the bed. Then, glancing quickly at his companions, he opened the table's only drawer.

It contained only a few toilet articles, a hand towel and a comb, a jar of pomade and a bottle of rosewater, a razor with a small dish for soap, the meaningless paraphernalia of life glinting in the light.

"Well, we didn't expect it to be easy," Hunt observed.

"No, but we had hoped," Tuckworth added, thinking to himself that now they must search in earnest, like true thieves.

Raphael and Hunt burrowed into the armoire, rifling through clothes and squinting into corners, while Tuckworth emptied the drawers of the bureau. Finding nothing but linens and shirts in perfect, neat piles, he turned his attention to the bed itself, throwing back the bedclothes and reaching blindly along the floor under the slats, hoping to bump into something solid amid the dust. But there was not even any dust. Wick had been a fastidiously clean man.

When they were all three finished, they looked stupidly at one another.

"Do we leave now?" Raphael asked.

Hunt sighed. "I don't think there's anything else to find here. I suppose we must."

But the dean shook his head. "We can't just come back here whenever we want," he said. "If we're going to discover anything, we're going to do it now."

"But what else can we do?" Hunt asked.

"We can look into the rooms as we go back down. If anything seems promising, we've time enough before dawn to investigate." The city chimes rang half past one as if in approval.

And so they made their retreat, opening every door they passed, and every door within every room, turning down halls and working back, determined that, at the very least, when morning came they would have laid their eyes on every inch of Price's home. Nothing aroused suspicion, however. Nothing seemed out of place or curious. All appeared perfectly proper for a bachelor living in London. A bit modest, perhaps, for a bachelor of such means, but proper.

They arrived finally at Price's bedchamber. Like the rest of the house, it looked to be as normal as Sunday morning, a simple, unpretentious room with a simple, unpretentious oaken bed and un-exceptional furnishings. The two armoires were empty, but Hunt had already reported on the mountain of baggage that Price had taken with him. Three doors led off from this room, the one they had just come through, one to a vacant dressing chamber, and a third that was locked. Hunt approached this last with his lock picks and soon they heard the familiar, satisfying click of the latch. From his knees, Hunt pushed the door open. Tuckworth went ahead with the lantern, and what he saw caused him to pause for a moment, confused, before catching his breath in horror.

It was a nursery, an elegant, whimsical playroom as lavish in its appointments as any monarch might wish for his pink and pow-dered heirs. Balls and blocks, dolls in finery, a wooden horse large enough for a child to ride upon, and regiments of tin soldiers were scattered about the plush decadence of the dark green and yellow rug. The walls were painted with a host of Jacks and Giants, Ra-punzels and blind princes, Red Riding Hoods and slathering wolves. A puppet theater rested in a corner with Punch and the Saracen draped lifelessly over its front. A delicate table and two small chairs sat in an alcove across the room under a painted window showing a vista of castles and cloud-topped mountains beyond. It was a dream of childhood, or would have been were it not for a large canopied bed in the center, vast and terrible for all its pretty lace and dainty ruffles.

Hunt and Tuckworth looked at each other in the partial glow of the lantern's beam, a sidelong glance that said everything. The scene was too awful for words, its meaning too certain, its sham innocence too complete. Without a sound they commenced their search. For an hour and more they picked over the room, hungry for anything that might incriminate Price and reveal his secret to the world. They poked in and around and about each corner, tugged at the rug, and would have torn up the floorboards if they could. Yet here again they found only a mockery of proof against circumstance, a clear and dreadful sign that pointed nowhere. All was as right as it might be, with nothing to show that the room was other than it seemed, as inexplicable as that was in a bachelor's home. It was a nursery, nothing more. And yet, for Tuckworth as for the others, it was a corruption of what a nursery should be, a perversion of childhood desire, a winsome nightmare.

Tuckworth would have remained and searched again. He would have defied his own reason and stayed in that room until its diabolical essence congealed into something, some scrap of evidence that might link it to its dread design. But the night was wearing on, and eventually even he had to admit the futility of their search. The room carried no mark of its awful past, no voice to witness what had happened in the secrecy of its walls, no tangible memory of sin. At last, Hunt placed a sympathetic hand on the dean's shoulder, and together the three men left the nursery behind, though written indelibly on their minds.

They continued their descent through the house, though disheartened now and dispirited. It was clear that Price had been careful of his secret, had known what precautions he must take and had taken them. As they peered behind every door Tuckworth was convinced that they would find nothing more, and nothing more they found.

They came down the staircase slowly to the ground floor, trooping in single file, their investigation now a retreat in earnest.

"We've done what we can for the time being," Hunt said as they gathered at the foot of the stairs, and Tuckworth only nodded in resignation. "It will be dawn soon. We'd best leave."

Suddenly, a beam of light shot out of the darkness and flashed in their eyes, blinding them.

"God, but you've took forever about it," a thick, irritated voice muttered from out of the darkness.

A spark of hope fired in Tuckworth's breast as he recognized the Bow Street inspector standing before them in the shadows holding a lantern of his own, still looking rumpled and disagreeable, yet a welcome sign that all was not lost, that justice still had an interest in this miserable affair.

Hunt stepped forward to greet the inspector. "Can't tell you how delighted we are—" he managed to say before the man struck him to the floor with a beefy fist. Tuckworth jumped to assist his friend, while Raphael leaped at their assailant, trying to grapple with the burly figure. A quick scuffle, and Raphael lay sprawled on the floor beside Hunt, struggling to hold on to consciousness.

"Now," the inspector said, taking a revolver from inside his coat, "we'll have no more of that." He did not bother to point the weapon at them, only held it as a warning against further trouble. Tuckworth helped his friends rise groggily to their feet and then confronted the inspector.

"Price put you up to this," he stated flatly.

"Still the smart one, aren't you," the man jeered, then waved his revolver toward the dean. "Step over here," he commanded.

Tuckworth glanced at the other two before nervously approaching. The inspector placed his lantern on the floor and then, with a speed that belied his size, hit Tuckworth a tremendous blow to the stomach. The dean doubled and dropped to his knees, retching and gasping for breath, and Hunt and Raphael struggled to his side as quickly as they were able.

The inspector calmly took up his lantern again and spoke as though they were all friends of long acquaintance. "Those are by way of instruction. Do as you're told and you won't get no more. Lie down on your faces and spread your arms wide."

Tuckworth felt Raphael's hand tense against his arm and saw the young man's eyes recede darkly below his pale brow. The dean knew enough about the rash temper of his friend to understand that some dire crisis was at hand. Placing his arm about the painter's shoulder, the dean lowered himself laboriously to the floor, keeping his knees curled slightly against the pain in his stomach. "Lie down, Raphael," he insisted. "You can't wrestle with a bullet."

"Right you are," the inspector agreed, and soon all three men were laid out at his feet. "Now, I'm going to search you, each one after the other, and we'll see what we find." The process took longer and was considerably rougher than it needed to be, but eventually the man had gone through their clothes and, aside from the lock picks and what little money they had about them (which he pocketed), found nothing to interest him. Then, stepping back, he ordered them all to stand.

Tuckworth rose slowly, keeping his weight on Raphael the whole time as a guard against disaster.

Hunt rose last. "So," he commented as he got to his feet, "Price knew we'd be here, did he?"

Tuckworth answered for the surly inspector. "Of course he did. He laid a trap for me last night, told me he'd be gone, and I fell into it and dragged the two of you with me."

The inspector smiled. "Not too smart now, eh, old sod?" he observed with some pleasure. "You been lawfully apprehended in a criminal act, my gents, and might spend the next few years in pokey, if you don't swing for it."

"But you're not going to hand us over to the constables, are you," Tuckworth stated coldly.

The man cast a dark look at the dean. "No," he admitted, "I ain't."

"You're going to let us go, but we have to leave London, is that it? We're being forced to give it up."

The inspector took a menacing step toward Tuckworth, but kept from striking out again. Evidently he was not going to exceed his orders.

"You two," he said to Tuckworth and Raphael, "there's a coach north tomorrow morning from the Saracen's Head Inn. Be on it. And I'll know if you ain't, so don't try nothing. You," and he waved the gun at Hunt, "I'll keep my eye on. You take a step in the direction of this house again, and I'll know that, too. Any one of you tries anything different, and I'm allowed to deal with you using my own discretion," and the man grinned at them, leaving no doubt where his discretion lay.

Tuckworth looked at his companions. "Come along, gentlemen," he said, trying to sound as confident and calm as the inspector. "I believe we're free to leave now." Yet he did not feel calm and confident. Far from it. As they all three trooped dejectedly through the morning mist, the sky glowing a pale orange with the dawning rays of the sun, he felt as thoroughly beaten as he ever had in his life.

CHAPTER XVI

RETREAT

Tuckworth was being sent home, penniless, frustrated, disgraced, a failure at the task he had been sent to do as well as the task that fate had dropped in his way. He lacked even the money to pay for his own fare. His passage aboard the coach, as he learned when he returned to Mrs. Terlanne's, had already been arranged for him by the forethought and charity of Hamlin Price, a final, smarting insult.

"So stupid!" he charged himself as he shuffled his feet in the coach yard the following morning, waiting for the end to his adventure as Raphael saw to their baggage and Hunt stood by, offering what comfort he could.

"Now, it's no disgrace our being outwitted for the moment," Hunt vainly reassured the dean. "Price is a close and clever fellow."

"And ruthless, Hunt," Tuckworth added. "That's been his greatest advantage over us in this. He'll do whatever he can to hide his secret from the world."

"Yes, and for the time, at least, that secret appears safe."

Both men stood silent for a moment, Tuckworth sullenly, Hunt awkwardly, as they each confronted again their failure.

Raphael came over to where they waited. "Time soon, sir," he said to Tuckworth, his voice softened by the sense of shame that enveloped him as well, his return to Bellminster a retreat from everything he had once thought himself capable of doing in the world, a move, it now appeared, not into the future, but toward the past.

"Hunt," the dean said suddenly, "do you feel capable of keeping an eye on that house?"

"Nothing simpler."

"Yes, but the inspector." With a supreme effort Tuckworth avoided glancing in the direction of the Bow Street detective, Price's strong arm in the city. The inspector was too large and arrogant a man to hide well, and Hunt had spotted him the moment they entered the yard of the Saracen's Head.

"He might follow me as close as he likes," Hunt asserted, "and he'll never catch me straying a foot in that direction. But that's not to say I can't have my eyes on the house," and he slid a knowing finger beside his nose and winked. It was all Tuckworth could do to keep from grinning, though he realized they were under observation. "If it's not too much to pry," Hunt continued, "what good do you think can be got from keeping watch over an abandoned house? Do you believe Price will return anytime soon?"

The dean shook his head. "I don't know. I don't expect he will, but I can't be certain. Anything's possible when you have nothing left to hope for. Still, I want to know exactly what his plans are for that house."

"Any particular reason?"

"I've been wondering all night why Price hasn't had the place cleaned since the dinner party. All those plates and pans lying about, untouched and festering."

"And what conclusion has your sleepless night produced?"

Tuckworth tried to appear casual as he spoke, for the inspector's sake. "I think it very possible that the body of Malcolm Wick is still within those walls."

Hunt tossed the notion around in his mind for a moment and

seemed to like it. "That would explain Price's reluctance to have servants hovering about everywhere. Naturally, with Quarles and Wick gone, he would have no one he could trust to dispose of the bodies for him."

"Yes, he must have been panicked with both corpses on his hands. So he devised a clever scheme to eliminate one and left the other somewhere safe for later, hopeful that he could make a way out of his predicament with time."

"But time was just the commodity we were depriving him of."

"Precisely."

"If Wick is still there," Hunt wondered, "why would Price allow the three of us to search at will?"

"But we didn't search at will, did we? The inspector was there the whole time, keeping us under a tighter rein than we knew, doubtless with instructions to stop our search at the ground floor."

"So is that where Wick is?"

Tuckworth shrugged. "That's what we don't know. He could be stuffed in a wall or in a pantry, or buried in the cellar under the coals. All we know with relative certainty is that he's not in the upper stories. Price would never have allowed us to get so close as that."

"Wouldn't Price be afraid that the inspector would stumble onto it?"

Tuckworth afforded himself a quick glimpse of the inspector, half hidden in the shadow of a doorway smoking a cigarette. "Would you be afraid of that man stumbling onto anything?"

Hunt smiled. "I take your point. Well, trust to me. I'll have the house watched night and day, and the inspector won't know a thing about it."

So they parted, better friends than their brief acquaintance might have allowed under kinder circumstances. Hunt waved to the dean and his young companion atop the coach as it carried them away, watched them sailing over the heads of the throng like mariners on a ship braving the waves of the open sea. He stayed until they disappeared around a sharp bend in the lane, and then, with a sigh, Hunt dived into the waters of humanity himself, swimming with the stream of traffic.

He did not move casually through the crowd, but stayed his course resolutely for some while, as though he had an important engagement to keep and was just in danger of missing his time. He held to the main thoroughfares, plodded with a sure and implacable stride until he was almost out of the city entirely, nearly to the clerks' poor houses of Islington and the ancient boundary of City Road. Then, with a smart turn to the west, he made his way through Somerstown to Regent's Park to spend an uneventful hour among the menagerie.

Tiring of the lions and camels, he turned back toward the city, down Tottenham Court Road to Holburn, to a favorite tavern where he might take a spare luncheon. He was well known by the proprietor and the waiter and was made much over as a welcome and too-infrequent guest. He sat right against the window overlooking the street, and every time he raised his head from the mustard pot and vinegar, his eye just caught a large shadow shifting in the alley across the way.

"Very well, Persistence," he mused as he chewed his beef and potatoes, nodding inwardly in the direction of the shade, "we'll try your patience some more after dinner." Hunt soon finished, and instructing his hosts to lay the charge to his account, at which they smiled, he wandered back out into the street, followed diligently by the shadow.

This two-man parade sauntered through the city streets as Hunt set off on a far-flung odyssey, walking as wide as Cheapside and over the river to Southwark, north again to Tyburn, passing Newgate on the way. He traveled with no sense of where he was, no destination in mind, no course or purpose, but only followed the whim of his feet. And his shadow followed him. His plan was certain, guaranteed of success. The surest way to thwart a shadow, he knew, was to bore it into nonexistence. Had he tried, even by the least sudden turn or trotting gait, to lose the inspector, he would have ensured himself of the man's company for another week. But keeping to his relentless purpose, he was confident that he would be rid of the man by nightfall.

Yet his time was not wasted while he walked. His mind hung to the same few patches of thought, circling and circling like some caged beast chained to a post. Where? Where might Price have gone? If there were some clue, some way to narrow the possibilities to even a few likely places, Hunt would have started off at once, lost the inspector within a quarter of an hour, and risked everything to run Price to earth. Those who knew Hunt only as he appeared to the world, as a shallow, senseless sponge, a ne'er-do-well and a spendthrift, might have been shocked at the sense of resolve slowly mustering within him. But others, those few intimates who knew him well, would only have shaken their heads and smiled, and asked what they might do to help.

Try though he might, however, his resolution could find no target for its purpose. Price was gone, and no one in the world could tell where. No one knew, no one save Price himself, Price and maybe . . .

Hunt pulled up to a sudden halt, and then set off again, at a quicker pace, somewhat jauntier, bouncing along the pavement, faster and faster through the rush of the crowd. Quickly he turned down a dark lane that led into an even darker alley. This wound about for a space before opening up again into a dreary court, with three identical alleys leading out of it. At a dead run, Hunt took the left path, and wove his way about for another three or four turns before ending in an even closer court with three narrower alleys. Again he ran almost at random and struck upon a twisting way. After several more turns, he seemed to satisfy himself. Pulling into a conveniently dark doorway, he waited for a space of time. No inspector followed.

Less than an hour after this, Leigh Hunt could be seen strolling down a busy thoroughfare hard by The Strand, where the great and the grand shared the pavement with their less noble relations. The day was hot and the dust of the streets choking, so that clouds raised by the sweeps at the corners were more irksome than otherwise. The young lads, some little more than babies to look at them, thin and haggard children dressed only in rags and dirt, scurried across the busy ways with their straw brooms, clearing the path of any offensive matter left by man or animal, then waiting in expectation of the penny tossed in absentminded payment.

At one corner somewhat busier than the rest, Hunt paused and, stepping back from the curb, leaned against a building and casually lit a cigarette.

"Got another?" a small voice chirped from below.

Hunt looked down into the rheumy eyes of an urchin. "Vile habit, Tuppy. I'm shocked that you possess so little self-discipline."

The child grinned before thrusting his hand into Hunt's coat pocket and removing a cigarette. "Light us a fag, wouldja?" he asked, placing the rolled paper between his chapped lips.

Hunt performed the service, then blew out a long cloud to mix with the miasma of the town about him. "So, Mr. Tuppman," he said at last while the child puffed languidly away, "what news?"

"Naught but what you knowed a-yestiday."

Tuppman was clearly a taciturn young gentleman, never wasting a breath that he might find useful later. This was one of his many recommendations.

"So our mark went off in a coach and never returned."

"Chap made off away like I tol' ya."

"Well, Mr. Tuppman," Hunt continued, "I need your inestimable services again. I want two things done, first the one and then the other."

Tuppman merely nodded in response.

"I want you to go back to that house and keep your eye on it. I want to know what happens there, even if nothing happens at all. Is that clear? Even if it just sits there empty for days, I want to know. I want you to look into it twice a day at least, and oftener if your schedule allows."

Again the quick, decisive nod.

"That's the second thing. The first is more delicate. I want you to shadow a party for me."

"Who's the mark?"

Hunt blew out another thick cloud into the air. "The same man who'll try to murder me this evening about eight."

Tuppman looked up and squinted, and his lips curled in an evil grin.

Several hours later, just as dusk was beginning to spread shadows into the corners of the world, a cab pulled up at the end of Caldecott Lane, and Leigh Hunt got out. Trying too hard to appear at ease, he strolled up and down the street with a stiff and halting stride, his arms pinched and close to his sides, his glance darting about. He paced nervously, trying to look as though he had a definite destination in mind, all the while going nowhere. After almost a quarter of an hour of this, he walked boldly up to number 18 and knocked at the door. He waited, and knocked again. Then, with another furtive look about the lane, he very conspicuously bent over and began to pick the lock.

He was interrupted by a cough. Jerking convulsively about, he saw the inspector emerge from the shadows just in time to raise an arm and deflect the fall of the cudgel against his skull. It glanced off his wrist and opened a cut along his cheek, felling him.

The inspector immediately knelt down and raised Hunt's head by the hair. "Now look, you," he whispered thickly. "I ain't got no wish to kill you, but I don't much care to keep you alive, either. So I'll give you this one last chance to save yourself. Don't you never come by this house again, not even in your dreams. It'll be your death if you do. Now, you believe me?"

Hunt stared at his assailant in terror and nodded his head.

The inspector nodded back and hefted his cowering victim to his feet. "All right, then. Here," and the man took out a handkerchief and pushed it into Hunt's hand. "Press that against the cut. Now, off." And he pushed Hunt down the steps and back into the street.

Hunt stumbled along like a drunken man until he could hail a cab. Once hidden within, however, all marks of distress melted away from him, and he rather gleefully gave the driver his address, wincing slightly at the pain in his cheek.

He arrived home, and after reassuring his wife that he was well, an assertion she was never too ready to believe but had given up on ever hearing otherwise, he retired to his bed with instructions to be roused at once should anyone ask for him.

He awoke on his own, without being roused. He breakfasted in peace, sat about his parlor all morning at leisure, and was just about to sit down to dinner before word came that a young person was waiting for him at the street door.

"Let him enter!" Hunt commanded, and soon Mr. Tuppman was sitting opposite him at the darkened hearth. "Any trouble, Tuppy?" Hunt asked, leaning forward hungrily.

Tuppman shook his head in derision of the inspector's powers. "Like follerin' a black cat through the snow. But 'e was forever to make 'is report like you wanted."

"Yes, he's not the most energetic fellow, though remarkably quick when he needs to be," and Hunt massaged the raw scar on his face. "But the report. You say he wrote it?"

Tuppy nodded. "Come out this morning and made straight to the Saracen's Head to post it with the mail coach. Saw 'im give it over to the driver 'imself."

"Any difficulty there?"

Tuppy smiled at this, broadly, and reached into his tattered shirt to remove the square of neatly folded paper.

Hunt snatched it away and looked closely at the subscription. The name meant nothing to him. "Mr. Caldecott." Certainly an alias Price used abroad. The direction that followed was likewise vague and obscure. "To be held until called for."

The last line caused Hunt to stop, however, as its lethal meaning became clear to him.

"The inn at Bellminster."

CHAPTER XVII
HOMECOMING

Y ou were sleeping so well, sir," Raphael said, "I thought not to disturb you. We're just another hour away at this rate."

Tuckworth stretched in his seat and his joints cracked comfortably. Home, he thought, and breathed in deeply the scent of familiar soil, the must of manure in the fields, the strident sweetness of bluebell and buttercup. And then he recalled all that he had left undone behind him, and the momentary respite of forgetfulness vanished like the mist in the morning.

He shook his head, determined not to allow such fretfulness to cloud his homecoming. As he caught first sight of the cathedral, however, he was shocked at the dreadful prospect it afforded. Of course he knew he would not find again that majesty of the lofty spire or the stolid architecture of the two stately towers as they broke from beneath the horizon in the distance. Yet neither was he prepared for the ruined, abject reality that confronted him, the burned-out hulk looking like some derelict vessel, abandoned amid the scorched bronze seas of chest-high corn surrounding the town on every side. He was home indeed, but it seemed a homecoming as alien as anything he had known in the city these few days past.

"I trust the rebuilding is going well," Raphael commented innocently.

"No," Tuckworth replied. "It's not going at all. I doubt you'll notice any difference in the cathedral."

Unsure what to say, Raphael only mentioned that it was a pity and then remained silent. The dean was intent on brooding, he could tell, and at such times it was best to let him brood.

The coach rumbled into Bellminster, pulled into the yard of the Granby Arms, and came to rest just as the setting sun was turning the western sky to orange behind the brown silhouette of the cathedral. Raphael tossed their bags to the waiting porter and helped the dean down from above to set foot at last on his home ground.

The innkeeper came bustling out, a small, quick, breathless sort of man, his apron streaked and smeared with the marks of his station, his day's growth of whiskers bristling in a welcoming grin. "Good to have you home again, vicar!" he called.

Tuckworth smiled. It was a hopeless cause, trying to get these people to recognize his new post, and frankly he liked the music of *vicar* better than that of *dean*. The word sounded more like himself, he thought.

"Good to be home, Taggart," he replied, taking his bag from the porter.

"And young painter!" Taggart exclaimed in surprise, seeing Raphael. "Didn't think to see you in Bellminster again. Figured a chap what's seen London don't never turn back."

"Well, sometimes he does, Mr. Taggart," Raphael confessed, shuffling his feet nervously. He didn't like the attention his return might occasion, looking as it did like failure, and he would have preferred to sneak unseen into the town, except for one pair of eyes he wanted desperately to be seen by.

"Any news while I've been away?" Tuckworth inquired casually, knowing that he could hope for no better source of gossip than the innkeeper, and wishing to hear some quaint bit of nothing to take his mind off his travels and settle him finally and immovably at home.

"News enough, I'm thinking," Taggart answered, "though you'll know what that is better'n I will."

"Will I?" the dean replied, but already Taggart had turned his attentions to other guests, and Tuckworth had no great care to pursue the matter. He wanted to be home, inside the comfort and coziness of the vicarage, just as soon as he might get there. He peered across the breadth of Cathedral Square to the dusky figures of the towers looming above, and taking Raphael by the arm he set off straightaway.

"Come on," he urged. "We can find lodgings for you after we've said our hellos, eh? Or you can curl up in a corner of the parlor. I don't think you'll mind that much." The dean smiled at his own facetious wit, and for some unaccountable reason he began to feel young once more, and eager, and happy to be home. This was Bellminster, after all, and its air was liquor to him. He was stopped again and again on his way by men and women willing to pause for a kind word, a warm greeting, and Tuckworth would have gladly shared his time, feeling revived by such friendly advances, if he had not felt more sharply the pang to be finished with his journey, truly finished.

"Yes, yes," he found himself repeating mechanically. "I'll tell you all about it." "Yes, stop by tomorrow. Or I'll visit you, how's that?" "Yes, certainly it's a great place. London is a great city." Though, great as it is, it's not this, he thought to himself. London is not Bellminster, and it's a pity for London that it isn't.

Finally he came near enough to the vicarage to be seen, and as if his approach had been foretold there stood Lucy in the doorway, Lucy looking as lovely—no, lovelier—as when he had left. She ran to her father and threw her arms about him and kissed his cheek, and he could have wished for no better welcome than that, not if the entire town had turned out.

She pulled away to look at him again, and then her eye fell on Raphael. She squealed, positively squealed, and blushed so that even in the gathering dusk her cheeks fairly glowed.

"Raphael, I didn't . . ." But her voice trailed off in confusion.

"Now, now, my dear," Tuckworth said, taking her arm and leading her back to the vicarage. "We'll have time enough to talk about how Raphael got here and why he's going to be staying for a very long time. But first I must get home and place my old bones into my own chair." He laughed, and it felt particularly good to laugh. "We'll have Mrs. Cutler bring us something cold from the larder and get some beer from the Arms and we'll have a long talk."

Tuckworth led the way into the vicarage and set his bag down by the door.

"I'm home, Mrs. Cutler!" he called, and turned into the parlor to rest himself at long, long last before his hearth.

"Good evening, Dean Tuckworth."

From across the room, Reverend Mortimer stood grinning a haughty, self-satisfied grin, and Tuckworth's heart rolled down into his boots. This was certainly not the homecoming he had looked for.

"Father," Lucy said excitedly as she entered the parlor, still clinging close to Raphael's side, "Reverend Mortimer stopped by with the most wonderful news from London."

"A trifle," the rector replied, waving his hand lazily in the air. "Miss Tuckworth makes more of my news than it deserves."

Lucy ignored this false modesty, however, and continued no less enthusiastically. "He's brought us a miracle. Five hundred pounds! Enough to raise the cross and shore up the floor. He's saved the crypt, Father!"

Tuckworth looked closely at Mortimer, and beneath the man's shell of magnanimity he detected the smug victory that the rector was only just trying to hide. "A remarkable gift, indeed," the dean offered as congratulations. "If I may ask, who is the author of this miracle?"

Mortimer smiled again, demurring. "I am afraid, Dean Tuckworth, that our benefactor requests that I preserve his anonymity. Of course we must respect his wish, if only to humor him. I must tell you, it required all my arts of persuasion to extract even the small sum mentioned. I say *small,* you understand, only in comparison to the whole. Five hundred pounds cannot be considered paltry on its own account."

"Of course not," Lucy enthused. "Semple got started today. They're building a scaffold over the cross, and setting timbers below in the crypt, and soon they'll bring in a great wagon and hoist the cross up on a chain and away it can go to be repaired!"

"How marvelous," Tuckworth said. "Tell me, Mortimer, how did you manage it?"

Mortimer shrugged as though he thought it was nothing. "I was tireless in my appeal, that is all, and finally won the gentleman over to our cause."

"I see," the dean commented, less gladly than his daughter might have hoped. "Well then, will you join us in a glass to celebrate?" Tuckworth knew that Mortimer never indulged.

"I fear I must be on my way," the rector replied, taking up his hat. "I only stopped in to see how the day's work has progressed. Miss Tuckworth is an admirable administrator of these matters, I must say." And the rector shot Lucy an ingratiating smile.

"Well, if you must go, then I'll show you out," Tuckworth said, taking Mortimer by the arm and ushering him quickly past Lucy and Raphael. When they were alone in the foyer, he spun the younger man about. "Look here, Mortimer," the dean began in a hushed voice, "you don't know what you're getting yourself in for. The less you have to do with that man, the better."

"And I can assure you, Mr. Tuckworth, that you have let yourself out of more than you know. Our anonymous friend only requires some special attention, a right which his generosity and resources more than warrant. If you are incapable of supplying that, then others will have to do it in your stead."

"Tell me, where is our anonymous friend today? I know he left London. Has he provided you with an address, some way to contact him?"

Mortimer shook his head. "And should I so readily betray the trust of one who is doing so much for you and your cathedral? I see you think very little of me, Mr. Tuckworth, to suppose that I would do anything so mean."

"You don't understand! You've thrown yourself in the middle—"

"I have positioned myself in the middle of an affair that desperately wants my services. The Lord will provide for the cathedral in the end, Mr. Tuckworth," Mortimer sniffed. "Where some may fail in their duty, others will step forward. Good evening."

Mortimer placed his hat upon his head, looked at himself in the glass quickly, and left. Behind him, the dean fumed silently and determined not to let this matter rest. Price had managed to place a spy in Bellminster, that was obvious, a ready source of information to keep tight reins upon Tuckworth. Some way must be found to open Mortimer's eyes. But the dean was too tired to think of a way that night. He went back inside and gave himself up to rest and ill-temper and Mrs. Cutler's cold meat pies.

The rector, however, did not go home, not at once. He marched a very straight path across Cathedral Square to the Granby Arms, where he strode righteously past the tavern and entered the inn. Taking a candle from the unattended desk, he ventured back into that labyrinth of dusty halls until he came to a weathered old door. Knocking softly twice, and then once, and then twice again, he waited.

The rector heard the bolt draw back, and he smiled at the eccentricities of the wealthy. The door opened an inch and stopped. An eye appeared at the crack, and the door then swung the rest of the way.

"Quick, quick," Price muttered.

Mortimer entered with a bow, as though he had been welcomed warmly. "Are you well, Mr. . . . um, Mr. Caldecott?"

"Fine." Price closed and bolted the door again, then retired to a worn old easy chair.

"Glad to know it, sir. The accommodations are meager, I daresay. Not what a gentleman must be accustomed to."

"A gentleman can grow accustomed to a great deal. I saw the dean arrive," he added nervously. "Well?"

"I have assured you, Mr. Caldecott, you need have no worry for Dean Tuckworth. He is no longer involved in the matter. All communications can move through me exclusively. The fact of the matter is, I have set things in motion that will materially alter the dean's position relative to the Cathedral Fund. Indeed, you should not be surprised to hear, in the near future, that Mr. Tuckworth has been relieved of that responsibility entirely." And Mortimer smiled at the thought of how he had spent his time in London, and the very satisfactory talk he had shared with the bishop.

Price nodded and seemed to relax slightly at the news, but only very slightly. Indeed, the redness about his eyes and the dank, wispy strands of his hair, the limp collar and his soiled cuffs indicated a severe lack of relaxation for some time. If Reverend Mortimer had looked upon his benefactor with open eyes, instead of through the softening lens of avarice, he might have wondered at Price's appearance and inquired after his health. To the rector's mind a rich man is ever healthy, however, and often good, and always right, so he noticed nothing.

"Very well," Price said at last, stepping back to the door. "I'll be expecting a letter within the next few days. See that you pick it up from the innkeeper and bring it here."

"Of course."

"Return tomorrow after dark."

"Yes."

Price unlocked the door and waited for Mortimer to make a move to leave. "What else?" he snapped.

"Are you not curious as to the progress of the cathedral?"

Price seemed to come to himself at this, and some of his old command returned. "Naturally, Reverend Mortimer, I am curious. I kept an eye on the proceedings all day from that window," and he motioned toward the closed curtains across the room. "Things are moving handsomely, I daresay. I wonder how they found so much timber so quickly."

"The millworks—"

"I must tell you, Mortimer, your activity in this business has been noted, and your sense of decorum is irreproachable." The rector bowed. "It grieves me to consider that, were it not for the slack attentions offered by some parties, I might never have discovered how invaluable you could be." Again Mortimer bowed, even lower than before.

"Duty—" he began, before Price cut him off.

"If you will excuse me now, I have work to attend to."

"At such an hour, too. My little industry, I confess, is as nothing next to yours, sir."

But Price had already opened the door and was waiting impatiently to let Mortimer out.

The rector left the inn as unnoticed as he had arrived. Making his way across Cathedral Square in the direction of the rectory, his own fine new house on the farther side of Bellminster, he looked up at the stars, and through the stars to something greater, and he smiled in smug certainty that he was serving a larger purpose here, one that was sure to reward his efforts as they deserved. "Duty," he murmured softly to the breeze. "Duty." And he disappeared into the night.

CHAPTER XVIII

THE CRYPT

D awn was hours away when Tuckworth rose from his bed, stiff and sore after a night of anxious tossing. He dressed in the dark, fumbling with his shoes and stuffing his clerical collar (which was becoming tighter with each passing year and now nearly choked him) into his pocket. As he descended the stairs, struggling against his weight to keep the floorboards from shrieking, he heard Raphael's soft snores from the parlor. They had made a later night of it than any of them had intended, a bad night. Raphael was constrained to account for his return in terms that made his doubts too apparent. Tuckworth lied again and again to his daughter, masking any reference to his troubles in a mundane account of London's sights. Poor Lucy was sure only that something was dreadfully wrong with both men, though she was unclear as to why they should be out of humor with so much good news to attend their return. And Mrs. Cutler had fretted over allowing Raphael to spend the night in the parlor, insisting that the sofa was no fit bed for a man.

And then there was the prayer. Lucy, in her ebullient spirits over the day's grand news, her overflow of enthusiasm that at last work was moving forward, the job of rebuilding started in good and earnest, had asked her father to lead them all in a prayer of thanksgiving.

"You know, dear," she had pressed nervously, "as we used to do."

Tuckworth had tried to beg off, to say he was tired, that the hour was late and his recent journey exhausting.

"Just a short prayer, Father," Lucy had replied, perplexed. "That's all."

He looked into her eyes, dark and questioning, confused yet loving and hopeful, always hopeful. "Yes, my dear," he said at last, and they all joined hands together in a circle in the parlor.

"May we all be truly thankful at these tidings," he prayed. "May we find the strength to labor, and the guidance to labor rightly, in the days to come. May we each follow the true path before us, and shun the false. And may we learn what is asked of us each to do, and have the will to carry it out."

A moment of heavy silence followed.

"In God's name," Lucy added, giving her father's hand a silent squeeze.

"In God's name," Raphael and Mrs. Cutler answered. Without another word, Tuckworth removed himself from the circle and went upstairs, feeling Lucy's eyes upon him all the way.

Yes, taken all together, it was a disastrous evening.

The dean quietly entered his study now, crossed the room, and left it again through the private door that led out into the open vastness of Bellminster Cathedral. Standing alone in the side aisle, he could believe he was truly inside the cathedral, the same place he had wandered tirelessly for years upon years, a place of solace, of comfort, even in these latter days, these doubting days. Moving out into the roofless nave, however, stepping around the toppled and topless columns, pews buried in melted lead or burned to charcoal, windows yawning empty and dreadful, he was no longer in his cathedral. He was in some netherworld, not here or there, neither inside nor outside. It was a sham sanctuary, more a piece of stagecraft than of worship. He had acted in amateur theatricals at university, and the sort of half-walls and pasteboard windows his fellow students had constructed for the purpose seemed to loom about him once more in the darkness, though on a grander scale.

Tuckworth meandered aimlessly around and about the place in a dream of timeless remembrance, every nook seeming right and yet wrong, a bad copy of a faulty memory, like a childhood home disparaged by fate and lived in now by unnamed strangers hording other times, other connections. And as he walked he thought, or rather dreamed, of his time in London, the terrible mess he had made of everything, the awful facts that clung to him like a stench. He had been bested by a murderer, a molester of children, a vile and ruthless monster. Was he angry now with moral outrage or injured pride? He hardly cared to consider the difference between the two. The truth remained that he was impotent now, unable to advance one step in any worthwhile direction.

But perhaps not helpless forever. Price had left himself one avenue of communication into Bellminster, a dark stream by which he might keep his eye on Tuckworth. Maybe, through Mortimer, the dean could break back upon his adversary, discover where Price had run and bring him to earth. Tuckworth almost chuckled at the thought of recruiting Mortimer as an ally. Still, one must be open to the good in men. It was always there, though buried deep sometimes, smothered with malice and greed, pride and raw ambition. Yes, even Mortimer might be made to help.

The dean stepped farther out into the nave, into the night, where the transept cut across the center aisle and the crypt opened at his feet, its stone stairway gaping below, a dark hole into eternity. That place had become his sanctuary lately, down in the earth where he might hide, out of the rain, out of the wind and the eyes of curious men, to bury his faith. He never told Lucy about his wanderings there, she would have worried so. It was too dark now to venture below into its mysteries. He should have brought a lantern, he realized. But the night was warm, if sticky, and the stars twinkled hazily amid layers of moist air above, so it was no hardship to be out-of-doors, even within Bellminster Cathedral.

While Tuckworth peered down into that shadowy hole, cut into the cracked and crumbling floor, something caught his eye, a flickering of the dark, not a light exactly, but an appearance of shadow where all should have been black. He squinted and stared more deeply still, trying to cut his way into the night. Nothing stirred. He looked askance, hoping the corner of his sight might detect something that was invisible to his more direct vision, and this time he thought he saw it again, a faint gray that swayed in the dark.

The dean descended into the crypt. The steps, though hidden by night, were known well enough to him. He could have managed blindfolded. But tonight there was no need. When he made his way down the twisting staircase he saw, in the distance stretching out beneath the nave, the pale glow of a smoldering lantern resting upon one of the dozen stately and imposing tombs.

"Hello?"

Tuckworth's voice shook against the ancient stones and died. The lantern flickered away, but no voice answered, no shape came forward.

"I see you there," the dean lied, trying to lure someone out. "You might as well answer me."

Silence still.

Tuckworth walked into the crypt toward the distant light. It was a dark lantern, the sort that he and Hunt and Raphael had so lately employed in their larcenous invasion of Price's house. The shutter had been left open but was pointing away from the stairs, so that Tuckworth moved now by the reflected light of the pale stone of tomb and pillar. He moved past cold, hard effigies, human figures prone in noble severity, resting in wait for the final days, a mimicry of repose as dry and empty as a row of hollowed gourds.

He reached the lantern, standing in solitary exile at the farthest reach of the crypt. The new timbers of the restoration lay strewn about, ready for the morrow's carpenters to raise them from floor to ceiling, propping up the sky above to save the dead beneath from a crushing second death. The dean picked up the lantern and looked at it. It might have been left by a workman, he thought. Did they use such lanterns? The flame within was burning low, the oil pan nearly empty. He opened the shutter full and blared its light about the crypt. Shadows swam in concert from left to right, then back again, but he saw nothing else that moved.

With the lantern in hand Tuckworth made his way back to the front of the crypt, back to the staircase. He closed the shutter as he went. The flame seemed a rude intrusion upon the solemnity of the scene about him, and he certainly had no need for its light. As he neared the stairs, however, he heard something that made him stop and bend his thoughts behind him. Without turning, he listened intently to the darkness. A scrabbling of pebbles, the sudden slip of a misplaced foot, the breathless gasp of a quick intake of air that is the opposite of a cry broke the stillness. Might have done, had he been listening for it. But now it might only be imagination, or the scurrying of rats, or the sound of the floor above settling into the space below. It might have been a hundred things.

He spun about. Nothing.

"All right," he called in a half whisper, respectful of the silence, "that's enough." He moved back into the crypt and opened the lantern again. "You're simply trying my patience now, whoever you are. This is not the hour and this is not the place to be fumbling about in the dark after . . . well, whatever it is you're after. I insist you show yourself."

Tuckworth waited, holding his breath for some revelation, his eyes darting over the shadows for the least movement. Was he speaking only to the stagnant air and the walls, the dust and the vermin? He began to feel very foolish. Besides, he had a recent history of nocturnal visitors to his cathedral, mysterious figures shrouded by night and dark. He had no relish to renew the experience.

"Suit yourself, then," he muttered, though unsure whether he was referring to himself or the silent intruder. He set the opened lantern on the corner of the nearest tomb.

"I'm leaving this for you. You might need it if you hope to find your way out of here." Without another glance backward, Tuckworth left the crypt and returned to the realm above.

An hour passed, and once more the world of the cathedral was grave and still, the silence broken by cricket and owl, the yelp of a fox and the fierce hiss of a stray cat, but not by human footsteps. The moon was swiftly falling from the sky, and soon the first pink of dawn would taint the black of the eastern night, when a figure rose out of the ground. A dark shape lifted itself out of the cathedral floor, climbing stealthily from the crypt, moving slowly, a cloaked figure, a patch of moving shade, a ghostly traveler. Once free of the earth, the figure pulled the cloak more firmly about itself and moved off in the direction of the Granby Arms. Passing beneath vast doorways that held nothing in, nothing out, drifting under the tympanum with its grotesque depiction of God's final vengeance and scant mercy, the figure quickened its step, walked briskly away from Bellminster Cathedral, over the square and into the sullen dark of the inn.

And as it moved, a pair of eyes followed its dark course. And when it was gone, a second figure emerged from the shadows of the side chapel, out into the moonlight. Tuckworth stood there until dawn could be seen over the rooftops of Bellminster, and as he stood he wondered, and he worried.

CHAPTER XIX
THE GAME RESUMED

oney? You come to me for money again?"

Hunt buried his head in his hands for just a moment before looking up. "It's not simply the money," he pleaded.

John Constable let out a scoffing laugh as he reached across the table in the dated opulence of his parlor, his own paintings surrounding him on the walls, testaments to a career now finished, and took up a small glass of yellow liquid. He sipped, and made a grousing face. "My doctors want to kill me," he insisted, setting the glass down again. "What else is it then, if not the money?"

Hunt steadied himself, preparing to make the same appeal he had made a half-dozen times already that day, to a half-dozen other scoffers. "I must go north to Bellminster. Tonight. Now. The night coach north leaves within the hour."

"Running from your creditors at last?" Constable chided. "We all knew it would come to this eventually, Hunt. You've been hopping about on one foot avoiding your debts for too long now. Begging loans that invariably get settled as gifts or actions in court. It was only a matter of time before they put the collar on you. Not that the Marshalsea wouldn't do you a bit of good, notwithstanding the inconvenience, of course."

"Yes, yes," Hunt conceded readily. "I am aware of my shortcomings better than any man alive, and better than any woman, too, save one. But this has nothing to do with myself."

Constable looked closely at his guest. Indeed, while he had been touched often enough by Hunt—as who hadn't?—there was something more frantic to this request. The man's youthful face seemed suddenly to show its age, the merry smile set by a grim and careworn determination. "It has nothing to do with you? But the money will go to you, correct?"

"Yes, John, it will, but it will not benefit me."

"Who then?"

"You recall the dean we dined with earlier this week."

"With the young friend?"

"That's him."

Constable grimaced again, and reached for the glass of medicine. "I haven't slept well since that young man spent the evening berating me with his theories. I don't like these disruptions to my life, Hunt. I'm past debate. I'm an old man and I just want to stroll slowly to the grave, but this turmoil undoes me." And he sipped again at the distasteful liquid, draining the glass with a sour grunt. "Vile."

"John," Hunt prompted gently. "The loan."

"That's right," Constable said, coming suddenly to life. "You owe me two pounds, seven and six from that dinner the other day."

"John!"

Constable leaned back in his chair with a look of condescension and an audible sigh. "Very well, tell me why you need this money so desperately."

Hunt leaned forward. "I fear that our friend, the dean, is in danger. He's being hounded by a desperate man, a man with no scruples or morals. The man's gone to Bellminster now, and the dean doesn't know."

"Write a letter."

"I would have written one if I'd known how hard it was to get coach fare and a few days' lodging money."

Constable laced his withered fingers together across his chest. "And why is it so hard?"

Leigh Hunt steadied himself and stared stolidly into his host's eyes. "It is hard because I am a wastrel and a vagabond."

The old man chuckled silently. "Very good. You are a vagabond, Hunt. It's good to hear you say it." Hunt merely spread his hands apart, the defendant in the dock confessing to his crime. "So," Constable continued, "you've already seen how many men about this loan?"

"Six."

"And they all turned you down."

"They none of them understood the seriousness of this business. A man's life may be in peril."

"Yes, a man none of them knows or has ever seen. It's hard to have sympathy for a name. And why am I number seven? Why not appeal to me first?"

Hunt looked boldly at his interrogator. "Because I sponged off you already this week."

"You did! And you are . . . ?"

Hunt sighed. "A vagabond."

The old man chuckled again. "So you've made your usual rounds and wound up back here."

"John," Hunt begged, staring desperately at his watch. "The coach leaves in three-quarters of an hour."

The older man squinted and looked up at the clock on the mantelpiece. "Well," he said at last, "you're lucky that I've met your friend the dean of Bellwether, or wherever. Nice chap. Sensible. What will you need?" And Constable rang for his butler.

Leigh Hunt laughed quietly in relief and gratitude. "A fiver should get me there and set me up until I can—"

"Until you can find someone else to sponge off of? No, thank you. I'll give you twenty to start, and if you want more, you write to me. I'll not send you off like a banshee to suck the life out of your dean."

"A vampire, you mean," Hunt corrected. And within the hour, he was settled aboard the night mail north from the Saracen's Head Inn, with nothing to occupy his mind but his fears and his thankfulness. And something else besides, something nearly approaching to shame. Leigh Hunt had never made any bones about his failings, or suffered many qualms about them. He had always been the first to accuse himself, and yet this confession to a man like Constable, an old and valued friend, stirred him to something like contrition. He was not so very contrite, however, but that he had booked a comfortable passage for himself inside the coach, and within a very few minutes he was sound asleep.

As Leigh Hunt slept, Dean Tuckworth roused himself from a satisfactory nap. Not that the day had been productive of anything very likely to make his slumber restful. Indeed, it had begun with a visit to Reverend Mortimer, which is to say it had begun badly. Tuckworth had tried every persuasive means within his power, every trick and trope he could devise to convince Mortimer to divulge Price's whereabouts. He hoped to visit Price again and renew his efforts, he said, to elicit further gifts. He wished to send Price a letter of thanks for his donation to the Cathedral Fund. He went so far as to express a desire to commemorate a side chapel in Price's name as the first great benefactor of the cathedral's rebirth. This last stratagem came nearest to success, and Mortimer went so far as to commend Tuckworth on finally thinking as he ought in the matter. But in the end, the rector declined to give up the address. So far as the dean knew, Price could be anywhere from Southampton to the Hebrides, and nothing he could think to do would clear away the obscuring mist that had dropped over the man.

Nor were the prospects of peace much more reassuring at the vicarage. True, work on the cathedral was progressing marvelously well. Abraham Semple and his men were busy below, upon, and above the earth, forcing timbers into position in the crypt to shore up the sagging nave above, hammering a scaffold into shape and erecting it into the sky over the Great Cross. Only the matter of a few days, or a week at most, should see their work accomplished.

Within the vicarage, however, matters appeared more somber. Raphael had gone off at first light, leaving Lucy behind. He needed to wander the fields and hills of Bellminster in solitude, he had said, "talking to the landscape." When Mrs. Cutler heard that, she almost shrieked at the insanity of it. And when she reported the incident to the dean, she had tapped her head meaningfully and whispered, "City vapors, get into the brain."

Tuckworth had no desire to educate the woman, so he allowed her to doubt Raphael's senses. Lucy was another matter, however, and after he rose from his nap he called her into the study and tried to relieve her concerns over the young painter.

"He only needs to find his way, Lucy," he assured her, though vainly. "There's nothing we can do to help him, outside of being pleasant to him when he's here and patient when he's not."

"But why would he come back and then act as if he wants to leave again? He doesn't seem like the same person at all that he was when he was here before."

"You must trust that he is, Lucy. Or at least trust that this new person owns all the good qualities still that you admired so much. Just give him time and I'm sure you'll see that he's not changed so much as all that."

"Yes," Lucy acknowledged, not convincingly. "But it's not Raphael alone."

Tuckworth looked at his daughter, stared deeply into her eyes for a moment, saw there the confusion and fear he had been avoiding, and looked away.

"Dear, what's been troubling you?" She asked the question softly, as though she were afraid of disturbing a bird she was intent to cage, and yet her words plunged into his heart with the chill effect of a cold needle.

"I'm not sure anything's been troubling me so greatly," he replied, trying to deflect her cares.

But they would not be put aside, not any longer. She had found a new strength in herself these past days, and she was bringing it to bear now where she needed most to feel its power. She reached out and grasped his wrist tenderly, yet firmly. It was a grasp he could not escape.

"What is it? What has it been?"

"Oh, just London putting me out of sorts."

"This isn't just about London. What is it?" She waited through his silence. "Is there something you're hiding, Father?"

"Hiding?" He could not keep his voice from shaking as he said the word, betrayed by his own breath.

"Tell me, dear."

He looked at her again, forced himself to see her soul, and what he found there gave him a moment of surprise. He saw her fear struggling to be hope, her hope trying to be strength. He saw in her a resolve he had never noticed before, and it shocked him.

"I really can't imagine. . . ." His voice trailed off helplessly.

"Tell me." She raised a hand to his shoulder and laid it delicately there. He placed his own on top. "Tell me. Is it Mother?"

Tuckworth folded his daughter into his arms and held her hard against him for a moment. Then he held her out again and saw the glowing joy of love radiating from her eyes and her smile and her glistening tears.

"Lucy—"

She held her fingers to his lips. "Don't worry, dear. Don't say anything, not if you don't want to. I don't want to force anything from you. I only want . . ." Her voice caught for a moment. "I only want you to know that I see you suffering. You don't have to tell me why. Just don't be afraid to show me. Don't be afraid of *me*." Tuckworth stood there, silent, dumbfounded at the maturity of her wisdom, the sudden truth of her love, the infinite capacity for forgiveness that dwelled in his child's heart. "I can't cure your troubles," she continued. "I understand that. But at least allow me to be a solace." And she reached up and brushed a tear from his cheek.

Tuckworth went out after supper, a feeling of lightness about him, a sense that there might be relief for him yet in the world, that his sins, compounded and unnameable as they were, might yet find a kind of absolution. When Raphael had returned from his wanderings even he had appeared in a better humor, and said that he would go back out tomorrow and take his paints with him, and Lucy might come along if she had no objection to watching him sketch. Their supper had been quite a merry meal.

And now Tuckworth hoped to relax a bit at the tavern and reacquaint himself with his home. Those few scant days away felt like months, and he needed the company of those who had never heard of Hamlin Price and had never seen the great city or dreamed of its awful secrets. For really, what else could he do? He found almost a relief in his helplessness now. Time enough tomorrow to feel frustrated.

He stepped inside the glow of the tavern, and every man there turned and smiled or nodded at him. He sat at the scarred old oaken bar and Taggart came over with three pints gripped in his fists.

"Vicar?"

"The sherry, Taggart."

The innkeeper-*cum*-barman nodded knowingly and went off, returning soon with a delicate glass of nutty brown-amber. Tuckworth sipped and looked about him.

"So, London?" Taggart commented from behind the dean.

"Yes, London."

"And's good to be home, then."

The dean turned and smiled. "That it is," he acknowledged. "You seem to be doing well," he commented idly, noting the crowd.

"Oh, aye. Well enough. Inn's proper busy, too. Can't complain on it."

"Lots of travelers stopping here?"

"Might say. Simon McTeach's old uncle and aunt, come for a visit. Another old couple touring the country."

"That reminds me," the dean said. "Someone was nosing about the crypt early this morning. You think it might have been one of your tourists?"

Taggart shook his head. "Nah. Not them. In bed early and up late to breakfast."

Tuckworth shrugged. "Well, when you see them, you might mention that the place is hardly safe at the moment. Don't want anyone buried alive down there. It might not be good for your trade, eh?"

"Dying ain't never good trade for an inn, that's certain. Afeard I might have a bit of that to worry over soon."

The dean sipped his glass again. "How so?"

"Chap stopped in three nights past looking like death itself, all hollow and empty like. Keeps to his room, takes his meals there but don't eat much. Don't drink much, neither. If he dies in them rooms, it'll be a bad business for me and thankless work for you."

It would not have been the first time Tuckworth might be asked to deliver services for some stranger at the inn, but he hoped things would not come to that. "Sounds like he's just feeling poorly. The road can do that to a man."

"But he traveled in his own great coach. Man should be used to his own. Friend of Mr. Mortimer's."

Something empty and cold crept through Tuckworth. "A friend of the rector's?"

"Aye. Brought him down from London himself. But he's kept to his room these two full days now. Don't even peek out the door."

The dean set his glass upon the bar. "His name, Taggart. What's his name?"

The innkeeper paused and thought for a moment. "Caldecott."

CHAPTER XX

A CRY IN THE NIGHT

T he Granby Arms splayed under the midnight moon, a rolling, tumbling collection of stone and mortar, timber and wattle and cracked panes of smoky glass, more a series of buildings pasted together with spit and nails than a bright, hospitable British inn. What was once a spacious but simple residence had slowly, through the whim of reckless ambition, transformed itself from livery to travelers' rest to waystation, reflecting its jaded past in the odd angles and querulous styles that struck Raphael with his artist's eye as something incomplete, the notion of an inn drawn with a careless hand and left to molder on the page. Its hallways, twisted and tangled by thoughtless design, gathered greasy dust in the folds of their shadows. Decay seemed always to be just out of sight within its rooms, buried in chilly hearths and damp beds, inhabiting the dim borders of vision, like a sty one cannot quite see and cannot ignore.

"Your accommodations are already settled," Tuckworth was telling his young friend, looking out at the Arms from the front gate of the vicarage. "Taggart gave us a room hard by Price's."

"Why do you think he followed us here?"

"He didn't follow us," Tuckworth pointed out, his brow furrowing in confused concern. "He got here before us, set up this entire charade before we ever arrived. I don't understand it."

"Do you think he means to threaten you?"

"He's already done that."

"To harm you?"

"He's managed to do that as well." They both knew what was left, though neither spoke it. And yet, Tuckworth himself was not convinced that Price would try to kill him, though he could not say exactly why at the moment. "I don't know what's brought him here. But I want to keep him close until we learn more about it. You've never seen him, and we're reasonably sure he doesn't know you, so just make yourself easy in your room and keep track of comings and goings. Nothing intrusive, you understand. Nothing rash. Just keep your eyes and ears open."

"What plan do you have to catch Price?" Raphael asked eagerly.

"I don't have a plan. I'm rather hoping to stumble onto one."

"But what if I should learn something? What if I can find evidence—"

"We're not looking for evidence just yet."

"If I could get into his room, get him away so I can look about—"

"Raphael!" Tuckworth controlled himself with an effort. "We've already tried that. We tried to force matters and you know what happened. We were lured into a trap."

Raphael wanted to speak, looked bursting to say something, but the dean silenced him with a stern glance.

"Patience. Nothing rash. Nothing foolish. Just watch and listen. Understood?"

It was not in the painter's nature to take orders so curtly given, but he made a grudging nod, and soon he was across the square and settled in his room. He left the door cracked to hear the least footfall in the passage, and, crawling between the sheets, he propped himself up with a mountain of pillows, took a book that he had borrowed from the dean, and read by the light of a discreet candle in the hopes of staying, if not entirely awake, at least alert.

And now Raphael lay in his bed, well past midnight, struggling with wakefulness, the candle at his side snuffed in its own drippings, the open book lying facedown upon his chest. His mind wandered in that realm between here and not here, his nostrils filling with a loamy rottenness, the images of the past week colliding in the close, airless antechamber of sleep, aware of dreamless visions, nightmares of murder and lost love, Lucy a nursemaid standing by and smiling coolly while he painted pictures of children who were not children. There was a presence in the room just out of sight that made the wee ones cry and he could not stop them from crying. It was nothing really, no danger at all. They were in a perfect nursery, a fairyland of childhood wonders. But the children's fears would not be silenced and they huddled in shadows so thick that only their bare feet and hands could be seen, their toes gripping at the carpet, their fingers clawing the air. Their tears were ruining his painting, streaking his colors, smearing his line. Wouldn't they like to stop their bawling? Wouldn't they like a nice sweet if they stopped and came out into the light? They must stop this foolishness now, children, or pay the penalty! Cajole and tease and scold as he might, they wept and huddled and wept some more amid the sparkling delights of that terrible nursery.

He jerked his head up from the sweated moistness of his pillow. What was that weeping? The sound receded into the distance of the night, and he laid his head down once more, closing his eyes, trying to find his way to a dreamless slumber, a sleep without weeping children.

A weeping child! Raphael leaned up and listened tensely, alertly. He swung his legs about and shot out from under the bedclothes, sat on the edge of his bed and strained to pierce the night through the whisper of the vagrant wind. Had he heard weeping? Was it real, or just the waking memory of his dream? Nothing, no sound from out of the black, only the low moaning from the ill-fitting windows. Is that what he had heard? No! It had been a child, undeniably a child!

He groped slowly for the candle, prepared to strike a match, but hesitated and listened again. Something not the wind, something more strident, less musical floated on the air. He put the match down unstruck and rose, creeping out into the hallway.

He knew which room was Price's, two doors down, and squinted against the darkness as though he might hear better if only he could see. Raphael took a deep breath, then inched along the corridor, one hand gently brushing the wall, dusting the rough plaster until he felt the raised wood of a jamb, touched the smooth panels of a door, and moved on quietly to the next. Reaching it, he waited and listened, strained against the senseless night, leaned his head so near the wood that he could feel its coolness. He heard something. It was a low moan, sudden and abrupt. The wind? Under the door? The sound rose and fell, then caught, choked, and rose again. Sobbing! Softly, just on the verge of silence, but sobbing, unquestionably sobbing!

What might he do? He turned his face to the dark. What must he do? He turned back. With a hand that trembled slightly Raphael reached for the doorknob. He grasped it, a firm, light touch, and turned it with an unsteady slowness. It clicked. The sound cracked the night's silence and the sobbing stopped. Raphael pushed against the door. Nothing. He pushed again. The door rattled at him, petulantly. Bolted, of course, and he cursed himself.

What now? He looked again into the unanswering black. Could he retreat? No. It was too late. With another deep breath, he raised his knuckles and tapped gently on the door.

"Is everything well in there?" he whispered, muffled by the dark.

He felt a complete fool, but what else could he do? No voice, no sound called back to him. He knocked again, harder, and the very idiocy of his position made him speak more forcefully.

"I say, is everything well? I heard something! Hello!"

A rustling and a creaking, and then silence once more.

Something like madness welled up inside him. As though he might make his actions seem more sensible if they were only louder, he pounded jarringly, using the fleshy part of his fist against the door's thick panel. "I insist you open up! I heard a child in distress! Open up!" He hammered against the door again. He beat at it and called and listened, and then beat at it once more. The very lunacy of his position fueled Raphael's folly, and soon he was shouting and demanding to be let in. But the door set immovably against him.

At last, the faint glow of a light came down the turning of the hallway, and Taggart appeared, clad in a loose dressing gown, his striped nightshirt opened wide at the collar and his middle-aged girth bulging forth from behind a length of corded fabric.

"What's the row?" he muttered as he came down the hall, with that resigned, suffering tone that innkeepers acquire through years of settling drunken debates. "Mr. Amaldi, I'm surprised at you!" he exclaimed when he saw who it was disturbing the night.

"There's a child in that room," Raphael explained, pulling himself up in indignation. "I heard a child weeping and I insist—"

The bolt on the other side of the door shot back with a dismissive click, and Hamlin Price thrust his head out into the hallway, his eyes thick and red, his cheeks sunken. "Innkeeper," he said calmly, "thank God you're here."

Raphael almost leaped at the door, pushing Price aside and charging forward. With the instincts of a confirmed gossip, Taggart followed with the light, against Price's useless protests.

The room appeared empty, notwithstanding. Against the far wall rose a sturdy mound of trunks and boxes piled neatly. The bedclothes were turned down and the room stifled in heat. The window must have been closed for the heavy curtains drooped stiffly from their rods in spite of a brisk wind outside and a pungent, human scent hung in the air. Bureau, nightstand, desk, and chair all seemed perfectly right, scattered with the odds and ends a single man might have about him when traveling.

"Now, what's about a child?" Taggart asked, sounding calm and slightly amused, the best remedy he knew for these disputes. "Come, Mr. Amaldi. You dreamed it."

Raphael looked about helplessly. He darted for the closet and threw it open as Price yelled for him to stop, but the closet was empty save for more trunks. Price slammed the door closed, glaring coldly at Raphael with that supreme control he effected so readily.

"Now, gentlemen," Taggart began. "Let's just say it were a misunderstanding, eh?" He looked at Price and jerked his head meaningfully at Raphael. "Young man's an artist," he observed, and tapped at his own temple. "They dream."

"The young man had best not dream of my room again," Price said, crossing to the door and opening the way out to the hallway.

Taggart muttered some reassuring nonsense and took Raphael by the arm to lead him away. The innkeeper sniffed at the air as he escorted his young charge and said, "Smell's like a mouse as has died nearby. Probably in the wainscoting. I'll send the maid up tomorrow."

"You will not," Price commanded, then added, "I smell nothing."

Taggart shrugged and moved on. As Raphael passed Price at the door, however, he looked closely at the man, looked past his stern form, his commanding mien, to peer into his heart with an artist's intuition. He saw there the firm resolve, the unassailable wall that held the world at bay. He noted the stiff composure and uneasy strength. And with the training of his craft, he noticed with some surprise the watery redness below the eyes, the flush of the cheeks, the sullen, haggard jowl streaked and discolored, so that he was struck forcibly by the certain knowledge that it was Price he had heard sobbing.

"It must have been, sir," he told Tuckworth the next morning, when he rather fearfully related the events of the night.

The dean was not pleased to hear of Raphael's rash adventure. "You were stupid and reckless," he scolded, taking great pains to sound angry. Nor was he more pleased as he looked across his study at the other visitor who had come calling that morning. "And you come traipsing in with the night mail when you knew that Price might see you."

"Yes," Hunt confessed. "I might have adopted an ingenious disguise, a mustache and a cloak, perhaps, but I felt that smacked of melodrama. Of course, I could have tried for a washerwoman, but then we'd have passed into the comical mode, and that hardly seemed fitting. Come, Dean Tuckworth," he said soothingly, "we are hardly in control of circumstances here. The lad acted as he thought right, as did I."

The dean looked from one to the other of his two coconspirators, the one seeming too nonchalant, the other too ardent, and he shook his head. "I know, I know," he replied, breathing deeply and allowing his anger to drain away. "We're all doing the best we can, floundering about with too little that's certain and too much at risk. I understand. But we can't stop Price until we know what he plans. We've got to know why he's here."

"Don't we know already?" Hunt asked, with a telling look at the dean.

"No," Tuckworth asserted. "We don't. He might have come here to silence me, it's true. But then why would he have come in company with Mortimer? Why make himself known to anyone here if his aim was murder?"

Hunt nodded. "A valid point," he confessed. "I'll entertain it for the moment."

"So," Tuckworth continued, "until we learn something certain, something that can help us form a plan, we've got to stay calm, stay patient, or we might lose him again."

Raphael rose suddenly and paced across the room. "So while we wait the time out, Price is free."

"Yes, for now."

"Free to molest children."

"Good God, Raphael!" exclaimed the dean, more frustrated because he felt Raphael's frustration. "Would you stop being so damn youthful for a moment and look at the thing coldly? We have no proof."

"Then we must get it!"

"We can't just beat a confession out of Price."

"I'm afraid the dean is correct," Hunt agreed.

"Why?"

Both men paused.

"What was that?" Tuckworth asked at last.

"Why not bring Constable Hopgood into it and just beat the truth out of the man? It would be as much mercy as he's shown his victims."

"That's not the way," Hunt cautioned.

"But if we know the truth—"

"That's not the way," Tuckworth said more sternly.

"Well, your way looks like no way!"

The dean hesitated. Is this what it had come to, then, not just Mortimer, but now even Raphael accusing him of inactivity. And not merely custodial incompetence, but a lethargy that might prove fatal to nameless, faceless victims. *Was* his way the right way?

"I don't know, Raphael," he said wearily at last. "It might be you're right and I'm wrong. I can only do what I think best. But please, please believe me, lad. Price may look like a soft man, a decadent man, but he will stand up against any beating you and Hopgood might lay on him. He will outlast your fists and your boot heels."

Raphael suddenly looked shocked. "I didn't mean anything so drastic."

"Then what did you mean?" Hunt asked, stepping forward. "My young friend, I've seen enough official beatings to know what they are. If you're going to follow your passions then you'd better be prepared, fully prepared, for where they lead you."

"Raphael," Tuckworth added, walking over and placing a hand on the painter's shoulder, "forgive me if I was too critical. Under similar circumstances, convinced that there was a child in danger, I can't say I would have acted differently. But we must be cautious, all of us. Price now knows he's discovered. Doubtless he came here for a purpose, but we don't know how strong a pull that purpose holds upon him. He might stay on in spite of all, or he might run tomorrow. But remember, there are more lives at stake here than we can imagine, future lives, the lives of victims likely as yet unborn."

"I would risk them all again to save one life today," Raphael answered, strong and obstinate, "and I only wish to have the opportunity again."

Tuckworth sighed, and was about to say something when a knock sounded at the study door. Turning aside, he opened it, and Mrs. Cutler handed him a letter. "From the inn," she said.

The dean closed the door again and the three men looked anxiously at one another. Tuckworth tore open the envelope and hurriedly read what was scrawled there in Price's quick, nervous hand.

"He wants to see me," the dean reported, looking up. "Tonight. In the crypt."

CHAPTER XXI
CITY OF THE DEAD

uch a day Tuckworth never hoped to live through again. After the first shock of Price's letter had settled into something like a ruthless fate advancing on them, they determined to abide the time as casually as possible. It was a doomed plan. Raphael went off to paint (after first revoking his invitation to Lucy), and never returned, slinking off with the petulance of a whipped puppy. Tuckworth would have lied to say he was not ashamed for the boy. Raphael's anger was painful to Lucy and difficult to explain. Still, Hunt did a masterful job of easing the tensions that pervaded the household all that day and into the evening. He enchanted Mrs. Cutler with his light graces and effusive compliments. He kept Adam Black and his sister Mary amused with thoughtful attentions. And even Lucy found herself delighting in his conversation, so full of humor and irreverence. Had Tuckworth not seen through Hunt's effortless charm to the dire need that compelled it, even he might have been put at ease. As it was, Hunt was shrewd enough to allow the dean to worry in relative peace, while relieving him of the burden that Lucy's well-meaning cares might have added to his troubles.

The two men retired after supper to the study and remained there in taut silence, measuring out the night in clock beats. Price had named two in the morning for their assignation, and the hours hobbled by on crippled minutes. They shared barely a word. None seemed fitting for the occasion. Each man knew the other's thoughts as well as he knew his own. Their mutual ignorance, the dim wish that some spark might soon light up their darkness, showing them for an instant the blighted landscape of this miserable affair, the faint hope that the elusive end they pursued might be, if not reached, at least begun by the time dawn broke—such musings they kept to themselves. It was wasted breath to speak them.

Finally the clock struck the hour, and Tuckworth rose and moved toward the door out into the chapel.

"One hour," Hunt stated in a voice heavy with all they had not said during the day. "One hour and then I'll come looking for you."

The dean only nodded and went out into the night. He did not take a lantern. He had no need for one. Nor did he provide himself with any weapon for his protection. He knew such a precaution would be useless. Price would never have attempted anything knowing that others were close-by to corner him. The dean simply went out as he might go to any meeting with anyone who requested his time, only the beating of his heart betraying the fear within him, and he alone was aware of that.

Tuckworth descended the stairs into the crypt. It was quite dark and he wondered for a moment whether he had not come before his time. A noise on his left, however, a soft scuttling let him know that something was there with him.

"Price?"

There was no answer.

"Hamlin Price? Are you there?"

"No, sir. It's me, sir."

"Raphael!"

"I'm here to ensure your safety," the young man announced from the total darkness that surrounded them both. "Price is a murderer and a fiend, and we know he wants to kill you."

"We know nothing of the kind! For God's sake, boy, clear out of here before he arrives!"

A third voice came from out of the black, and a light shone brilliantly about the two men. "But he is here already, Dean Tuckworth."

The dean squinted into the rays of the lantern, but he could make out only the slimmest suggestion of a shadow. Still, it was Price. That was certain. "I had no idea the boy was here," Tuckworth insisted.

"Had you not?" Price answered, clearly not believing this denial. "I suspected you of some treachery. I arrived at midnight. Your man got here at one. I've been sitting here for the past hour listening to him breathe. Don't think you can overpower me now, either. I am armed." A metallic click echoed about the vaults.

Tuckworth turned to Raphael, and he had no time to manage his anger. "Get out of here, Raphael!" he commanded in hushed fury. "Get out now! Hunt's in the study! Go there at once, or so help me, you'll never see my daughter again!"

Raphael looked defiantly into the light, and for a moment Tuckworth feared what he might try. The dean grasped the painter by the shoulders and shoved him forcibly toward the stairs. "Go!" Raphael glanced at the dean once in hurt confusion, then darted upward.

Tuckworth took two deep breaths to steady himself. "I'm sorry about that, Price. The lad is rash."

"Youth will be rash, but what excuse do *you* have for such a foolish plan?"

It was useless to stand there and repeat his denial. Even Tuckworth realized how compromised he appeared. So he did not bother to try. "You wanted this meeting," he said. "What have you to tell me?"

Price opened the narrow beam of his lantern now, flooding the crypt, illuminating a scene as ancient as the millennium, as old and as reverent as man's fear of God. Stone pillars carved in faint relief, only lightly weathered by light or life, by wind or word these centuries past, extended into the darkness to uphold the low ceiling, standing like squat sentries beside the pale yellow of new timbers. The dry, sere scent of history mingled with the green woodiness of resurrection, while abandoned posts, hammers, and a few kegs of nails littered the floor.

Rough-hewn figures, blocky dukes and duchesses and petty noblemen, lay rigid upon their biers in pantomime repose. Iron enclosures of ornate and elaborate design rose here and there in the distance, their black tracery imposing the inviolable caste of death. Unfluttering banners and heraldic displays declared the supremacy of those who slept within these cages over their less happy kinsmen, mute beneath such tattered austerity. All else was silence and the grave. Armor and gown, silk and steel alike lay frozen by an unseen art, their majesty fit only for the eyes of Death itself to judge. Death and the dean, for Tuckworth was a frequent visitor to this dark world.

"The history of England, eh? The country is planted with dead aristocrats," Price observed with a sweep of his hand as he stepped forward, replacing his pistol in the folds of his cloak and raising his lantern to some knight's stony chest. "Who's this?"

Tuckworth stepped up to Price and looked at the dry, whiskered face encased in its semblance of mail. "That's the first Duke of Granby. He fought with Lancaster against York."

"Lancaster and York? And that's his duchess?"

"Yes." Tuckworth walked farther out into the crypt and approached the lady where she lay beside her husband, reciting her tale by rote as he had many times before to pilgrims more welcome than Price. "Lady Penelope. Like her namesake in ancient Greece, she was a symbol of faithfulness, a confidante and almost-sister to Lady Anne. When that unfortunate woman betrayed her dead lord and married King Richard, Lady Penelope refused to follow. Richard locked her in the Tower, but after his defeat at Bosworth Fields, Henry the Seventh rewarded Penelope's loyalty with marriage to

Sir Vincent Clapham, one of his chief knights, and made them duke and duchess."

The dean looked into the empty eyes of the first Duchess of Granby. He had always felt a fondness for her, a tender affection mingled with the pang of guilt and the ache of a past sin left unforgiven. She seemed so like his Eleanor.

"I was never one for history," Price confessed, straining to sound at ease. "Old stories about dead kings. The greatest impediment to success in this country is an overwrought fascination with the past." Price turned away and began to weave through the labyrinth of tombs. Tuckworth took one last look into the face of Lady Penelope, then followed.

Conversation hung between them like the monuments they wandered among, something massive and dread. Tuckworth was bound to let Price lead him on, to bring their unspoken subject to light. He was determined to torment Price with patience, knowing (as he felt certain he knew) that the man wanted to talk, that he longed to be understood, to display the scabbed surface of his sin like a boy with a fresh scar. Tomb after tomb drifted slowly by as they progressed into the farthest reaches of the crypt, Price asking the names of various slumberers, displaying a marked interest for a man who professed no love of history. A side passage opened on their left, separated by plain bars and a gate chained and locked. Price stopped to shine his light within.

"Some special family vault?" he asked.

"Final resting place for the bishops of Bellminster."

"Ah," Price murmured knowingly. "I understand from Mr. Mortimer that your bishop lives in London, rather a truant shepherd." Tuckworth merely nodded. "Well, it's good to know you've a place reserved for him here at last. And the deans, where do they reside?"

"Above, in the churchyard."

"Poor country cousins, eh?" And Price laughed nervously at his own dense wit before continuing, going farther and deeper into the earth, beneath the long expanse of the nave, asking about this duke, that earl, until at last the crypt ended.

He turned his attention to the final monument, a stone slab with no image of its occupant, no name or title etched upon its surface, more a table than a tomb. "And this is?" he asked, setting his lantern down upon the flat top.

"The Baronet Sir Philip Dorsay, youngest brother of the fifth duke."

"Really?" Price passed his hand delicately, almost lovingly down the length of the sarcophagus. "Why such modesty for a baronet?"

"He chose the wrong side in the Civil War. Threw in his lot with Parliament."

Price shook his head and made a sour face. "More history," he muttered. With nowhere to go now but back, he turned, and in turning came face-to-face with the dean. They stood for a moment, regarding each other, and for the first time Tuckworth could mark the change that had fallen over Price. It was more than his appearance, so haggard and pale. His very nature seemed altered. The commanding man was still there, the man of business, the controlled man. But chinks had begun to peek through his wall. The man beneath, the awkward, fearful man so horrified at the death of a dog, so desperate to prove himself strong, was making his way to the surface, no longer smothered under a weight of worldly ambition.

"You're suddenly a very patient man, Mr. Tuckworth," Price commented at last, sounding vexed.

"Am I?"

"Patient and dull. Nothing but talk of the dead."

"Give me a better topic," the dean offered.

A cloud fell upon Price, a darkness that enveloped him. "Death seems to be the only fit topic for us," he admitted, and his voice echoed plaintively in the sullen emptiness of the crypt.

Tuckworth urged the moment on. "Then let's talk of death."

"Of murder!" Price uttered harshly, feverishly as though the word scalded him. *Murder* reverberated against the coolness of the stone walls, rolled against the hardness of the crypt, then fell dead and still. "Murder," Price repeated in the ringing silence. "Isn't that what you mean?"

The dean only looked at him, a dry look that said nothing, asked nothing.

"You've been hounding me," he went on. "You and the others, dogging my footsteps, snapping at my heels. You've set yourselves against me. Why? What have I done to you?"

The dean stayed silent, stayed calm.

Price turned away. "I'm no murderer."

Tuckworth's silence came as a force of will, charged and clean like the air before a storm. He waited, a minute, two minutes, willing the storm to burst forth at last. Like a pot just before it boils, Price must be let alone, the heat of his need working on him. But the moment was agony.

Price suddenly turned back to Tuckworth, confronted him with the mad fire of anguish in his eyes, spittle jumping from his lips like trapped steam erupting. "I killed Quarles! But not Wick! I didn't kill Wick!"

Tuckworth held his breath, refused to show the least emotion, but stared at Price with eyes as dead and stony as those others around them who heard this confession. He must not judge, not now, not yet, only listen and be present and allow Price to open that place within his heart where his sin dwelled.

"Quarles did it himself. He attacked Wick," Price went on more easily, more in command now that the first awful truth had been burned away from his heart. "They struggled. I tried to help. I picked up something, I don't know what it was, something heavy, and struck Quarles with it. He died before he hit the floor. I could hear his skull crack beneath the blow like dry wood being broken! Wick was already dead, stabbed under the ribs, straight through to his heart. Quarles carried a stiletto with him. *That* was easy enough to dispose of," Price added with a sorrowful laugh.

The wall had been breeched, the secret place revealed, and now Tuckworth pressed at the wound, probing gently, like a surgeon. "Where did they die?"

"My study."

"What of the blood?"

Price shuddered. "On the rug. I burned it and replaced it with another." He grinned a sickly grin. "You never noticed the change."

"When did it happen?"

"I don't remember when. On that day, that afternoon or morning. It was before lunch, I remember. They came before lunch. Cook had gone. Wick made certain of that."

"Why did he make certain? What were they there for?"

"For blackmail," Price said, with almost a hint of injured pride, as though he would prove to Tuckworth that he was the victim in this, the abused party to be treated mildly, with respect for his suffering.

"Blackmail how? With what?"

But Price ignored the question and carried on with his narrative as he had rehearsed it over and over again all day, locked in the stifling heat of his lonely room. "Wick let me know that Quarles wanted to see me, insisted on coming in the middle of the day. He'd never done that before, had always come only when bidden. I should have known. Quarles was a devil. Men must do business with the devil at times. Wick had been acting strangely, too. I saw that afterwards. Short-tempered and furtive. But I thought nothing of it, or nothing much. I was the master of my world, and these little bumps in the road, these bits of unfortunate business, Wick had dealt with them before. How should I know what they were doing to the man, how they were wearing away at him? His weakness! His damn, common weakness!"

Price was talking to himself now, or to nothing at all, or maybe to

Malcolm Wick. Tuckworth tried not to move, not to make a sound, not even to breathe. The dean stood like one of the dead figures frozen about him, only his eyes and ears alive, tingling to catch it all.

"Wick brought him in. Brought him into the study, then refused to leave when I dismissed him. Quarles got right to his business. Spoke of wages, let me know my peril if I refused, exposure and scandal and arrest. Told me what his silence would cost. *Their* silence, for Wick stood by the whole time, tense, sweating, a party to the whole filthy business."

Price began pacing about the stark tomb of the baronet, circling aimlessly as he recalled the scene again, and Tuckworth wondered how many times he had relived it in his solitude. "What could I do? What power had I, with all my resources, to fight them off? Not then, but later, I thought. Appease them now, meet their demands, and then come at them subtly, secretly, when they couldn't expect it. I'm not violent. But a man must protect his own, must preserve what he is, what he's made. I began to write out an order on my bank. Five hundred pounds. A start, Quarles called it. But as I did, something went wrong with their plans.

"Quarles should have known he couldn't trust Wick. The man had no blood in his veins. Oh, he was proper. Always proper. The perfect secretary. But when it came down to it, he had no stomach. He began to cry as he stood there, whimper like a child. Quarles tried to ignore him. Told him to shut up. But soon the man burst out, sobbing. Said he couldn't go on. Called us vile beasts, sick and depraved. He would go to the authorities. He didn't want the money, he said. Didn't want his share of five hundred. He only wanted it to stop. Wanted me to stop! The effrontery! He was as thick into it as anyone! And why not? He'd as much as engineered the thing! It was all his planning, his doing! I'd been lost without him! He made it all possible!"

Price gasped as the tide of his emotions overwhelmed him, clutching at the bare tomb to steady himself and weeping, tears dropping to the ageless dust. Tuckworth realized that the man was telling more than he had meant to, had moved beyond rehearsal into the shadowy realm of truth. With surprise, the dean realized that he was digging his nails into the flesh of his palms, and he relaxed his grip, wincing at the pain.

After a very few moments, Price regained his control, his sublime and terrible control. "Going to the authorities, that's what set Quarles off. He might have tried to reason with Wick, but the man was already dashing for the door. Quarles pulled out the knife and caught him, here," and Price pushed up into his own ribs from below with his finger. "Wick crumpled like a dry leaf."

There is a weight to silence that sometimes can be felt. Tuckworth felt it now, crushing his chest, his lungs, pressing on his temples. He could feel his heart pulsing in his chest, and he knew if he tried to move he would fall under the weight. Price bent over now, spreading his arms across the tomb. "What could I do?" Price confessed, limp and breathless, his long race run, his body spent. "What could I do?"

"So you made a plan."

"You know the plan," he snapped, looking up sharply, a wild hunger still in his eyes. "I planned too well. You saw through it too easily."

"I only saw what was there to see. Nature never leaves things so pat. She's sloppy."

"Yes, next time I kill a man I'll keep that in mind." Price stood up now, already recovering and possessed of himself again. He straightened his coat. "Now you know. I am no murderer."

"Yet you killed—"

"I killed a fiend! I killed a man whose death was a blessing!"

"Why did you kill him?"

Price pulled himself up even straighter. "I've told you."

"What did they know?" Tuckworth went on. "How were they blackmailing you?"

The man's eyes narrowed. "I've told you all you need. I am no murderer! Now stop tormenting me!"

Tuckworth sighed, and steeled himself. "The children, Price. What of them?"

The two men stood on opposite sides of the tomb, one glaring and defiant, the other merely sad. They stood there without moving, scarcely breathing, afraid to upset the world's balance.

"What children?" Price whispered at last, eyeing his adversary.

"Price—"

"You can prove nothing! You have nothing!" he hissed, his voice a suppressed shriek ringing breathlessly about them. He almost panted in his fury, hurt and filled with hatred, his darkest self exposed to the light.

"You can't go on, Price," Tuckworth said, though knowing his words carried no force.

Price eyed him, judging within himself how far he might go now, how much he could confess. At last, he saw that he had gone too far already to turn back. "Tell me, Mr. Tuckworth," he began, "what is your darkest secret?"

The dean could not help the sudden spark of pain that flashed across his face, the surge of his sin within him.

Price almost laughed. "Something, I see. Dip into the charity box, perhaps? Abuse a bit of the clerical power? Or maybe there's a romantic indiscretion in your past?"

Murder, Tuckworth thought. Murder, murder, murder!

"We all have it. Don't distress yourself. That place inside ourselves where we hide the worst we are." And Tuckworth's mind flew back to the Devil's Acre. "Who put it there, eh? Who made that place?"

"It doesn't matter who made it."

"Doesn't it?" Price spat out. "Doesn't it matter? I'll tell you, I think you're right. It doesn't matter. I fought for years against who I am, what I am. I struggled and wept and cursed myself. I told myself I was at fault, that these stirrings in me were somehow mine to suppress. How many times did I revile myself and deny myself, only to fail in the end, every time, fail and return to my desires. And then, one day, I found myself rich. Do you know what wealth is, Mr. Tuckworth? Wealth is God. It puts you on a par with the Almighty. It frees you. It makes you see the world for what it is. If I am depraved in the world's eyes, who made me depraved? Who made me desire what I desire? Who made me love? God shares my sin, Mr. Tuckworth, as surely as he shares your own."

"It's not love, the thing you feel."

Price leaned forward, pressing his hands against the tomb that separated them, his voice rising again in defiance of the darkness. "You know nothing of love, don't you see that? Nothing of a love that burns with no quenching, a love that devours. I have always been what I am! I always will be!"

Some settling of the crypt about them, a shifting of stone reverberated in the shadows. It might have been a rat. It might have been anything. Price's eyes darted off toward the far end of the crypt. He tensed, a look of startled panic coming over his sweated brow. He glared back at Tuckworth, once more the fearful, panicked man. Then, with a spasmodic jerk and a strangled oath, he swept an arm across the top of the tomb and knocked the lantern into blackness.

Tuckworth stepped calmly away from where he had been, a dozen steps, his breath silent, his heart pounding. He crouched slightly at the knee, kept his back straight, was ready and attentive. He knew Price might attempt anything now, now that he felt cornered.

But nothing came. Soon the dean heard footsteps, soft, padding, trying to hide their progress. Price stumbled, cursed, went on, a man struggling through the dark, tripping and falling and rising again to step and stumble again. Finally, the sounds of Price's dreadful retreat receded into black silence.

The dean waited several minutes longer, then calmly made his way back through the dead, out into the living world.

CHAPTER XXII
STALEMATE

S o he is not the murderer we thought him to be," Hunt said.
"It would appear not, if we are to take him at his word."
"And are we?"

Tuckworth considered for a long moment. There had been some-thing about Price, a frantic, desperate air that made it all appear too likely. The man was no killer, not the sort they had imagined. "Yes," the dean answered at last. "Yes, I think we can believe him. Our investigation has been headed the wrong way all along."

"Yet there still remains this other business."

"I know." And here was the crux of the matter, the sickening feeling that had been sweeping slowly over the dean since he had left the crypt behind, the central point around which all revolved now like the flotsam of a wrecked ship about the maelstrom. Price's other crime, his depraved appetites, upon which they had stumbled almost by accident, what now of those? Price was no murderer, it was true, but he was something worse. "And we have no proof."

"None," Hunt conceded.

So they had reached a stalemate, mired in indecision and im-potence. Yet Price was stuck as well, or so it soon appeared. The following day, and the night and day after that, for three days to-gether the man kept entirely to his room, never emerging once, and Tuckworth and Hunt bided the hours impatiently.

Not as impatiently, however, as Raphael. For the young painter, this term of watching and waiting appeared useless, unmanly, and oppressive. "We must act, sir!" he had told the dean as they all three sat in the vicarage study one evening before supper, brooding over the plodding time.

"Act upon what?" he had been answered curtly. "What proof have we?"

"What proof do we need beyond our own conviction to stop such a fiend?"

"It will take more than *our* conviction to ensure Price's," jested Hunt, and receiving a pair of nasty glances for his pains, he coughed and rose from his chair. "If you'll excuse me, I think I'll go try Miss Tuckworth's company." This term of inactivity was weighing on all their spirits.

"Raphael," the dean said when they were alone, trying not to sound too paternal, "we must be patient. This new state of affairs, these revelations, they've set all our work at naught."

"Then we must work harder! We must do something!"

"Do what?"

"Anything!"

"Well, your *anything* doesn't do us a damn lot of good," the dean snorted, unable to mask his irritation. "I'm glad you seem so certain how to deal with all of this. I'm not. Not yet."

"Even after seeing that devilish nursery?"

"And what should we do with this knowledge? Break down Price's door? Force him to confront his crime? Take his punishment into our own hands? How can we do that, Raphael? Or haven't you thought that far ahead?"

"But we can't simply wait! When we know what he's capable of, the things he might do, how can we?"

Tuckworth slammed his open palm down amid the clutter of his desk, sending up a puff of dust. "We can because we must! Because we have no alternative but to wait! I know what Price might do as well as you. We're keeping as close an eye upon him as we dare. You and Hunt are both at the inn. Taggart tells me what he knows. But that's all we dare attempt or we might scare him off completely. If you can't see that, it's too bad. I'm tired of explaining myself, to you or to anyone."

"Why doesn't he run, then?" Raphael asked, and placed his finger on the very puzzle most troubling to the dean. "If he's made his confession, come clean to you about the murders, what is he waiting for?"

Tuckworth shook his head. "That I can't tell you," he muttered. "I don't know."

Raphael left soon after, not precisely storming out, but departing in a gloomy cloud of frustration and smarting temper that mirrored the banks of storm-laden clouds gathering on the horizon. In such a mood, there was nothing he could do but draw. Returning to the inn, therefore, he went inside and emerged shortly with a scratched and scarred wooden box. He settled in a corner of the coach yard wall overlooking the square and set himself to observe the ruin of the cathedral in the dimming twilight. He unpacked his sketch pad and pastels. He tried to capture the grandeur of the towers and the remaining walls in all their disarray, light and shadow speaking to his heart of fallen glory and the past's dreadful beauty. But his fingers would not answer his will. Bellminster Cathedral loomed from the page before him, not the true and noble friend of the year before, subject of a score of heartfelt studies. Something in him transformed its towering splendor into a dark and dreary travesty, blighted and forbidding.

He let his colors run freely over the page, released his mind and tried to forget himself in the moment, or rather, forget the moment in his own sullen soul. How else could he capture such a vision unless he were made a part of it, after all? The world was what it was, but on the canvas and the paper and in the mind's eye it must be a reflection of his spirit, like looking at a landscape through a window and seeing the phantom of your face looking back at you. They none of them understood that.

His fingers flew feverishly now. For the first time in months he loosed the reins that had been holding them back and allowed them to gallop, to race across the sheet. Great sweeping lines and looming shades filled the page from corner to corner. Reds and crimsons streaked the crippled towers in the dying light, ghosts of that terrible fire that had consumed them. Blue-black sky framed gray-blue clouds, drifting by in wisps of remembrance. At the base, brown and ocher, black and umber tied the cathedral to the square, dropping deep roots from wall to earth, spreading out and away and off the edge of the sheet.

Raphael paused and looked at what he had accomplished, a formless smudge, a void where before him rose a temple. How little he seemed to recall of his dear old friend, the cathedral. How easily he forgot that spark that had drawn him and held him for months in Bellminster. He sighed. Was this a mistake, coming back? Was he returning to his true art, or retreating to a secure and safe memory?

Rising to his feet, Raphael tore the sheet from his sketchbook and cast it aside into the filth of the coach yard, then leaned back against the wall and folded his arms about himself, the image of a dark intent. He was so consumed with his woes that he failed to hear the footsteps coming up to him, or the sound of fingers picking up his discarded sketch and spreading it out again.

"This really deserves a better fate than you'd give it," Hunt commented, looking at the sketch intently, eyeing it from several angles in the dim twilight.

Raphael cast a glance in Hunt's direction, then turned back to his sullen brooding. "It's only scrap from my imagination. Not worth twopence for kindling."

"Well, that's very true. Still," Hunt opined easily, "you've captured something here I've not seen in your work before. Something dreadful." Raphael laughed scoffingly. "Come now, Raphael, you know just what I mean. You've caught an attitude in those towers that speaks of their suffering."

"But that's not what I meant to put there," Raphael insisted, spinning about and snatching the page from Hunt's fingers. "At least, it's not what I feel when I look at the cathedral. Where is the grandeur? Where is the nobility from centuries past, those parts of the cathedral I carry within me?"

"But any common draftsman can make us feel what he feels in a scene, make a happy picture when he's happy and a sad picture when he's sad. You've shown me how the cathedral feels, and that's infinitely more interesting."

Raphael considered. He looked at the sketch more closely again before handing it back to Hunt. "Keep it if you want."

Hunt folded the paper up small and put it in his pocket. "You're trying too hard to find something here that's not here anymore, Raphael," the older man said with the certain air of a doctor giving a diagnosis, a very wise and kindly physician. "The world won't wait for you to find your proper vision. You must go out and meet the world as it is."

"You think I should leave Bellminster again?"

Hunt shook his head. "Your world is here as clearly as anyplace else. But the world changes, and men change, and often enough they do not change along sympathetic paths."

"Now you sound like Constable, telling me to resist placing any of myself into my painting, that I want to use art to fix the world."

"And Constable wasn't wrong to tell you that, either. Nor was he right." Hunt took a step closer to Raphael as dusk settled over the square. "Life's not a right or wrong proposition, Raphael. And advice should rarely be taken with the conviction that it must be all or nothing. Listen to what those who have gone before tell you. If they are good men, by which I mean true men, they'll have wisdom to profit you. But then you must act according to your own dictates. Now, that's my advice to you. Take any part of it that seems appealing and toss the rest in the dust."

Raphael gave a quizzical glance, as though the things Hunt was saying echoed off of some hard matter within him. "The dean thinks I'm too rash," he muttered.

"And so you are. The dean offers you good advice, but you're not the dean. Listen to what he says, and do everything you can that he advises. But follow your own way, too. It will all come out right."

Raphael glanced back over his shoulder once more but said nothing and seemed to fall even more deeply into his dark mood. Soon Hunt left him alone to go find Tuckworth.

The dean had his own youthful concerns to contend with, however. Raphael's mercurial spirits were having their effect on Lucy, the painter's despair over his confused prospects tangling itself in her openhearted affection. She had already faced her worst fears, that Raphael's return was merely a prelude to his leaving forever, and now she covered over her pain with a grim and stoic resolve. The strength she had begun to find within she put to use against the turmoil of her heart, and only Tuckworth noted the war battling within her. He watched her now, moving firmly about the vicarage, getting supper ready like a general supervising the troops, worrying Mrs. Cutler with her questions and commands and receiving any sideways glance as a covert questioning of her authority. And as the dean watched his daughter try so hard not to show her fear, try to smother her feelings for Raphael under a steady and officious front, he hurt all the more, knowing that she had learned such tricks from him, watching him hide his pain day after day, a pain he would never speak of. Without warning he suddenly saw himself in his child, and he loathed what he saw.

Tuckworth walked over to where she was rearranging the dishes on the supper table and took her hand, patting it gently in his own.

"Try not to worry, dear," he told her. "It will be right before long." She looked at him and a quick and overwhelming panic coursed wildly across her face, the surge of emotion she had been holding back. She mastered it just as quickly, however, and offered her father a safe, suffering smile, the sort of smile he knew too well.

"I'm going for a stroll before supper," he told her, and the dean went out into the cathedral, where he met Hunt returning from the Granby Arms.

Hunt read Tuckworth's worried brow with ease. "It's strange," he said, his voice falling into a natural and respectful hush, "amid all these dire trials, the domestic cares of family and friends remain somehow paramount."

"Not so strange, I think," the dean replied.

"You know, it might not be inadvisable to let Miss Tuckworth know—"

Tuckworth shook his head violently. "Out of the question."

"She deserves to know."

"I won't have Price add her name to his list of enemies. He'll not have cause to pursue her."

"Yet you said yourself, you don't think the man capable of murder."

Tuckworth paused. "It's true," he confessed. "I said that. But I might be wrong."

They walked on for a few steps together before Hunt continued. "I have to tell you, I've given it some thought and I think you're right. He's not a murderer."

"I'm still not going to tell Lucy anything. The child has troubles enough of her own."

"She's a woman, Tuckworth. And I'll warrant her troubles all stem from this other business, only she doesn't know it. She deserves to face this thing in its full light."

Now Tuckworth was silent, remembering Lucy's sudden look of confusion and panic, remembering her transparent bravery in the face of things she did not understand. Could he protect her better than she could protect herself? Shouldn't they all confront their fears together?

"Perhaps—" Tuckworth began, before Hunt gave a cry and pushed him to the cathedral floor as an explosion shook the space about them.

The dean raised his head and looked about. A stone had dropped from the height of the clerestory, the tops of the walls standing stern and gaping above them. He turned about and there lay Hunt, severely shaken but starting to rise until his leg collapsed beneath him and he cried out.

"Don't move," Tuckworth said, getting to his feet and preparing to go for help.

"No," Hunt said with surprising calm. "Don't leave me alone out here." And he gave a darting glance up the sides of the walls, a glance that told Tuckworth everything.

"You saw him?"

Hunt nodded.

"Let me just make it to the chapel," the dean said. "I won't let you out of my sight."

Hunt grasped Tuckworth's wrist to keep him from going. "You'd be in greater danger than I would."

Tuckworth realized the truth in this. Price might be hiding now in the shadows, waiting for him to leave Hunt's side.

"I'm afraid, my friend, that we are reduced to a theatrical absurdity," Hunt told the dean, and then, clearing his throat, he cried out in a stentorian voice, "Help!"

"Lucy!" Tuckworth called. "Mrs. Cutler!"

But it was Adam Black who heard them, walking home to the apartment he shared with his sister close-by the cathedral, and it was Adam who carried Hunt into the vicarage and went for Dr. Warrick of the Municipal Hospital, returning in less than half an hour with the doctor panting behind.

"No break," Warrick announced after a hurried yet methodical examination. "The ankle looks sprained, though. Not much walking about for you, Mr. Hunt." And after applying a sturdy wrapping about the wounded ankle and dispensing a few drops of something into a glass of water to help Hunt rest, the doctor departed for more serious cases.

"So it would appear," Hunt told Tuckworth in private, lying on the parlor sofa while the women gathered everything necessary for their guest's comfort, "that Price has managed to remove one of us from the chase."

"Don't be ridiculous. You're just as valuable lying here in my parlor as you would be by my side."

"Am I?"

Tuckworth knew what Hunt was saying. The evil they were battling was more dangerous now. Once again, all their conjectures and speculations had been proven wrong. Price was very capable of murder, after all. "We still have Raphael," the dean said, trying to sound encouraging. "I'll send over a note right away, tell him what's happened. He'll keep a sharp eye on Price."

"You'll have to rely on that young man more than ever now. On his rashness as well as his strength."

The dean shook his head slowly. "That rashness concerns me."

"Don't let it," Hunt advised. "We've been very cautious until now. Maybe too cautious. I think a little rashness might serve us well."

CHAPTER XXIII
RESURRECTION

The solid bank of clouds, sullen gray and dingy white at their peaks, flashing black and green beneath, advanced on Bellminster with a speed that made men cross themselves in uneasy jest, and children stop their games and watch in mute amazement. By nine, the wind rose up to wrap the town in dust. By half past ten, the moon was swallowed in the rumbling gullet of the skies. By ten-thirty, the sky itself was a boiling mass. An unexpected lull, and then at eleven the deluge burst.

A sea of rain poured down on Bellminster in the space of an hour, the pent-up fury of a summer-long drought. The earth sopped the tempest's first fall, drinking deep with an interminable thirst. But the rains kept up their onslaught well past midnight, and soon the streets splashed with the overflow, cascades rushing down cobbled ways, lanes become rivulets become streams become rivers feeding the Medwin with their tributary waters, swelling her banks, transforming the tired flow of the ford into an angry, stygian surge. Each flash of lightning captured for an instant the liquid landscape roiling on the surface of the flood, a brown-white torrent at the bottom of the town, hills and valleys and white-capped mountains of water shifting and raging, flying upward to splintering peaks before collapsing, washing the depths of Bellminster in violence.

Close to the Medwin the flood's roar drowned the thunder to a rushing silence, the deafening numbness of incessant, unvarying sound. Up by the cathedral, however, every slashing, ragged arc of light brought with it a clash as palpable to the skin as a leap into cold water. Try as he might to prepare himself for each explosion, Tuckworth jerked in his bed time after time, his heart jumping, his jaw grinding in anticipation, sweat matting his straggled locks, the bedclothes sticking in patches to his damp flesh. One particularly rending peal caused a reaction in him so violent that he yelped like a whipped mongrel, until there was nothing more the dean could do but laugh at his childish fear, laugh at the supernatural storm, the eerie flashes, the dull hope that the sun would shine again. He laughed, and covered himself with the sheets.

Tuckworth woke to the sound of birds bravely announcing that they had not been drowned in the night or carried off on the whirlwind. He opened his window to a world made new, with no sunlight perhaps, and a persistent fall of drizzling damp, but a pleasing glow from the murky sky and the fresh, wormy smell of saturated life.

The noise of a great bustling downstairs caught his attention, and dressing quickly he descended the stairs to find his daughter and Mrs. Cutler scurrying about the parlor, the one upturning cushions and peeking behind chairs, the other reaching with a broom handle under the furniture. In the middle of this activity Hunt, in a red velvet dressing gown with threadbare patches on the elbows, was sitting up on the sofa looking over a letter, quite oblivious to the ladies and their frantic searching.

"Something lost?" the dean asked, and Lucy turned to him with teary eyes that carried all the care and worry that he failed to feel.

"Nothing," she lied, and stood there. Tuckworth waited until the lie should drift away and leave the truth behind. "The accounts ledger," she confessed, and with a guttering sob that she would not let escape she turned back to her quest.

"Good morning, Tuckworth!" Hunt called gaily, and motioned for his friend to approach.

"A moment," Tuckworth answered and disappeared into his study, from which he emerged an instant later with the ledger raised in his hand. "I was going over the details of our mysterious contribution," he said in answer to the accusatory gaze his daughter leveled at him. "Mortimer seems unusually specific about how our benefactor wants the money to be spent."

"Don't frighten me like that again," Lucy chided, snatching the book away. "Tell me when you want to look at the accounts and I'll help you."

"I'm sorry, my dear. Is it so important? There's little enough recorded there."

"Important?" Mrs. Cutler cried in disbelief from the floor, where she continued to pluck at invisible dust balls from the corners and under the furniture.

"Father," Lucy explained, "Mr. Mortimer has made a request to go over the books with us this afternoon. He really has no business with it," she added in a churlish tone, "but since he's acting for our benefactor, I can't think of a good reason to refuse him."

"It's all quite right, I'm sure," Tuckworth said, clearly not engaged in Lucy's problems just now. He looked at Hunt, who displayed through his eyes and a quick, jerking nod of his head a certain urgency to be alone with the dean.

"Well," Tuckworth continued. "You and Mrs. Cutler have plenty of things to occupy you, I'm sure. I'll just sit here and keep Hunt company."

Mrs. Cutler stood up and huffed, as though to say that men were only good for so much anyway, and it was a blessing to have them out of the way when there was work to be done. Reaching into the pocket of her apron, she plucked out a letter and handed it to the dean. "From the bishop," she informed him. "Come in the mail coach yesterday morning and just made its way across the square today, and if that man Taggart ain't the laziest man in all of England and Wales, then I don't know who is." Saying which, she left.

Lucy stayed, however, her eyes wide in surprise and a certain dread. "The bishop?" was all she said.

Tuckworth was eager to confer privately with Hunt, but it was clear that he must deal with this unexpected message first, for Lucy's sake if for no other good reason. Unfolding the envelope, he looked the letter over quickly, a cursory glance telling him all he needed to know.

"What is it, dear?" Lucy asked, her voice anxious, her eyes questioning.

Tuckworth managed a casual smile and a cavalier wave of his hand, neither of which was especially effective. "Nothing. Nothing really."

Lucy remained silent, but her eyes spoke her growing fear.

Tuckworth sighed. "Mortimer's trip to London," he admitted. "It seems the rector was lodging a fervent complaint against the way I've been handling the Cathedral Fund. Not malfeasance, you understand. Nothing so sinister. Just incompetence."

Lucy's eyes narrowed as she listened. Her fists clenched, and she seethed to hear her father maligned. "Of all the presumptuous, stupid, mean—"

"Charity, my dear," he advised her, but her indignation was such that she could only express it with a suppressed and explosive scream.

"The man's an ass, Father!"

"Lucy!"

"So *that's* why he wants his fingers on the books. To get evidence against you! He knows how impossible it is to get people to donate to the fund in these times. Money's *that* tight."

"I have been rather lax."

"Nonsense! Look at all the work progressing now!"

"Actually, it would appear that Mortimer arranged for the donation himself before leaving London. The bishop is very effusive in his praise of Mortimer's industry. Oh, he doesn't blame me for anything," Tuckworth went on, folding the letter and burying it in his pocket dismissively. "It's not exactly a threat to my position here. Call it the threat of a threat. The bishop merely says I might be led by the example of a younger, more active man."

Lucy stared in disbelief, and expressed herself in another stifled scream before raging off to vent her fury in domestic warfare.

Tuckworth turned at last to Hunt.

"Well, it seems the noose it tightening all around," the invalid commented. "I'm sorry for you."

Tuckworth waved a hand in the air again as though he were clearing away a wispy cloud. "This is nothing," he said. "What have you got there?"

Hunt held up the letter. "From Mrs. Hunt, a report made by the lad I set to watch Price's house. The gist of it is that, two days following my departure from London, an army of domestics assaulted Price's home. At least a dozen healthy, red-faced Irish maids and matrons, it says here. They set about scouring the place to virtual nonexistence. It would appear that Price contemplates an extended absence."

Tuckworth sat motionless for a moment, absorbing this new fact, trying to find a place for it among all he knew. Then, with a quick jerk, he sat bolt upright. "Mrs. Culter!" he called, and the housekeeper materialized from the kitchen in her usual cloud of flour. "Run over to the inn at once and tell Raphael I need to see him."

"But the loaves is just—"

"Mrs. Cutler, *please!*"

She knew that tone of voice, and even she saw better than to question it a second time. Off she scurried, doubly fast for the loaves' sake, and soon Raphael was sitting with the others in the dean's study, where Hunt had managed to hobble on Tuckworth's arm.

"Consider it," the dean was explaining. "We saw the state of Price's house before we left London. Nothing moved. No one allowed in. Dishes and pots and pans left to sit without a finger raised to clean them. Clearly the man was afraid of some kind of discovery."

"He doesn't seem to be afraid of it anymore," Raphael observed, "letting all those women into his house."

Tuckworth looked sharply at his young associate. "Doesn't he? Think of how he's lived here in Bellminster."

A dim light sparked in Raphael's brain. "I see, sir. The same as in London."

"Precisely. So whatever he was hiding there, he has brought with him here."

"Then all we must do is search his rooms at the inn!" Raphael exclaimed triumphantly. "That shouldn't be difficult to arrange. Constable Hopgood would do it if you asked."

The dean glanced ruefully at his young companion. "You tried that once," he said.

"But that was only a quick look, with no freedom to—"

The dean shook his head. "It's still too risky."

"Why?"

"Because we can't go to the local authorities until we have something definite. Hopgood would do anything I ask, it's true. Once. One time he'd conduct a search, but if we come up with nothing," the dean confessed, shrugging, "I doubt he'd be so amenable again. Besides, I don't think there's anything to find anymore."

"Why not?"

Hunt snapped to life. "Last night, of course! He'd never have attempted anything so bold if he were afraid of some discovery later. As long as he was frightened of what we might do, he was captive."

"But now," Raphael said, joining in the game, "he feels free to act and move about, if only at night."

They were all silent for a moment.

"So, what do we do?" Hunt asked.

Again, they were silent.

"I'll tell you what's been troubling me about this whole business," Tuckworth said at last, in that far-off voice that seemed to be speaking only to itself. "Why Bellminster?"

"Because you are here," Hunt observed, "and the man was driven to tell you that he wasn't guilty, that he didn't murder Wick."

"But why stay on? What is there about Bellminster that keeps him here? What does he know about the place?"

"Only what you told him in London," Raphael answered.

Tuckworth's brow clouded over as he tried to recall. "What did I tell him in London? The sort of town Bellminster is. The state of things with the mill so woefully underemployed. What is there in that?"

"Nothing," admitted Hunt.

The dean looked up suddenly at his compatriots, a triumphant light sparkling in his eyes. "Mortimer!" he cried. "Mortimer told the bishop that he acquired Price's donation *before* leaving London. Of course, that's why they came down together. He must have told Price something that fit into the man's plans."

Raphael looked about excitedly. "But what could it have been?"

"What, indeed?" repeated Hunt. "That's what we must ask Mr. Mortimer."

And so, when the rector arrived at the vicarage that afternoon with the purpose of going over the books, sitting at table with Lucy, the dean, and Abraham Semple, Tuckworth had his own interests to pursue.

"I can't say as I'm happy with this rush, Mr. Mortimer," Semple said after they had made a minute examination of the costs and heard from the rector what schedule he expected them to follow.

"And why should it concern you, Semple?" Mortimer asked. "I think your men have been dawdling about the business long enough. Things appear to be in readiness, and tomorrow is none too soon to begin our work."

"Aye, we might move tomorrow, without tryin' the equipment first," Semple agreed. "We might save two days' time, but if aught goes awry with that cross, it won't save your cathedral. You'll lose cross, crypt, and all."

"But surely there's scant danger of a disaster," Mortimer insisted.

"Scant ain't none," Semple declared with that air of fatalism that marks a good foreman.

Even the essential design of the scaffold was called into question, so that Semple had to detail the procedure twice before the rector appeared satisfied, announcing finally that he looked forward to seeing the Great Cross flying high over Bellminster the following day.

"Don't know as how high she'll fly," Semple observed laconically. "Just enough to back a wagon under her will do for me."

As Mortimer was about to leave, however, Tuckworth pulled him aside into his study. The younger man looked warily at the older. He was prepared for some nastiness, it seemed, and as he stood there he pulled himself up. The rector was taller than the dean, slimmer, straighter, appearing superior in every way that counted to the world.

Tuckworth closed the door firmly. "Honestly, Mortimer, if you had a problem with the way I'm managing the cathedral, I wish you'd have brought your concerns to me first," he began, a hint of paternal reprimand in his voice.

It was just the sort of tone to irritate a man like Mortimer. "I'm sure you wish I had, but that's irrelevant now."

The dean coughed. "I suppose you're right. The bishop suggests I learn a few tricks from you. Tell me, then, how did you convince Price to come to Bellminster and undertake the restoration?"

Mortimer appeared stricken by the question, so honest and innocent. He was prepared for a battle, and as usual Tuckworth denied him one. "I only did what any man of determination might have done. I described in very moving detail the state of affairs here, the impoverished appearance of God's house, the shame which that state reflects upon the entire community, not just of Bellminster, mind you, but of the Church of England at large. When there are men of means, men of influence and station who might assist, when such men demur, when they deflect their duty, when men debar the brighter for the darker way, then God's call is surely falling upon deaf ears."

The rector was always marvelous at the impromptu sermon. "How clever of you to be so determined. And how did you describe the state of affairs here?"

Appearing stiff and uncomfortable, Mortimer looked up into the cobwebbed corners of the study. "I will tell you straightforwardly, I informed him of what I consider to be your less than energetic efforts. I let him know that the situation was far more critical than you doubtless expressed it."

Tuckworth breathed evenly, finding his own temper beginning to flare at such posturing, but managed a soft smile. "Yes, we've already been over your opinion in that regard. I meant physically, how did you describe the cathedral to him?"

The rector was not certain at first how to answer such a question, it seemed so far afield of the dramatic recriminations he had expected, the dean's necessary defense of his conduct, and his own withering rebuttals so carefully prepared. "I told him of the Great Cross, and the need to raise it," he said at last.

"Why that particularly?"

"My dear Mr. Tuckworth," Mortimer explained, with a tutorial air that he clearly relished, "I reasoned, and I think rather successfully, that Mr. Price is a man of business, not charity. I therefore presented him with a single task, something that his businessman's mind could grasp and imagine being accomplished. I fear it is asking too much of his imagination to see the entire project at once, as a staggering whole, or to ask that he give his money to some empty promise of good works. No, he responded to the immediate need of resurrecting the cross and saving the crypt. He responded to the tune of five hundred pounds, I might inform you," and the man glowed in self-satisfied rapture.

"The crypt," Tuckworth repeated. "Yes, he seemed remarkably interested in the crypt the other day."

"I am not surprised. I painted for him a rather affecting picture of its peril. The sagging ceiling, the risk of losing all beneath the rubble and devastation, the irreparable damage to faith and to history should that revered ancestry be lost forever. It moved him very deeply."

"So," Hunt said later when the dean related his exchange with the rector, "it's the crypt that brought him here. But why?"

"That is the question," Tuckworth acknowledged. "Why?"

They paused, trapped in the same musing silence that had ensnared them now for days. Tuckworth shook his head. "I'm stepping outside to have a look about," he announced. "I want to try to see what Price is seeing in all of this."

"Excellent," Hunt agreed. "Action, that's the remedy to all this wretched thinking. Move the limbs about." And he adjusted himself upon the sofa and groaned.

Tuckworth stepped out into the misty afternoon, struck at once by the flurry of activity going on throughout the nave. Semple was busy directing his men as they swarmed over the Great Cross and the tall scaffold that stretched above it. When the foreman noticed the dean, however, he came to meet him at once.

"That rector is a pinch-penny," Semple muttered in disgust,

"afraid to pay one extra day's wages. I just want you to know, if aught goes ill tomorrow, it won't be for lack of me warnin' him. Senseless haste makes shoddy work, that's what I told him from the start."

Something began to stir in the back of Tuckworth's mind, a confluence of thoughts trickling together, so that he hardly heard the foreman's complaints. "Certainly, Semple," he commented in an offhanded fashion. "Quite correct, I'm sure."

"It's the crypt I'm worried about, vicar," he went on. "Anythin' happens, ought goes awry, and that cross'll come down to bury your crypt for good and all. Good and all, Mr. Tuckworth."

"Yes, certainly," was all Tuckworth said.

Semple looked offended at the dean's casual manner. "Well, if it don't matter to others then it don't matter to me," he sniffed, feeling unheard and unappreciated. "Leave the dead for the dead, that's what I says."

Tuckworth suddenly jerked his head out of its reverie and stared at the foreman. "What was that?"

"Just leave the dead to the dead, is all. If you want to go about losin' your crypt, I doubt them present occupants will raise a stir for some time to come."

Tuckworth's mind fired now and his body caught the flame and burst into action. Without a word he darted to the crypt, shot past Adam Black, who stopped his labors and instantly fell in behind, dived into that flickering world below where men were putting the final touches on their work, preparing all for the task ahead.

The dead for the dead. The words reverberated within him as he paused at the foot of the stairs, grabbed a nearby lantern, and began to search about. He passed the light here and there, back and forth before him. Others came up behind, curious laborers wondering at the dean's mad behavior, but none disturbed him as he hunted. For what? Even Tuckworth could not be certain, not exactly. Some sign. Some telltale mark. He proceeded farther into the earth, looking carefully at each tomb, examining the timbers set up as supports, stopping to run his hand over rough stone, rasping wood, past duke and earl, duchess and bishop.

He came to the end at last, the pale, sullen tomb of Sir Philip Dorsay. Tuckworth looked up at the cracked, distended ceiling. The cross must be directly overhead, he realized. He glanced about at the wooden posts erected around the tomb, sturdy pillars to preserve Bellminster's past. He stopped. There! The dean knelt and ran his fingers across a fine layer of sawdust at the foot of one of the posts. He rose and looked about again. There! And there! The same thin residue on the floor. He felt along the face of one of these timbers, until his fingertips detected the hairline cut, each post sawn halfway through at a sharp angle.

He turned his attention to the tomb, rubbing his hands along the top, brushing it, peering close to spy . . . There! The marks of a crowbar!

He pulled back now and noticed for the first time the little knot of people gathered around him.

"Here," he ordered, pointing to the tomb. "Open that." They all stood about silently, casting odd glances at one another.

Adam stepped forward and grasping a corner of the heavy slab in his hard fingers, slid it aside, grinding, grating, slowly inching it sideways. Quickly, the tomb was open enough to peer into. Tuckworth raised his lantern and leaned over the open darkness that enveloped the physical remains of Sir Philip, the woebegone brother.

The baronet's bones lay stately and awful in the dust of eternity. Beside him, seeming almost hale and plump by comparison, another body, naked, yellow, rested on its side.

The others drew back as every eye turned to Tuckworth, who merely nodded his head in dull triumph.

"Malcolm Wick," was all he said.

CHAPTER XXIV

SCHEMES

Five men, surrounded by a pale halo of light at the end of the crypt, stood warily about the open tomb. Four of them stared, eager and attentive, at the pair of grisly figures, one desiccated and brown, little more than bones and the ragged threads of antique cloth, the other yellow and bloated, its nakedness a testament to the great indignity of death, and the face, crushed and misshapen beyond all recognition. The fifth man held himself against the wall just outside the flickering glow of the lantern, lost in a web of plots and schemes.

"What would you say, doctor?" Hunt asked, leaning over the tomb in macabre fascination. "Dead a week?"

Dr. Warrick reached deep within the black recesses before him, his head disappearing from view, his voice emerging from the darkness like the call of death. "Not much more than that. Of course, the fellow's kept well, but he's still in wretched poor condition. Been brutally handled."

"Excuse me, vicar," Chief Constable Hopgood interjected, appearing almost embarrassed to interrupt Tuckworth where he stood in the shadows, thinking. "You say this man was murdered in London and transported here? Why would someone go to all that trouble?"

"I can't say for certain," Tuckworth stated, "but I expect Price was lost without Wick here to manage such things for him. It's not unusual, really. A man caught in a crisis rarely trusts the simple, direct way."

"Why not just sneak him out at night and dump him in the river?"

Hunt provided an answer, leaning upon the makeshift crutch that Raphael had fashioned for him. "London's not like Bellminster, Mr. Hopgood. It never rests, never slumbers. And Price is deathly afraid of discovery."

"So he brought the man all this way?"

"All this way," Hunt replied.

"And you're willing to state for a fact, Mr. Tuckworth, that this is," and the chief constable referred to the jottings in his notebook, "Malcolm Wick?"

"I can't imagine who else it might be," the dean answered pettishly, too aware of the doubt in Hopgood's question and the delicacy in his manner. Tuckworth had already given a fair report of the matter thus far, seconded on several key points by Hunt and Raphael, who stood by, eager to serve now that there was something to be done. Still, the dean recognized that every hard-won answer he was able to uncover in this business only led to more questions, more difficulties, and they were all turning to him to show the way.

Tuckworth removed his spectacles and wiped his weary eyes. It was tiresome, this perpetual claim upon his mind, this desire that others had to be led. Why could no one else see what he saw, make the connections he made? It was all there. They had only to fit the pieces together as he had fitted them together. Tuckworth put his spectacles back on and looked at the four men, willing, active, but lost. Yes, even Hunt was looking to him, and he realized with dismay that they could not piece it together, try as they might. It was his gift, like it or not, to see what lay invisible to others. He sighed.

"Tell us, doctor," Tuckworth continued now, drawn out of his worried musings at last, "would you say a hammer did that damage to his face?"

"More like a mallet," the doctor answered, motioning the chief constable to hold the lantern closer while he reached in and turned the head from side to side. "The blows were restricted to the face, and I think were administered here in the crypt. Would have taken, oh, a great many of them. The bone is pulverized, exposed in spots, here and here, and there are a few chips off the lower mandible here. It was a thorough job. Yes, probably a workman's mallet. Whatever it was, though, it's not what killed him. There's no swelling or discoloration."

"No," Tuckworth agreed distractedly. "Wick was stabbed to death. You'll find a knife wound just below the left breast."

Dr. Warrick probed about for a moment. "Straight to the heart. Didn't even touch the ribs. Whoever did this knew his business, all right."

The dean shivered, though not from the damp chill of the crypt.

"Very good," Hopgood affirmed, still nervously. "We know what did this, but back to the question of who he is."

"He was brought here in a trunk, wouldn't you think?" Raphael offered, ignoring the constable's inquiry.

Tuckworth nodded. "A trunk filled with lime. You can still see the powder in some of the folds about the man's neck and torso. He was probably lying just a few feet away from you, Raphael, when you burst into Price's room that night."

The doctor dipped into the tomb and emerged again, a thick, white powder adhering to his fingertips. "Lime, all right. That would certainly make the job less messy," he remarked. "The lime would absorb any fluids, and fluids are a great source of your odor and decay."

"But how can we be sure this is the man the dean says he is?" Hopgood demanded at last, bringing out into the open the question that had been nagging at Tuckworth these past hours. No identification could be made from the victim's face, that was certain. Price had been careful about that. But already Tuckworth was working his way through that difficulty, slowly, in his certain fashion.

"If you'll bear with me, gentlemen," he explained. "Without asking you to believe that Mr. Price is at the center of all of this—"

"If you say this man Price is our likeliest suspect, I'll go along for now," Hopgood assented readily.

"Good man, chief constable," Hunt encouraged.

"But I need to know how we can hope to prove this poor chap is your Malcolm Wick."

"Thank you for your confidence, Hopgood," Tuckworth said, and he felt suddenly gratified, very sincerely gratified to be home again in Bellminster, where his word carried at least a little weight. "But, ignoring the 'who' of this case for a moment, I think we now have a good idea of the 'why.' " Four blank faces stared back at him. "Where better to hide a body than buried beneath ten tons of stone surrounded by a dozen other corpses?" he explained. "Several of these posts have been cut halfway through, and I daresay if we have a look at that scaffold above, we'll find the same cuts made along its supports."

All four of the dean's companions looked above with tense, searching gazes, and the crypt seemed suddenly smaller.

"It's safe, isn't it?" the doctor asked, giving voice to their immediate fears.

"Yes," Tuckworth reassured them, then looked nervously at the ceiling. "Yes, of course it is, for now. But as soon as that scaffold collapsed, as it undoubtedly would have done when the cross was aloft, all of this," and the dean spread his arms wide to embrace the whole history and tradition, the very foundation of his beloved cathedral, "would have been lost."

"Not to mention him," Hunt added, tilting his head toward the tomb.

"Precisely. So Price has been sitting in his room all this time with Wick for company, poor Malcolm Wick stuffed in a trunk, covered in lime, waiting for the right moment to be put to rest."

"And last night's rain would have been the perfect time," Raphael realized.

"A moonless night would have done well," the dean remarked. "That's doubtless what Price was waiting for. But last night was an opportunity he couldn't miss. And now he's in the devil's own hurry to finish the job and get away from here."

"So that's it, then!" Raphael announced triumphantly. "We have cause, victim, and opportunity! We've got him!" He quickly noticed that no one else was sharing his triumph. "Haven't we?"

Tuckworth sighed. "Not quite, I'm afraid." And the dean asked Hopgood to point out the problem they still faced.

"There's no way we can attach this mangled thing to your Mr. Price as yet," the chief constable stated flatly. "I'm sorry for't, heartily sorry, but it's true."

"Can't we search his rooms?" Raphael insisted. "Surely there's something there. The empty trunk! That would prove it!"

The dean snapped at Raphael irritably. "Stop being so eager to search rooms! We tried that in London," and Tuckworth's hand massaged his stomach at the memory of their disastrous crime. "My boy, we can't allow an uncertain hope to lead us. We must try to eliminate the possibility of failure. The trunk might still be in Price's rooms, or it might be bounding down the Medwin, or sunk beneath its waves, but wherever it is I'm sure it's washed out and useless to us. There are too many possibilities, and we've seen how resourceful Price can be."

"Then we're at a dead end once more," Raphael muttered, thoroughly crestfallen.

"Not quite dead," and Tuckworth sounded guardedly gleeful as the various possibilities before him began to converge into a plan.

"No, all the evidence we need is right here. If we can prove this is Malcolm Wick, then we'll have tied Price to the murder in bonds he can't easily break."

"But *can* we prove it?" Hopgood asked.

Tuckworth turned to the doctor. "Tell me, in lieu of a face," and he coughed at his own morbid words, "in lieu of that, how can a body be rightly identified?"

"By physical marks, naturally. This fellow," and Dr. Warrick leaned in again, "has a mole on his left shoulder, another inside his left thigh, an old scar from some burn on his abdomen, likely a childhood mishap, and once we roll him over I'm certain we'll find a few more identifying marks on his back."

"Hopgood, if we can produce someone capable of identifying these marks, would that hold up at an inquest?"

The chief constable considered the point for a moment, before nodding. "Yes. Yes, I think it would. If there was a plausible reason for the witness to know about these here marks, and if he could give a blind description, without examining the victim, I'd say it'd hold up."

"Good," the dean asserted. "Now, Price is expecting Semple to raise the cross tomorrow. He's staying on here for that very reason, to see the fruition of his plans, to assure himself of his own safety."

"But can Semple repair this damage by then?" asked Hunt, looking uneasily at the posts standing their uncertain guard on every hand.

"It doesn't matter if he can. We don't want him to."

"Why in heaven's name not?" exclaimed Hopgood.

"Because then Price would know his plan is discovered, and it's the last we'd see of him."

All four heads nodded.

"So," Tuckworth continued, "we've got to distract Price, make him think that something else is causing the delay. Semple can devise some story. Locating a wagon sturdy enough to take the cross, perhaps, or a team strong enough to pull it. The man's own natural obstinacy to test the scaffold might be reason enough. But we need something that will give us two or three days at least while we keep Price occupied."

"Occupied with what?" the chief constable asked.

"I have an idea about that," the dean replied, a grim twinkle in his eye as he thought of the mischief he was about to set in motion.

"And why two or three days?" Raphael added, his spirits starting to revive.

"Because," Tuckworth added, with a piercing glance at Raphael, "that's how long it will take you to get to London and back."

Hunt turned to the dean. "The cook?" he asked.

"The cook."

An hour later found Tuckworth in the office of the mayor of Bellminster, a close, airless little cell buried somewhere in the labyrinthine corridors of the Town Hall. Mayor Winston, a stuffy little man who seemed peculiarly unfit for his close surroundings, was blustering uncontrollably at the news the dean had brought him, and his two assistants, the Messrs. Bick and Bates, blustered emphatically on either side of him.

"Do you . . . do you mean to say," the mayor stammered, "that this man is funding your renovation on his own? With private funds?"

"Private?" echoed Bick.

"Funds?" extemporized Bates.

"Not the entire renovation, you understand," Tuckworth went on. "At least, not yet. We have hopes, of course, great hopes that Mr. Price will ultimately back the whole job."

"But that would cost thousands," the mayor proclaimed in disbelief. "Tens of thousands."

"A hundred thousand, at last estimate. Which is why we're beginning slowly. Just the Great Cross, for now, but Mr. Price is certainly capable of undertaking the rest of it, if he's so inclined."

The mayor leaned back knowingly and laced his hands across his massive breadth of waistcoat. "I see, I see. Testing the waters, eh?" And he glanced at his pair of assistants, a glint of avarice in his eye. The thought of someone with such resources in Bellminster, a man of such clear eminence, made their three mouths water.

"Yes, you might put it that way," the dean conceded. "Once the cross is successfully removed, I believe it's Mr. Mortimer's intention to interest Mr. Price in some other project. Restoring the crypt or replacing the floor of the nave, some single, specific task that he can undertake."

"Yes," the mayor mused. "Yes, I understand you. Do the thing piecemeal, as it were . . . piecemeal. A bit here . . . a bit there. Then, before the man realizes it, he's sunk in too deep to back out again." And he lost himself in a moment of acquisitive reverie. "Tell me, Dean Tuckworth," he continued, "this anonymity Mr. Price guards so closely. Might it be . . ." The mayor searched for the word.

"Got over?" offered Bates.

"Circumvented?" tried Bick.

"Circum . . . circumvented," enthused the mayor. "That's it. Can this anonymity be circumvented?"

The dean smiled vaguely. "I'm not certain what you mean."

"Dash it all, can the man be approached?"

"Ah, I see your point," Tuckworth exclaimed. "You wish to approach Mr. Price to offer him some honorarium on behalf of the town, some recognition for what he has begun here."

"Honor . . . honorarium, that's it!"

"I suppose you'll give him a tour of Bellminster. Perhaps have the town band perform for him in the evening. Dine him handsomely. Might even take him to the mill to see that great work. It's a shame no friendly investor can be found to fund *that* project."

The gleam suddenly went out of the mayor's eye, and a suspicious leer took its place. But he said nothing.

"Mr. Price is a very private man," Tuckworth went on, oblivious to this sudden chill in the atmosphere of the room. "However, I don't suppose any man of business objects to being recognized for his munificence. Of course," the dean added, "you mustn't interfere with his interest in the cathedral."

The mayor laughed loudly at such an absurd notion, though the suspicious leer remained in his eye, brightening perceptibly. "Of course not," he assured Tuckworth. "Taking money from the cathedral to finance the mill? It's laughable . . . laughable." And in evidence of that fact, he laughed again, more loudly still.

The dean looked at the mayor, and then at Bick, who had already taken up the good humor of his superior, and then at Bates, who was not far behind. Tuckworth smiled at their merriment, and then grinned, and then chuckled quietly to himself.

A minute later, back out on the sidewalk, the day drizzling with its own gentle humor, Dean Tuckworth looked about him. It was too early yet to feel confident, he knew. Too much might happen, too much go wrong. But one thing he could feel confident of: Things had been going along in the dark for far too long. It was time to bring them out into the light.

CHAPTER XXV
OUT OF HIDING

D ean Tuckworth and Hamlin Price stared at each other across a dense checkerboard of yammering faces on a damp, depressing afternoon. The sun shone through a tattered quilt of clouds just often enough to leech the moisture from the earth that it might hang thickly in the air, and all about men were dabbing and swiping their faces. Tuckworth and Price had spent the morning in determined avoidance, and yet for the space of time it takes to draw a breath, the dean and the philanthropist set the world at naught and stared openly at each other. Price, cunning and incisive, delved with his eyes into the dean's motives, his schemes, his plots and stratagems, tried to burrow to the heart of the man to fathom him. Tuckworth looked back, bold, unflinching, but frightened and anxious as well, fraught with worry and suspicion, care and the pain of imminent failure. At least, that's how the dean hoped he looked.

About them massed Bellminster's leading figures, men of station and more than moderate wealth, huddling like a swarm of penitents set upon a pilgrimage. The mayor and his traveling show of sycophants and aldermen formed the nucleus of this party, bustling about the courtyard of the millworks, pointing off here and out there, marking this feature or that which was sure to entice their hoped-for friend, their fellow industrialist. They offered up like a sacrifice the expansive grounds looked over by rows of grimy windows, the sturdy construction with stables and outbuildings, the modern waterwheel turning and tumbling endlessly in the renewed flood of the Medwin, the pipes for moving water to the furnaces crossing above gradually dwindling mountains of coal and slag, the single smokestack belching its black clouds, its two companions staring idly on. Some ten or a dozen happy acolytes of industry puffed their chests with pride and contended with one another in effusive praise of this commercial miracle.

In the midst of it all, Hamlin Price looked with an impassive eye, a frozen smile, a stiff and commanding presence. Yet he saved one meaningful glare for Tuckworth, and in that glance, the dean caught the unmistakable signs, the nervous twitching about the corner of the mouth, the pale brow that seemed too furrowed by secret woes, the chin held up in grim defiance of nothing, the ill-shaved jaw and the lank collar, certain marks that his wall was cracking, that Price's sublime control was shivering and breaking apart.

"Are you certain it's wise, sir?" Raphael had asked the night before at the livery, saddling his hired horse. "Price is certain to be suspicious if he sees you among the crowd."

"That's just the point," Tuckworth had explained. "We need him to be suspicious. I must look false, as if I want him to think I know less than I know."

Raphael glanced up from cinching the animal's girth strap long enough to convey his utter confusion.

Tuckworth tried again. "Price is already suspicious. He's afraid to stay but unwilling to leave until he sees this thing through. That's how we must keep him. Unbalanced. Uncertain. We have to seem desperate. Which means we have to *look* desperate. Do you see?"

Raphael nodded noncommittally, and shortly after he mounted and rode off with a melodramatic flourish that almost tumbled him to the muck, sneaking away through a steady fall of rain in a hissing darkness with the promise to return in three days at the latest. But

Tuckworth wondered now, as he stood among the many clean, well-moneyed faces of Bellminster. Raphael was far from being an accomplished rider, and the road was slick and dangerous. Could he make it to London and back in time?

"Gentlemen!" the mayor announced over the ceaseless hum of the factory and the cackle of his party.

"Gentlemen! Gentlemen!" Bates cried.

"Gentlemen!" called Bick.

The mayor coughed. "Let us take Mr. Price to the heart . . . the heart of the factory, shall we? Into the mill! And let's show him what Bellminster can be!" With an approving murmur and a flurry of nods, they all trooped together out of a sudden fall of spitting rain and into the millworks.

They were greeted by the clatter of the great machinery within, the scalding smell of steam and human sweat, the frightful blur of belts and bands rushing on their endless course from engine to machine and back again, the rumbling of the floor shooting vibrations through their vitals, the mechanical fingers of the looms clawing and pulling, twisting and grasping anything that came in their way. A temple to business, a holy shrine to commerce, the mill breathed and gasped and cried like a living thing. Yet the whole busy place was only half as busy as it might be, laboring along at but a fraction of its capacity. The mayor struggled to explain that the entire factory was managed from afar by indifferent heirs, relations of the former owner who were eager to sell and collect the profit of their relative's bad fortune. A word here and there managed to creep through the blanket of noise surrounding them. "Modern!" "Profit!" "Returns!" "Labor!" But the scream of the steam engines, the bitter whine of the belts, the machinery's low growl, the whole vast, hellish cacophony drowned the mayor's words in a discordant sea.

Such lost eloquence hardly mattered, the dean thought. As they filed by those fortunate workers who still found employment at the mill, the happy few with dead, hollow eyes and sickly pale skin turned yellow or blue or red with the errant fluff of the thread, women and children darting in and out of the scrabbling looms, to tug and gather the cloth, to dance in a mad riot of commerce, as all of this dramatic show played out before the admiring eyes of Bellminster's great men, it seemed very clear what a remarkable opportunity this business presented. A rare opportunity indeed.

Tuckworth looked down and saw that tufts of colored thread were gathering now on the muddy brown splotches that soiled his trousers and boots, giving him the odd appearance of a semiharlequin, half clown and half clergyman. The sight of his muddy boots caused him to think again of the plots he had devised that morning with Semple after the dawn's early downpour.

"This rain has left the roads a quagmire," the dean reported as he and the foreman looked on at the cathedral and the dissembling activity of laborers trying not to labor, the work that was not work going on about them.

"Aye, mess and muck," Semple agreed. "What of it?"

"Do you think we might have trouble bringing a suitable wagon to town through such a swamp?"

The foreman thought for less than a moment, then winked slyly at the dean. "Long as this wet keeps up, don't know when we'll be able to get a wagon here," he pronounced with a conspiratorial leer that Tuckworth hoped might have been more circumspect.

The dean was pleased with this scheming. Every delay, every obstacle meant precious hours to them now, and as the party continued through the factory, his mind toiled over further plans to cheat time. They stopped to nod approvingly at a lethal-looking contraption whose purpose escaped Tuckworth entirely. A shirtless girl, no more than six, stood nearby, serving the machine in some arcane rite, staring into its oily hot interior, her stringy, ill-fed body slick with sweat and covered with collected fuzz from the air like a soft fur. The dean moved over and placed his hand on the child's grimy head, desperate to offer some consolation for a life laid waste by inhuman occupation. The girl ignored him, her every fiber intent upon her mechanical master.

Tuckworth looked up to find Hamlin Price staring at the child, and in his gaze the dean saw something besides calculation. He saw hunger there, a compassion beyond human feeling, a quick, lustful longing, importunate and possessive. It was gone in a moment, suppressed by that supreme mastery of self-control, and the dean was left to wonder in horror. Was this what Price called love? Could any human spirit distort itself so thoroughly as to call that sordid desire affection? Having seen it once, bare and unrestrained, Tuckworth could now find its marks in the man, in the corners of his eyes and his hard, cruel mouth, spy its telltale signs like a caged thing pacing behind bars, ever prowling, ready always for that instant of release. Could such bestial passion be some form of human love? Perhaps, Tuckworth thought. Perhaps to Price's mind it felt like love, this fire within him. But the dean also knew, knew from his own dire experience, how even love can be turned to pain. Even love can destroy.

The tour was over presently. Price went off for a private supper with the mayor and a few select associates, a prelude to the following day when the same crowd would troop together to view the living quarters of New Town, wretched hovels designed and built as stalls for human cattle, each one identical to its neighbor, half of them boarded up and abandoned. And then afterward, the crowning event of this hurried courtship, a great banquet in the Town Hall, Bellminster feasting her honored guest. Tuckworth went home to the cathedral, surprised that his day's dissimulation, this shadow game, should be so taxing. He was far more weary and depressed than he felt he had cause to be.

He was met, upon his return to the mock bustle of Semple and his men, by the barely suppressed fury of Reverend Mortimer. The rector had been awaiting the dean's arrival for some time, it seemed, and his eyes burned cold and keen, with a temper kept barely in check by the austere practice of a relentless spirit. Without the least show of polite greeting, he launched into his accusations.

"I have had report of your meeting with the mayor, Mr. Tuckworth," he began as he stood amid the ruins of Bellminster Cathedral. "Am I to understand that you betrayed Mr. Price's confidence? Do you know how the mayor is laughing at your innocence, your absurd naiveté? Do you truly expect me to believe that you had no idea the mayor and his pack of pharisaical cronies would forgo chasing after Mr. Price's purse strings just because you asked them not to?"

Tuckworth looked at the rector with all the dull and lifeless stare he could muster. "I'll tell you in all honesty, Mortimer," he replied. "The mayor hasn't a chance of interesting Price in that mill. Believe me, if I thought he had, I never would have uttered a word."

This admission failed to address the question, however, or to assuage the rector's ire. Mortimer's eyes folded into dark slits, his nostrils peaked, and the veins at his temples twitched as he adopted a severe, almost biblical posture. "I regret the action you force me to take at this juncture, Mr. Tuckworth," he announced, the crisp precision of his words and the clicking of his tongue upon his teeth clear signals of the passion surging within him.

The dean only nodded, his mind momentarily preoccupied with the senseless labor going on about them, a half-dozen men employed to unravel the chain from its web of blocks and pulleys, the insane business of nailing nails that had already been nailed, securing joints that were already tight. Word of Price's sabotage had spread. The men were working nervously, tiptoeing about the scaffold, afraid of every footfall, casting anxious stares about, and trying to speak caution with their eyes, and Tuckworth worried that Price would see through their playacting, would know he had been discovered.

"I am afraid," the rector went on, "that I must report this latest lapse in judgment to the bishop. I daresay," he sniffed, "that it will be the final error you will be allowed to make."

The dean heaved a sigh. He dreaded saying what he was about to say, but he could not avoid it any longer. His conscience would not allow him to stay silent, and he steeled himself for the inevitable bother.

"Mortimer," he began, trying to sound friendly without being fatherly, "I really don't think you should pursue Mr. Price's purse so aggressively."

The rector pulled himself up straight (or straighter) and a thin smile of open condescension creased his dry lips. "Do you not?" he asked.

"Look, Price is . . . well, he's not what he appears to be. If you could just sit quietly for a couple of days and do nothing—"

"Do nothing, is that your advice?" sneered the rector. "It seems that inaction has become a matter of policy for you."

Tuckworth removed his spectacles and rubbed the bridge of his nose. "I'm only trying to give you a friendly warning—"

"And I will warn you, sir. Prepare yourself for retirement from your public duties. I daresay you will soon find yourself relieved of any last attachments you may have with your cathedral." And with that, Mortimer turned sharply and strode off.

Well, he had tried, Tuckworth thought, but the realization gave his conscience no solace. Perhaps he had not tried hard enough. He turned and went back into the vicarage to escape for a time his fears and demons, to try to catch a moment of repose before he was forced again to wage his private, invisible battle with Price.

He shared a quick conference with Hunt, told him how matters stood ("We plod," Hunt had said encouragingly, "but even our plodding serves"), and then retired to the privacy of his study. No sooner was he settled, however, than he was greeted by Lucy, who appeared all mad charm and merry spirits. She seemed too happy, in fact, and Tuckworth knew at once that she was suffering, suffering terribly. "Father," she said, a quaver in her voice belying its musical lilt, "Mr. Hunt tells me Raphael has gone off to London."

Tuckworth winced. "Yes, he hired a horse and rode off last night. Some business left unfinished that he had to . . ." The dean's words trailed off as his daughter's merry mask dissolved into tears. He held out his arms and she fell into his embrace, burying her sobs in the crook of his neck, holding herself on his shoulders. Tuckworth let her weep, and as she wept he weighed a host of fears, the danger and the deadly risk against her strength and cunning. He tried to find a balance to her woes and his worries, and failing that, he came at last to an irrevocable resolution.

He grasped Lucy's shoulders and held her out before him, leaning down to catch her eye and telling her through his somber expression that he had news. She sniffed, and dried her streaming tears, and nodded.

He told her all, from the start, from his first meeting with Price, the calamitous supper party, his reluctance to involve himself and his growing certainty that he must, the threats and recriminations, his own crime, turning burglar in pursuit of a murderer, the dread he felt at knowing Price was there, in Bellminster, everything up to that moment. He revealed it all, and as she listened, he could see her mind grow dark.

"And you knew of this all along," she said when he was finished, "and you never told me?"

"I only tried to protect you, my dear," he replied, suddenly feeling wrong.

"I'm not a child anymore," she declared, trying to control her outrage.

"But, my dear—"

"I have been managing the Cathedral Fund for months now," she stated, her voice rising. "I've supervised Semple and his work, taken on the duties you don't want, and I'm glad to do it. But I will not be considered a helpless little girl anymore, Father. I'm sorry, but I won't."

Suddenly, Tuckworth realized just how wrong he had been, and the contrition written upon his face caused Lucy's growing anger to vanish, leaving their small family strangely adrift. She had a right to know the truth, he now saw. She no longer needed his protection, not the way he was accustomed to protecting her. He could not find any longer the darling of his heart, the little girl who came running to him with a skinned knee or a bruised toe. He saw only a woman he did not really know. Life was growing so different so quickly, he thought. "I was afraid of how Price might use you if he suspected you were with us. He's desperate and violent."

Lucy shook her head. "Desperate, perhaps, but not violent."

Tuckworth paused. "Excuse me?"

"You just said yourself he didn't murder those men. He only killed Quarles to save Wick."

The dean paused again. "He tried to kill Hunt and me in the cathedral."

"Throwing one stone at two men in the near darkness? That was desperation, not violence. He's a vile creature, true enough, but I have to wonder if he's as violent as you think he is. I think, perhaps, your cares for my safety have clouded your judgment."

Tuckworth hesitated, considered, thought over again everything he knew, everything he thought he knew about Price. He had argued that same position once, that Price was not a violent man. At last the dean shook his head. "We can't risk that he isn't dangerous," he said. "But at least now you know."

Lucy leaned over and kissed him, once more her forgiving nature supplying what was wanted. "Of course, dear. Now you rest in here. Raphael will be back in a day or two, and we'll have the truth out soon enough." And with those comforting words, the first genuine comfort Tuckworth had received in this matter since it began, Lucy left him, her spirits restored, happy now to be aware, to know, to understand. Understanding, Tuckworth thought as she closed the door behind her and he sat in the solitude of his study. Maybe that's all there is to it, peace in spirit, peace at heart, the eternal balm, not of forgiveness or of mercy, but only to be understood by those you love, who love you. He sighed a heartfelt, hopeful sigh and closed his eyes.

CHAPTER XXVI
ENDGAME

The bird peered down from its perch atop the dark mahogany bookcase crammed with its overflow of books and papers, bric-a-brac and oddities. It sat there, sat motionless, frozen, watching Tuckworth, marking him, noting his breath, his fears, his pain, its black, unblinking eyes like dark crystals, shining but inscrutable, allowing no meaning to escape, no message to illuminate the thoughts behind their blank opacity. Full and yet empty, knowing and unknowable, they delved into Tuckworth's heart and saw the murder nesting at its core.

Tuckworth tried to return its gaze, tried to be strong and withstand this onslaught on his soul, but he was no match for the mystery behind that dark angel. Some power beyond itself informed the creature, acted as its aegis and its muse. It was out in the cathedral now, that power, dreadful and irrevocable, carrying its onus of sin and guilt and penance, out there waiting for him to emerge. The bird's dark god waited for him, but he could not move.

Suddenly, the bird fluttered down from its perch and dropped heavily, too heavily, on the dean's shoulder. The ebony beak bent to his ear and whispered with a hot breath, "He's here."

Tuckworth brought himself awake and saw Lucy's dark eyes, filled with care and caution, as she leaned down to him. He felt her steady hand upon his arm, gripping him tightly against the coming shock. The door of the study swung open. The dean looked up from Lucy to this impatient visitor, and there, framed in the warm glow of the parlor, stood Hamlin Price.

He was disheveled and distraught, his clothes marred by the rain that was now pattering against the windows, his collar limp and soiled with perspiration. Moisture clung to his face and hair, a porcelain gleam that made his skin appear too delicate to stay long uncracked. His eyes were watery, too, with red and scraggling veins stark against the pale yellow of what should have been white. It was clear that the man's unyielding command was on the very verge of collapse.

Lucy gave her father's arm a secret squeeze and stood up, her demeanor all warm smiles and tenderness. "Father, a gentleman is here to see you," she chimed, sounding easy and musical, walking to a nearby lamp and lighting it, filling the room with her gentle manner. Tuckworth felt a strange sort of awe at his daughter's command in the face of what she knew, her self-control an equal to Price's. She was calm and natural, a beautiful dissembler, and at that moment a vicious pang of guilt struck the dean as he inwardly mourned her need to dissemble, the danger he had brought into their lives.

"Now," Lucy went on, moving toward the door and ushering Mr. Price in, "you two have a nice chat, and let me know if there's anything you require. I'll be sitting right out here, with Mr. Hunt. He's been so active today, I expect him to be running about in no time." And she was artfully, breezily gone, leaving only a sweet scent of violets on the air behind her.

Tuckworth was fully awake now, alert and aware. He had not been expecting this, though he had been trying not to expect anything, to be ready for every eventuality, any move his opponent might play. He was willing now to let Price state his business, eager to see what might come.

Price stood for a long minute staring at the dean, oblivious to his surroundings, to the clutter of the study and its homely comfort. He stood and watched, something crazed yet helpless in his look, as if sanity had run its course at last and was left with nowhere, not even madness, to retreat to. He seemed to glow with a luminous tension, fear and doubt vibrating through him, giving to his stolid presence an animated energy.

Almost without moving his lips, Price whispered, "What are you doing?"

Tuckworth spoke calmly and distinctly, his words sounding strange and distant. "I'm doing what I must do."

"To what purpose?" hissed Price. "To torment me? To force my hand? To exercise your will against mine?"

"To keep you here."

"So you can find a way to get at me, is that your game? Keep me here until I trip and fall, till the trap springs open and you're there to watch the noose tighten around my neck!" He raised a hand to his throat, grasping at an imaginary rope. "I told you, I'm no murderer!"

"I believe you."

He spread his arms wide to encompass Bellminster. "Then why all of this?"

"To rescue you." Tuckworth had not been certain, not until he voiced the words, that this was his intent. Yes, he wanted to save the children, Price's victims, but to do so he suddenly realized that he must help Price. So many years a spiritual guide, a confidant and adviser, so many confessions heard, so many sinners reclaimed and so many lost, had made service a second nature to the dean. And so when he spoke, made this desire real with the utterance, he was surprised not to have realized it before.

Price did not appear surprised, however. He only looked as he had ever looked, searching, testing this information, marking it and fitting it into the picture of his strife, the twisted landscape his life had become. "You want to rescue me," he repeated dully.

"Yes."

"From my sin."

"Yes."

"You're a greater fool than I ever imagined."

Tuckworth thought for a moment, and then said, "Yes, I suppose I am."

"You think I can be redeemed? You think I care to be?"

"No," the dean answered, honesty now his only recourse, his sole scheme. "No, I don't imagine you can be redeemed, not by me. Not by anyone. Redemption, that's too much for my poor abilities. I only want to rescue you from yourself, so you can recover the freedom you've lost."

"Freedom? What freedom have I lost?"

"Freedom to live your life outside this prison you've built, these inescapable bars you carry about with you everywhere. Freedom to do the good in the world you want to do, that I know you want to do, the enormous good that you're capable of. Good for its own sake, not as penance or atonement."

Price moved cautiously about the edge of the room and found an old, disused chair piled high with books and papers in a shadowy corner. He pushed these to the floor with a riffling thump and sat down, never taking his eyes from the dean. Odd, Tuckworth thought, his mind for some reason calm and entirely collected. He'd almost forgotten that chair existed.

"Is my freedom your gift to give?" Price asked, a forced edge of scorn cutting through his voice.

"No, I can't give you freedom. But I can help you to find it."

"Through God?"

The dean shook his head. "I'd never presume."

"How then?"

"By forcing you to leave your prison."

"How?"

"By making it impossible for you to stay."

Price paused for a moment, looked keenly at Tuckworth, weighing the dean's words, their sincerity and likelihood. Yes, he realized, the truth slowly dawning on him. Yes, there was possibly a way out, if only he would take it. "You're a fool," he muttered.

"I've already told you that's very likely."

"And I've told you once, God made me what I am! He made me love the way I love! He tempts me with innocence, don't you see? He makes me hunger after purity!"

"Hunger, yes. Hunger, but not love. Look, Price, I don't know who or what made you how you are. But I know you have the power to resist it. I've seen your command, your strength of character."

Price laughed a sick, tormented laugh as a few sorry tears began to well up and overflow his raw, weary eyes. "Strength? There's not enough strength in a hundred souls to resist what God has placed in my heart. I've tried! Don't you understand? I've tried to resist, tried to stop! I've resolved a thousand times, never again! And a thousand times I will see sweet innocence before me, hear its laughter in the streets, watch it from a distance, and I will succumb! God—"

"It's not God, Price."

"Do you imagine I did it myself? Would I have chosen such a life? The fear, the terror of discovery, of shame and scandal? Would this have been my choice? You don't understand."

"No," the dean conceded. "I don't understand. I've tried and I don't. But you don't understand, either. You keep saying God did this to you, but He didn't. And neither did you."

"Then who—"

"It doesn't matter who. It doesn't matter why. If you believe it's God doing this to you, fine. Then set God at defiance. If you think it's the devil, then defy the devil. It doesn't matter. It only matters that it stop, now, tonight. From this moment, you must end this madness, this terrible lust that's devouring you and all those who come near you. I thought once you were a monster, Price, but you're not. You're only a man, confused and lost, but a man, that's all. And you must fight this as a man."

Price stared at Tuckworth, a troubled, open look that seemed to carry with it the fear of hope. "How?" he asked in soft derision. "How? Through prayer?"

The dean began to think the problem through. "No," he answered, unaware that he had a plan until it came to him. "Not through prayer. Through money." Price looked suddenly shocked, and Tuckworth went on to explain. "You've set yourself apart from the world, surrounded yourself with men who cater to your desire." Price nodded. "Then you must do the opposite. Bring those into your world who will help you fight against this desire. Pay them, as you paid Quarles and Wick, to assist you. Use your money to buy your release."

A sudden look of defeat swept over Price. "Money," he muttered. "No, it's too late for that."

"It's not too late—"

"It is! You don't understand! I've paid for my privacy. I've paid for my sin. Now, I'm doomed to keep paying."

"But you can pay for redemption."

"I tell you it's too late," Price spat out, his words final and horrible, and Tuckworth knew that he could do nothing more now. "I've come here for a purpose," Price went on, his steely reserve returning, if only as a mask too grotesque to hide his anguish any longer. "I'm warning you, a last warning. You have no idea what danger you're in. You can't stir from this house again, not as long as I'm in Bellminster. Do you understand? Just let this be as it must be, as it's ordained to be, and in a few days I'll go and you can have your precious Bellminster back again. Have your cathedral. Good God, grant me this peace and I'll build your damn cathedral for you, all of it! Just leave me be!"

Without waiting for another word, Price turned and fled out the cathedral door, out into the night.

The moment the door slammed shut, the other door, which led into the vicarage, opened, and Hunt hobbled in with Lucy close behind.

"I heard all," Hunt said.

"There must be some way to help him, Hunt," the dean insisted.

"If there is, I don't know what it could be. I'm afraid money is an ineffectual savior. It corrupts before it can redeem."

"But he wants to end this. I know it."

Hunt sat down and stretched a hand out through the air as Lucy came up beside her father and threw an arm about him. "We must just let all plans play out now as they are meant to do," Hunt advised. "Afterwards, after Price is safe behind bars, there will be time to redeem him."

Tuckworth nodded slowly, and recognized that then Price might have a more adept confessor to whom he could appeal. Perhaps that was his only hope. But at least he had tried. It seemed to be his only consolation anymore, that he tried, but it was oddly satisfying.

Early the next morning, in the hour before dawn, his usual time for waking, the dean came down the stairs of the vicarage. He had not slept well. He never did anymore. But at least he had not been haunted by fears of failure. His thoughts had turned away from schemes and traps, plots to ensnare a villain. Instead, he was filled with hope, the hope for a troubled soul soothed, a man shown that there might be another way. He had known such a feeling before, the pleasure of good works, but it had been a long time. And it mattered nothing to him now, in the faithlessness of his later years, that there should be no God hovering overhead to reward such service. It almost felt better to act on behalf of the good with no hope of reward.

Tuckworth wandered into the study quietly so as not to disturb

Hunt sleeping in the parlor and made his way to the cathedral door. It creaked softly as he opened it, the familiar whisper that had bid him good morning these many years. He took two steps out into the cathedral, and abruptly a black shape loomed up behind him and clapped a single broad hand across his mouth, pinching his nose shut in the crook between thumb and finger, stopping the air. Tuckworth struggled to raise both hands against his attacker, but the man pinned one arm to his side. With his remaining hand, the dean clawed at the man's fingers, dug and scraped at the merciless grip. His lungs began to ache as he convulsed, trying vainly to draw air through the wall of flesh. He jerked his head back and forth as though he might shake off this assault as he would a spider's web, but the hand only held him tighter. He ceased his wild struggling and cleared his mind. Calm, that's what he needed. Calm. His lungs burned. Stay calm. He raised his boot and tried to drive his heel into the other man's foot, but to no avail. He only stamped uselessly against the stones of the cathedral. A fire raged in his body. With his one free hand, he dug deep into his pocket and came across something long and thin and smooth. He took out the toothpick, gripped it tight in his fingers, and stabbed down into the hand across his face. Tuckworth heard a sharp cry by his ear as his attacker tried to raise his other hand to defend himself, but now it was the dean's turn to pin his assailant's arm. Still grasping the toothpick, Tuckworth spun it like a drill and drove it deeper into the flesh, pushing it in halfway along its ivory length.

The man let go at last, and Tuckworth fell to his knees, sobbing in great gulps of air. But he could not rest. Without even rising, he scrambled on his hands and knees, retreated back into the study, hurried to slam the door behind him. But it would not close. He glanced down. A foot wedged in the space between door and jamb. A great weight threw itself against the door, trying to force it open. The dean raised his heel again, and this time he did not miss but brought his full force down upon his attacker's toes. With a grunt the man pulled away, and Tuckworth closed and locked the door.

For a second only he sat against it, drinking air. Then, he stood and hurried on wobbling legs to lock the other doors of the house. He roused Hunt and checked the windows in the parlor, lit candles and lamps in every room, took a knife from the kitchen, and sat himself down at last, shaking and exhausted. And as he sat, the truth dawned slowly upon him. He was alone now, without Hunt, who could only limp about, without Raphael, gone off to London. Now it was only he and Price, alone.

And against the sofa Leigh Hunt sat, aware of the dean's fear, anxious and frustrated and, for a time, without a word to utter in comfort.

CHAPTER XXVII
CHECK

The Banquet Chamber in the Town Hall of Bellminster, generally a dark, drafty cavern, shone with the glow of two hundred candles mounted in sparkling candelabra positioned down each side and along a brightly laid table that stretched the length of the room, sparkling with pewter and crystal, silver and immaculate linen, redolent with twisting summer garlands hung from the rafters and the stiff scent of starch and lye in the air. Much had been done in the last forty-eight hours to prepare for this auspicious feast, and as Tuckworth looked out over the milling crowd of luminaries, keeping his eye ever on Hamlin Price, he was cautious not to appear too troubled.

Yet he was troubled, gravely so. Since that morning, when Mrs. Cutler, rising with the dawn, had found him still sitting silently in the parlor with Hunt and screamed to see her best carving knife angled across the dean's lap, his life had been a tumble of frights and starts. He had told Lucy about the attack, of course. No sense holding back the truth from her any longer. He let her know the very palpable danger they were in. But he was determined not to be held prisoner in his home, and she understood that. Once the sky had lightened, once the solid bank of clouds overhead had changed from black to gray to sullen white and started to unleash their damp burden, the moment dawn was finished with the world and day could be said in truth to begin, the dean ventured out the door.

"No illusions now, Tuckworth," Hunt had told him, a shy, apologetic smile on his lips. "I'll not tell you this is the right or the wrong thing to do. It's your life in peril, and a poor invalid has no right to counsel. But I am proud to know you."

"Very good of you," the dean had replied, "but I'm still afraid."

"I'm glad you're afraid," Lucy told him, straightening his collar before he went out and reading the fear in his face and his nervous hands. "It will keep you careful."

"I'm glad I'm afraid, too, my dear," he answered, giving her a kiss on her moist cheek, not dried yet from her worried tears.

She pulled him tightly to her, giving him the sort of ferocious hug only children ever freely give, and whispered in his ear, "I'm sorry."

"Whatever for?" he asked, surprised.

"I'm sorry for offering advice that proved so dreadfully wrong. Mr. Price is not as far beyond violence as I had thought."

The dean considered for a moment before replying. "It would seem not."

That first step past the garden gate was the most terrible, and he felt no shame in his fear. Neither did he feel particularly brave for going out. There was really no choice. He must do it, make a show of himself for the audience he knew to be watching. He must keep the game alive, see this thing through until Raphael might return. Indeed, he was not so certain that he could stop now even if wisdom dictated otherwise. He could not put into words why it was so. He simply knew that his going forward was inevitable, his fate propelling him like a leaf caught in a current. He knew it with a surety he neither doubted nor questioned. He only felt troubled. And anxious. And afraid.

He joined the tour of New Town and saw Price there, and was seen by him. It was a fitting landscape for such a secret battle, the one place in all Bellminster that never failed to depress the dean's spirits. Blocks of monotonous flats three and four stories high piled one upon another, laid out straight like dull red serpents, unnaturally cumbrous and uniform. Row after row of brick houses molded their sinuous line to the earth, shoddy structures that were painted and pretty once, but in just a very few years had grown shabby, unkempt, unloved, mere hovels for men to breathe in and die in. A white door, chipped and peeling, one window below, two windows above, behind a small envelope of a garden banked by high wooden fences, the same on either side and on either side beyond that and beyond that, an unending mockery of domestic life fit only as a place to rest and eat between shifts at the mill.

Here families sprawled and grew, forging life in a place not meant to be lived in, only inhabited. Children ran up and down the filthy, muddy streets, leaping over the stream of ordure that flowed down the middle, hiding and screaming and leaping about, giving the dean more than one breathless start. Tuckworth kept his eye on Price throughout this journey, and what he noted caused him some confusion. The man seemed lonelier and more distant than ever, unsmiling, immovable, proof against any human approach. He was a wan and pathetic figure amid these self-important potentates, the dean thought. He hardly seemed a killer at all.

The mayor noted Price's aloof spirits and unleashed a torrent of enthusiasm upon the man, trying to elicit some encouraging mark of his intentions.

"As you can see, Mr. Price," he explained, "our families live with every mod . . . modern comfort. The wealth of windows, you notice. Light has a most efficacious influence . . . most efficacious . . . on the workers' health. Keeps their tempers pleasant and amenable. And the chimneys. Very modern. Cheap . . . cheap to erect, of course, but remarkably efficient. One family can warm itself all winter on . . ." His voice trailed off as he struggled to dredge up the statistics from his memory.

"Five hundredweight," offered Bates.

"Three," corrected Bick.

"Three hundredweight of coal! Purchased from the mill, naturally," the mayor concluded, and they walked on. It was a mystery how they kept from getting lost in that maze, where every street looked like every other, where each corner was identical to its three brethren and all vistas were the same. And, in fact, they must have made a wrong turn somewhere in their travels, for they found themselves in a small neighborhood devoid of any human pretense. Shutters were closed and nailed shut, and the few windows that remained open were open in earnest, smashed and empty. Notices fluttered on a few doors, warnings of eviction and dismissal, harsh clues to harsher futures, lives cast off on the sea of insolvency and ruin. Only the wealthy come to be known as bankrupts, Tuckworth had thought. The poor are merely poorer still.

With the assistance of Mr. Bates, who knew these streets better than the dean might have expected, they extricated themselves and went on with their dismal tour. Through it all, Price kept to himself, only muttered answers to direct questions, looking as though he were from some alien land, some place outside this world. It was only when their party broke up that Tuckworth noticed how Price had never once looked at him.

That had been the afternoon. Since then, the dean had returned home to the vicarage, told what little he might tell to Hunt (who cursed his lame ankle in passionate terms), assured himself through Lucy and Mrs. Cutler that all had been well and quiet for them that morning, reassured himself of this fact through Mary Black and Adam, conferred briefly with Semple to learn that no cart could get through the muddy streets for at least another day, tried to compose himself when the foreman actually nudged him and gave a too-knowing leer, and went off to the official reception of Mr. Hamlin Price by Bellminster's commercial society.

The rains had begun to fall with a sterner purpose as he made his way to the Town Hall, so that now Tuckworth was dripping slightly on the polished floor, watching Price where he stood like some ancient and severe stoic beside the enthusiastic mayor, not caring for what the man had to say, for the gallery of faces he was forced to meet, the names that went past him and through him with no hint of interest on his part. Indeed, it was evident to most there that Price's presence was purely formal, that he had no desire to bring his money to Bellminster. Only the mayor seemed entirely blind to the fact.

Still, a feast is a feast, and cause enough for pleasure. The soft murmur of important talk rose to the high ceiling, into the dark, smoky reaches just out of the candlelight's glow. The town's bankers, barristers, financiers, and men of industry stood in distinct audience here and there, while lesser notables, merchants and aldermen, swarmed like moths about the great lights of the town. Mortimer was missing, no doubt in protest against this kidnaping of Price from the parochial vault. The greatest light of all, Lord Granby, stood in one corner like an affable sultan, tall and stately, and despite the crowd jockeying about him, he had one twinkling glance and a wave to spare for the dean. Tuckworth waved back and wondered if a meeting of Parliament felt half as important as this provincial reception.

Out of the corner of his eye, the dean noticed an elderly servant in livery motioning energetically for him. He walked over to the man.

"Forgive me, vicar," the old man said, looking extremely concerned. "Don't mean to call you away."

"Nonsense, William," the dean replied. "I didn't recognize you in your, um . . . grandeur."

"Aye," the man beamed proudly, straightening his green-checked coat over the red waistcoat. "Anyways, there's a young feller below says he's got to see you."

Tuckworth's blood surged within him at the news. He left in a blink, careful not to run at first, but outside the chamber he bounded down the stairs and would have greeted Raphael with a warm embrace, had the lad not been covered from top to toe in mud.

"You've not come a second too soon, my boy," the dean informed him excitedly. "How did you get here so quickly?"

"It was the lady, sir," Raphael answered breathlessly, looking as though he had run the whole way to London and back. "I went straight to the address you gave me, and once she knew my business, I don't think four strong men together could have kept her away. She'd never ridden before in her life, yet we made the entire journey through this rain and she never complained except once, and that was just carping at our slow pace. She's a remarkable woman, sir."

"I hope she is," Tuckworth replied. "Where did you leave her?"

"I took her straight to the vicarage. She's there now."

The vicarage. A vague misgiving passed over the dean for a moment and was gone. "Fine," he said. "Well done. Now, there's work yet to do, and we must hurry about it."

"Is Price still here, sir?"

"That he is, and I think he's more dangerous than ever."

Raphael nodded. "Lucy told me. Are you well?"

"Right enough," the dean demurred, feeling unduly proud of his adventure. "Now, you run off to the hospital and fetch Dr. Warrick. He should be there. And then pick up Hopgood on your way by the Constabulary House. They're both ready for the call. Bring them to the vicarage right away. With luck, this will all be resolved this evening."

Raphael raced into the dusky twilight, back into the wet and mud of the coming night, and Tuckworth set off for home. Perhaps, he thought as he padded through puddles and raised his collar against the rain, perhaps tonight it will be done.

When he got to the vicarage, he dashed immediately into the parlor, where he found Lucy and Mrs. Cutler administering warmth, comfort, and soup to their guest, while Hunt entertained them all with his easy manner.

"Dean Tuckworth," Hunt called as they heard the door open and close again, "our visitor is arrived and in a perfect mind to assist us."

"Mrs. Merton," Tuckworth said as he entered, "you have no idea how grateful we are to see you."

The women turned now to look at him, and Mrs. Cutler screamed and pointed a horrified finger at the floor.

"Muddy boots!" she shrieked.

Tuckworth stumbled to a chair, more shaken by his housekeeper's indignant rage than he cared to show, and set about removing the offensive boots.

"You're not half so grateful to see me, sir, as I'm grateful to you for calling me here," Dolly Merton informed him. She spoke the words with a dire and serious intent, and the dean could see at once that she understood all and grasped the gravity of the role she was to play. She was still somewhat bedraggled-looking, though Lucy and Mrs. Cutler had seen to her needs quite admirably and helped her straighten and wash herself as best as they could. Still, there was something sad and noble about this woman, and brave.

"It's terrible to ask this service of you, I know," Tuckworth said, putting aside his boots and catching his breath, not realizing until now how tired he was.

Mrs. Merton nodded her head decisively. "I told you I'd do anythin' for Malcolm Wick," she answered, her eyes going suddenly dark and proud. "I meant it."

Leigh Hunt reached out and patted the woman on the hand. "We always knew you did, my dear," he said.

CHAPTER XXVIII

THE TABLES TURNED

They awaited Raphael impatiently, anxious and expectant, Lucy and Mrs. Cutler hovering tenderly over their guest and offering her every comfort. Hunt prattled away as though they were all enjoying a marvelous time over tea, while Tuckworth paced nervously up and down the room, watching the clock on the wall as their chance ticked by. Why was he so distraught, so frightened of failure when success had never been closer? He wondered at this success that lay within his reach at last, and it left a taste of iron and grit in his mouth, a taste no different from the failure he had been forced to swallow since this whole affair began.

Raphael arrived at last, with Hopgood and Warrick in tow (the doctor explaining, not very apologetically, that he had been detained with cases of his own). The two men appeared solemn and ready to begin, however, and Tuckworth ushered them, along with Hunt, into his study, then turned to Raphael with a fierce and determined expression.

"Go back to the Town Hall. Keep your eye on Price," the dean ordered. "Tell the doorman you're there under my instructions. It's Will Asher, so I doubt he'll offer any objection. Don't let Price out of your sight, not for a second. He'll spot you, no mistake, but so long as you don't lose him, we should be all right when the time comes to bring him in. Hopgood," Tuckworth continued, turning to the chief constable, "do you feel up to making an arrest in the midst of that crowd, with the mayor looking on?"

Hopgood glanced about nervously at the others. "Well, if a scene could be avoided—"

"Yes, of course," the dean responded testily. "But once we get a reliable identification, once we know for an absolute fact that's Malcolm Wick, you'll have enough to detain Price, won't you?"

"Detain? Yes, I think that will warrant bringing him in to be questioned. Outside the Town Hall," the chief constable added with a dry cough, "in the street."

"Good," the dean said. "Raphael, keep Price at a distance, but don't let him off alone. We should be ready to bring him in the moment he leaves," and his young friend nodded energetically. "Go!" Tuckworth urged, pushing Raphael toward the door. Without a further word, Raphael turned and bolted out into the darkening twilight and rain.

"Now, gentlemen," the dean said, returning his attention to the others in the study, "are we ready to begin our interrogation?"

Hopgood nodded, Warrick took out a small notepad and a pencil, and Hunt crossed his hands before himself excitedly. Tuckworth left the room, returning momentarily with Mrs. Merton on his arm. "This is our chief constable, Mr. Hopgood, and Dr. Warrick," he said by way of introduction. "Mr. Hunt you know. Gentlemen, this is Mrs. Dolly Merton, formerly the household cook for Hamlin Price."

"Mrs. Merton," Hopgood began after they were all seated, taking a stern and authoritative tone that he deemed appropriate to the proceedings, "this is an official inquiry, in advance of the magistrate's inquest, into the identity of a deceased person, unknown, found in the crypt of Bellminster Cathedral." Hopgood hemmed, very formally, and continued. "Now, ma'am, if you don't mind me asking, has the dean here or young Mr. Amaldi or Mr. Hunt told you ought of what we're after?"

"Young man told me you'd found Malcolm and needed someone to identify him." She spoke the words proudly, as a sort of final act she was honored to perform. "Take me there, and I'll tell you true if it's him."

Hopgood looked about at the others. "Yes, well. It ain't quite that simple, Mrs. Merton. The body we found is, well . . ." The chief constable was unsure how to proceed.

"It's unrecognizable, my dear," Hunt interjected, trusting to the woman's strength. "The face has been beaten beyond anything human."

They saw her wince slightly. "Is that how he died?"

"No, thankfully," Tuckworth said. "His end was swift. A knife to the heart."

She nodded and heaved a silent sigh. "The less violence, the better for him. He was a peaceful man, himself."

"We were only wondering," the doctor spoke up now, "whether you might be able to describe any marks that would clearly identify this man as Malcolm Wick."

"He was a short one," she offered. "Not puny, but small. Not quite five and a half feet, I imagine, and didn't weigh no more'n eight stone, if that. I used to tell him as he'd earn more bein' a jockey than a secretary," and she smiled the wistful smile of memory.

"Yes, we have a general description from the dean that fits what we know, but anything more . . ." Warrick hesitated, awkward and embarrassed. "Something more intimate would be welcome."

She looked knowingly at the four pairs of eyes studying her. "I see," she said, understanding at once, and she leaned back in her chair. She stayed there for a moment, strangely serene, eyes shut, and Tuckworth knew too well what she was doing, conjuring the image of Malcolm Wick before her, giving life once more to the man she loved. Another smile, less sad, glided across her full lips. "He had a scar on his belly," she said softly. "A burn. He got it when he was a young'un, leaning up against a hot stove. But children will do that, you know." She thought again, dreaming of days past. "A mole. On his shoulder. His left one. No," she corrected, "my left, his right. His right shoulder. It's shaped like a heart, and the man was that embarrassed by it, God only knows why." Again her gentle musing look, her mild reminiscence. "A scar on his bum." She chuckled. "Forgive me, gen'lemen. His backside. He had a flask in his hip pocket, he told me. Took to carrying it about in his days at university. Made him feel rakish. Sat down and busted it one night. Chewed his flesh ragged. Never took to drink again after that." She sat up straight, opening her eyes at last. "And he's missing the nail of his left small toe."

"I didn't notice the toe," Warrick announced.

"Well, look closer," Dolly Merton insisted. "If that's Malcolm Wick, he'll be without that nail. Smashed his foot movin' a box of books in his room. Nail turned black and dropped off a week later."

They all sat for a moment, exchanging looks, hopeful yet tentative, afraid to think they might finally have what they sought.

"So, doctor," Tuckworth said finally. "Will this serve, do you think?"

Warrick nodded gravely. "I like the toenail, especially. None of the rest of us saw that. If it proves true, I'll testify that this is certainly Malcolm Wick."

"Hopgood?"

"Doctor's word carries all the weight I need. I'd say your Mr. Price will have to explain a great deal before this night is finished."

Tuckworth sat back in his chair and released a deep and sorrowful sigh. "That's fine, then," he muttered, not certain why he felt so dispirited at the news of triumph. "Thank you, Mrs. Merton. If you'll wait outside, I'd like to confer a bit with these men. Mrs. Cutler will see to a bed for you this evening."

The woman rose and took a step toward the door, then turned back, her eyes moist, her lashes catching her tears. "Catch him, sir," she whispered to Tuckworth. "Catch him and hang him, please." And then she turned again and left the study.

Hopgood coughed once more and shook his head. "It's something, no doubt. But enough to hang a man of his position? I'm not so certain of that."

"I don't want to see Hamlin Price hang," Tuckworth stated.

"What?" asked Hunt, more surprised than the others.

"I thought that's what this was about," exclaimed Warrick, "to bring justice to a murderer."

"But he didn't murder Malcolm Wick."

Hopgood sputtered a bit. "Well, that's true, I suppose. But he killed that other chap."

"Defending Wick. I don't think a man should hang for that. I'm not even sure he should rightly be called a murderer."

The dean's companions glanced confusedly at one another before Leigh Hunt threw his arms up in exasperation. "Well, what the hell have we been about, then?"

"I'm sorry, Hunt," the dean said. "I should have told you earlier, but I've only just come to the realization myself. We can't convict Hamlin Price for murder. Nor, I am afraid, do we have evidence of his other, more despicable crimes."

Hunt muttered a curse. "There must be someway to implicate the man."

The dean glanced at Hopgood, who shook his head sadly. "Mr. Price was bein' blackmailed by the only two chaps who might testify against him, and they're both dead. Unless we can catch him in the act of molestation—"

"Which we'll never do," Tuckworth announced.

They all sat for a moment, mortified and dejected.

Hunt turned to Tuckworth slowly, a suspicion of something growing slowly within him. "You have some plan, haven't you? What is it?"

"I'm determined to force Price to give up his depravity."

"Now how do you propose to do that without evidence?" Hopgood asked.

"I'm convinced Price wants to give it up." The other men looked doubtfully at one another. "I understand how ludicrous that sounds. He's given no proof of wanting to reform himself. But I know he's tortured by his lusts. I know he feels helpless against them. He only needs . . ." Tuckworth paused to consider what word best fitted. *Sponsor? Warden?* "A friend. He wants a friend to help him."

Hunt looked on, disbelieving, bewildered. "But how can you hope to befriend that?" he uttered. "What of the children he has ruined? What of the victims this monster has left in his wake?"

"If I could find them I would assist them, as well," the dean exclaimed pettishly, angry with himself at what he knew sounded foolhardy and vain. "I won't insult us all by supposing that Price is as great a victim as those poor ones he's abused. He isn't. But he is a victim of something beyond his control, and I mean to help him see a way to the end of this."

"All right then," Hopgood declared. "How?"

"I only want the threat of an investigation, a public inquiry."

"You want to destroy the man with scandal?" Warrick asked.

"No, I don't want to destroy him. I want to give him sufficient cause to stop. We're agreed that there isn't the evidence to convict him of his crimes. Very well. Then I want to hang Damocles' sword over his head and let him live under the perpetual threat of discovery. His fear will curb his desire."

"You hope," Warrick added.

Tuckworth sighed. "Yes, doctor. I hope."

"Yet you know how dangerous he is," Hopgood reminded the dean. "He's twice tried to kill you."

Tuckworth considered for a long moment. "I can hardly explain it," he admitted finally. "The man I've seen on the street these past days, he doesn't strike me as a killer."

"What?" exclaimed Warrick.

"It's as if all this violence, this sickness, exists outside of him. It's not a part of who he is. He'd abandon it if he had cause. I think the man can be made—can be forced—to abandon it."

"It can't work," Hunt stated flatly, and a little sadly.

The dean had no answer for such a sure statement.

"So, if you'll forgive me," Hopgood ventured, having mulled over the dean's purpose, "what you're saying is you want to blackmail Hamlin Price yourself."

Tuckworth was taken aback by the accusation, but he could not deny its essential truth. Yes, he wanted to blackmail Price, exactly as Quarles and Wick had tried to do. But the cost of his extortion was not to be had in currency. He wanted Price's soul in return for his own silence. This had all been a game to him before, like chess, a game with a winner and a loser. But it was no game, and he was wrong, horribly wrong to have approached it like one.

Just then, a commotion outside in the hallway stopped the dean's thoughts, and all three men stood and turned to the door, through which Raphael burst suddenly.

"He's gone!"

"What?" the dean shouted.

"He was gone when I got there. No one remembers him leaving. The mayor left his side for a moment and couldn't find him after that. Will Asher never saw him leave out the front door. He must have sneaked out." Raphael glanced ruefully about the room. "I've been to the inn. His coach is missing."

CHAPTER XXIX
FLIGHT

*H*orses!" the dean was shouting in the rain-spattered muck of the coach yard. Where Price's coach had been sitting for several days a great hole gaped at him in ridicule. "Hopgood, we'll need horses and riders! He can't go very far in this! The sooner we get after him . . ." But Hopgood was speaking to Raphael, oblivious to the dean's instructions. "Hopgood!"

The chief constable turned to the dean with a stifled grin. "Not so much haste, I think, vicar," he said, oddly confident of himself.

"What? He's getting away as we stand here!"

Raphael stepped forward. "He's not getting so far as he intends, sir," he said.

"What?" Tuckworth asked again. "What does this mean? What have you done?"

The young painter looked suddenly sheepish before the dean, but he knew even this moment could not be wasted, so he stated the case quickly. "I cut the traces, Mr. Tuckworth."

"You cut . . . ?"

"The coach traces, sir. The other night, when I was being so . . . so rash, sir. I just felt I had to do something, so after the sun was down and things quiet, I slipped out here and trimmed the traces. I didn't want to give Price the chance to get away unnoted, and I reasoned, if things turned out for the worse, you could just blame me. I don't think the coach could get very far before the horses run right out from under it."

Now it was the dean's turn to waste their time in silence before erupting in a short burst of laughter. "Bless your rashness, Raphael!" he cried, slapping the lad firmly on the shoulders, and then turning back to Hopgood. "How soon can you get a search party together?"

"Get a dozen men here in less than an hour, and I daresay we'll gather more as we search. Folks'll join in ready enough. Nothin' like a good search—"

"Good, good!" Tuckworth shouted over the storm. "You do just that. Hunt!" the dean called as his friend came hobbling into the coach yard. "He's trapped here, in Bellminster. Can't get out without . . ." Tuckworth's voice trailed off suddenly. "Raphael! Run to the livery! Rouse Cubbins! Make certain his horses are safe, the stable secure. That's the first place they'll try to get to!" Without a word Raphael ran off into the night toward the livery, while Hopgood trotted off in the other direction to raise his forces. "Hunt," Tuckworth commanded, "you come with me. I want to have a talk with Taggart and take a look into Price's room."

"Anything particular to be found there?"

Tuckworth helped Hunt along as he explained. "We've been a couple of dolts, Hunt."

"I don't doubt it. How so?"

"Price had an accomplice, of course! Someone here to help him."

"Who would—"

"The coachman, Hunt! The coachman! He came here with a coachman and we forgot all about him!"

"How do you think—"

But they had reached the tavern by then, and Tuckworth immediately called the innkeeper over.

"Coachman?" Taggart said, musing very noticeably, his brow crinkling and his eyes squinting and a look of enormous concentration spreading across his face. "Aye, might be some'at I know about a coachman, but it could take some time to call it all to mind."

The dean knew Taggart well enough to know that he was offering a fair barter. The man was a commercial animal, through and through. "Time is precious to us, Taggart," Tuckworth said wearily, too aware of the minutes he had at his disposal before the search must begin in earnest. "I'll stand us all a beer or two and we'll think this through together."

They settled along a far corner of the bar, where Taggart could keep a greedy eye on the night's custom.

"Now," Tuckworth continued as the innkeeper pulled three pots from the tap and dumped them sloppily on the table, "what can you tell us about the man who brought Hamlin Price here?"

"Ah, it's *him* you want to know about. Great fat feller, handsome appetite and an endless thirst." Taggart's eyes twinkled at the memory of the bills the man had run up.

"Was he long in Price's service?"

Taggart considered. "Can't say he was, as you mention it. Said he was a hired man. Never been so far from London afore, he told me, which don't seem so far to the likes of us, eh? Chap made Bellminster out to be north of north."

"A hired man?" Tuckworth considered hopefully. Certainly no hired man would be a reliable accomplice in such a venture.

"Aye," went on Taggart, drinking deeply from his pint. "A fine customer. Sorry to see him leave."

"In a great hurry to go, I imagine," Hunt observed.

Taggart looked confused for a moment. "Not particular. Though his master was in a hurry to see him leave."

Tuckworth's eyes narrowed. "How's that?"

"I mean Mr. Price, he sacked the first coachman I just was tellin' you of. He left days ago."

Tuckworth leaned forward. "*First* coachman?"

"First coachman. You asked after the chap as brought Mr. Price here. That was the first coachman. But Mr. Price's own man must have got here soon after, 'cause that first chap got sent back to London."

Tuckworth felt a chill spill across his spine. A second man, called specifically by Price, perhaps, called to Bellminster for some special service. "What do you know of the second coachman?"

Taggart shook his head. "Hardly nothin' at all. Rarely saw him or his master."

"You never saw this second man?" Hunt asked.

"Once or twice from a distance. Shadowy, if you get my meanin'. He was a big chap, I'll tell you that. Sturdy-lookin'. But he didn't eat overmuch and drank nothin' at all."

"His face?"

"Naw. Always kept his hat pulled down, head lowered. I'm not one to go about another feller's business when I know he don't want that business known." Taggart nodded his head sharply to emphasize this point of honor and drained his pint.

"Tell me, Taggart, could you take me to this second fellow's room? I'd like to have a look about."

Taggart was willing, and curious, so the three men left the pub and began to wind through the serpentine halls of the Granby Arms. The innkeeper might have asked what it was about, why the dean and his crippled friend seemed so interested in these matters, but something in Tuckworth's attitude told him to find such answers elsewhere, and indeed, the dean was lost in his own thoughts. A new portrait was taking shape before him, a new picture of Hamlin Price forming as he walked behind Taggart. Price's warnings, his confessions, his tortured, anguished appeals painted a dark shadow that loomed behind the figure of Price.

"So," Hunt whispered as they moved slowly along, "it was this other fellow who tried to kill you."

Tuckworth nodded.

"And cast that stone down upon us?"

Another nod.

A moment of hesitant silence, and then Hunt tossed his final thought into the air. "The inspector?"

Tuckworth did not answer. "Clearly," he muttered with a sickening sense of having missed the point all along. "Clearly there was someone else to fear in all of this, someone more desperate than Price, or merely more ruthless." And suddenly Tuckworth saw in Price's actions of the past day, his wan detachment, his blank severity, not the resolution of a cornered animal nor the despair of a soul in torment, but the emptiness of a man who has given up his will, who is only being moved about, acted upon by an unseen hand. The hand of the mysterious coachman? Who was really in command of the situation now? he wondered. Master, or man?

"Here we are," Taggart announced, shocking the dean from his disturbed reverie. "Yonder there's young painter's room," he said, pointing back down the hall. "That there was Mr. Price's you know, and this across from it was second coachman's."

The innkeeper handed Tuckworth the candle and unlocked the door, which swung open silently, revealing a room in riotous disarray. Bedclothes were flung about, drawers pulled and fallen to the floor, a plain armoire with doors thrown open looking gutted and savaged.

"Gent was in a hurry, true enough," Taggart observed.

Tuckworth took a step into the room, and his foot fell upon something soft. He pulled back, bumping into Hunt who advanced behind him. The dean looked at the floor. For a moment, his mind failed to grasp what it was, this small bundle of cloth and yarn. He reached down and picked it up, holding it before his eyes.

It was a rag doll.

CHAPTER XXX
PURSUIT

T hey have a child with them, Hopgood! A child!"

The chief constable stared blearily at Tuckworth and Hunt through sheets of water. "We can't search faster than we can search, vicar," he explained officially. "We found the coach not four streets over, but no sign of your Mr. Price. Dogs is no good in this. We've got to go door to door. Get more help that way, too. We'll get your men, sure enough."

Hunt stepped forward. "This is not just a matter of catching them anymore, chief constable. Time is everything."

"So's this rain everything," Hopgood replied. "A search has got to be done methodical, or we might just skip by what we're looking for."

Hunt turned back to the dean. They knew Hopgood was right, but something more must be accomplished.

"Listen, Hopgood," Tuckworth said, "what if we can narrow down the places they might go into hiding? There are only a few where Price will feel safe, a few spots in Bellminster that he's familiar with. The cathedral and the mill we can rule out. Too much going on there. And anything this side of the Medwin is too close."

"Where then?"

"New Town."

Hopgood nodded his agreement. "It's removed. Whole streets is abandoned now."

"And Price got a private tour this morning," Hunt added.

The chief constable appeared to warm to the idea, before shaking his head vigorously. "That ain't the way for a search to progress. Now, if they're in New Town, we'll get to them soon enough. And if they try to head across country, we'll have riders after them to-morrow."

"Tomorrow!" the dean cried, exasperated. Then, another idea occurred to him. "Hopgood, can you spare me any men? Just a few to start at the far edge of New Town and work back this way. That's methodical, isn't it? Catch Price in a pincer!"

The chief constable hesitated for just one moment longer.

"He has a child," Hunt said softly.

A child. So did the chief constable. "Jaggers!" he shouted, and a tall, thin young man came bustling over.

"Yes, chief constable?"

"How many do we have searching already?"

"The whole constabulary, sir. A dozen regulars and as many more volunteers."

"And how many men are handy for a detached duty?"

Jaggers considered. "There's four of us right close-by, chief constable. Me, Harbury, Fallstone, and Jackson."

"You get that lot together, then, and go on with vicar here to New Town."

"Do the men have firearms, Hopgood?" Tuckworth asked. The chief constable stared at the dean, a dour, baleful stare. "It's the coachman," he explained, refusing to feel guilty at his increasing demands. "I'm afraid the man is dangerous. He'll almost certainly have a gun himself."

Hopgood turned back to Jaggers. "You heard the vicar!" he shouted. "Pistols! And move, man! There's a child to rescue."

"Hunt," Tuckworth said, turning now to his friend, "I'm afraid—"

"Nothing of it," Hunt replied before the dean could finish. "You hurry, though! I'll stay here."

A quarter of an hour later, and five men carrying five dark lanterns were gathered together in the brick wasteland of New Town, rain falling about them in billowing sheets that streamed off the bowing roofs and overflowed the gutters. They appeared to be stark, slender demons in their glistening weatherproofs, all except the dean, who was somewhat too short and stout to look threatening.

"You keep the shutter open just a bit, you see?" Harbury was needlessly explaining to Tuckworth, showing him the mechanism that kept the dark lantern's light secret, its beam a sliver in the night. "Try not to wave it about as you walk. And here." He handed the dean a pistol. "Keep this handy."

Tuckworth had never considered that, in suggesting they carry firearms, they would *all* carry firearms. But it was too late now to object. The night was moving swiftly on the wings of the storm, and every moment was precious.

They split up, each man taking a row of houses down parallel lanes. They were to walk up to each house, try the door, peer through a window, and then move on. The party would reassemble at the end of each street, then go off again in a new direction.

At first, Jaggers wanted to stay with the dean, showing him the proper way to search, but Tuckworth would not hear of it. "I might as well not be here at all, in that case," he insisted, and so he found himself wandering alone, or as nearly alone on such a night as the rain and the dark left him feeling, through a deserted town on a desperate quest. It all felt so hopeless to him now that he was actually doing it, moving from door to door, slowly, almost mechanically. Test the knob, shine the lantern, peer through the window, so easy to miss something, to neglect for one instant the single clue that would bring this all to an end. He got only half as far as the others before they were forced to come down the street for him.

"Not so cautious, sir," Harbury chided him gently. "We've got to make time."

"I'm afraid I'll miss something," Tuckworth explained, though no one listened. They were off again quickly down other streets, searching about other houses.

The dean had no idea what it was he should be watching for as he looked into the windows. The slithering beam of light that shot from his lantern made everything within appear strange and alien, unlike anything he would call usual. Sticks of broken furniture and crumpled sheets and mounds of mysterious refuse looked like so many odd formations in a subterranean vault. A man could hide so easily in such a landscape. And what of the upper floors? Who was searching there? So many avenues of escape. So many ways yet to lose Price.

Tuckworth walked up to another door and tried the latch. It clicked and opened noiselessly in the dark.

What should he do? Jaggers had never mentioned open doors. Should he call the others? But that would waste time, the dean reasoned, and besides, he was there to search. He walked, short, nervous, tiptoeing steps, into the empty house.

The drumming sound of rain as it spattered on the roof made the place feel even more desolate than it might have seemed in daylight. The single room Tuckworth found himself in was hardly more than a cell, and as he swung his lantern about, it felt impossible to him that a family of any size might have been able to fit in such a space, much less live there.

Suddenly, Tuckworth heard a scrabbling at the back, from without the door. He glanced at the cracked, wooden panels, tried to peer through them with his ears, his eyes. He walked as bravely as he could across the creaking floor and leaned his head against it to listen. Something was there, muttering in a high-pitched voice. He opened the door swiftly in a single, sudden, sweeping jerk. A family of cats, huddling from the rain, broke apart like leaves before the wind and scampered off.

Tuckworth looked about the back garden, a muddy little puddle of a space, entombed within its dilapidating fence, a coffin of wooden planks. The sight of this secluded poverty made him consider. Was it not more likely that someone might sneak into a house from the rear entrance than the front? If they were looking for an open door, a mark of entry, some sign of habitation, weren't they going about it the wrong way?

He determined to continue his search from the gardens, at the rear of the houses, and he went back out into the night alone. The lane seemed longer this way, however, and the way more twisted than it looked from the front. It took more time to maneuver the decaying gates and weed-eaten paths, and when he arrived finally at what he thought would be the end of the street, he could not see his fellow seekers anywhere. Had he made a wrong turn in going down the back way? He retraced his steps, stopping to look in at the odd garden as he went, recognizing little that he had passed before, continuing his search even as he came to realize that he had succeeded only in losing himself.

Lightning began to split the darkness of the night, and thunder exploded close overhead. The dean came suddenly to a sort of back-alley crossroads he didn't remember seeing before. Unsure which direction to take, he simply chose one that looked grimmer and more abandoned than the others and forged on. He would wander into each garden, try the doors, which were often open, peek inside, and then move on, finding his way slowly but feeling now that he was making earnest work of so haphazard a game.

He kept the light from his lantern turned downward as he walked, to avoid treading in puddles and onto glass, and so, as he came up to a doorstep that looked like any number of doorsteps he had already seen, he was able to mark the difference and stop himself before proceeding.

A muddy footprint stared up at him, left upon the threshold just under the eave where the rain had not washed it away. Someone had passed in here, and had done so this very night. Tuckworth backed slowly away from the door and stepped over to the shuttered window. Without using his lantern, he strained to see through the slats, to tell if there was anyone inside. Lightning flashed for a moment, illuminating everything without and about him, and the dean had to wait for his eyes to grow accustomed to the dark once more. Once they did, however, he saw two figures, huddled together and shadowy in the wasted interior of that hovel, mere silhouettes suggesting human form amid refuse and decay.

He pulled back. What must he do? He could manage nothing alone. Could he mark this place and return later when he had found his companions? But who knew what might happen by then? He reached into the pocket of his weatherproof and fingered the slick smoothness of the pistol weighing heavily there. Could he hope to do anything on his own?

From out of the dark behind him, a black figure rose up, reached out, and tried to clap the dean about the throat. Tuckworth's weatherproof was slick, however, and ill-fitting, and the dean managed to slip out of his assailant's grasp. He fumbled in his pocket for the pistol, pulled it out, and felt his heart stop as it slid awkwardly from his fingers and fell with a wet thud to the ground. The other man reached quickly down and recovered the revolver. Standing again, his face was caught by the light from Tuckworth's now open lantern, a large face under a slouching hat, a tired-looking face with a limp, tired-looking mustache.

"Hello, inspector," Tuckworth said calmly. "I thought it might be you."

CHAPTER XXXI
MASTER AND MAN

T he room was stark and cold, the air damp and heavy with mildew. The only light was a thin stream that shone out of the dark lantern from where it sat on the hard floor, next to the inspector. Across the room from him sat Hamlin Price, looking numb and lifeless in the shadows. In a corner of the room, ignored for now and quiet, rested a child, a girl in a dirty dress with un-combed hair. She was small and fair-haired, yet in the darkness she might have been any age from four to ten. She was not whimpering or crying, and she seemed almost unconcerned by her plight, pos-sessed of a mature resignation that appeared diabolical in one so young. She hardly moved, and only her head turned from here to there at times, to watch the shadowy figures around her.

Tuckworth observed all of this from his place by the dripping hearth, a puddle of water forming about his feet, drafty breezes sweeping down the chimney, as far from the door as he might be placed. He was not bound or held by any constraint other than the watchful eye of the inspector, cradling the dean's gun absently in his fist.

Tuckworth could tell the man's thoughts with ease, as easily as he had before in London, a brutish, stupid man with only enough raw intelligence to follow in the rutted paths others had left. He had stepped beyond his powers almost as soon as he formulated his scheme, to operate as Price's man, to take up where Wick and Quarles had been left, to make himself procurer and protector. The inspector was thinking now, running through the ways of escape still available to him, the avenues yet open. Light sparked outside, casting strips of brilliance about the room, and a crash of thunder shook the panes of dirty glass in the windows.

"Two dozen men, inspector," Tuckworth said.

"Shut up or I'll brain you now," the man answered, not angrily but truly. The dean found it far too easy to imagine the fellow a murderer. He must be careful how he dealt with him, the way he exposed the futility of the inspector's position, how flight was now impossible, all escape forestalled. He must be careful, lest the inspector simply kill him to silence him, before he had a chance to get through to Price.

The inspector rose suddenly and groaned. "Old parson's right about one thing," he mumbled, more to himself than to Price. "We can't stay here no more. Head out over open country, maybe. Find a nice quiet farmhouse and invite ourselves for a stay." He held Tuckworth's pistol in front of him, comparing it to the one he carried himself, the small revolver he produced from the folds of his coat. "Here," he said, walking over and dropping the larger gun in Price's lap. "Get used to the feel of that in your pocket." Price only sat there, however, and the inspector shrugged as though he were accustomed to such behavior by now.

"Tell me, inspector," the dean inquired, casually, as though they were speaking over tea cakes, "when did you first see your opportunity? Was it after you threw us out of Price's house?"

The inspector cast a darting eye at Tuckworth, and then back at Price. He shrugged, as though it mattered little what he told the dean anymore. "I had a quick look about the place," he replied. "It weren't hard for a man to make it out."

"Not once we had shown the way. Did Price know you let us

search the entire upper stories? You were supposed to send us packing the moment we broke in, I imagine."

The inspector only eyed Tuckworth with a hostile suspicion. "Shut up," he muttered.

Tuckworth turned his comments to Price. "You must have sent for him as soon as you knew you'd been discovered. And the inspector saw his chance right off, of course. Was it blackmail he wanted at first?"

"I ain't no blackmailer," the inspector said darkly.

"He probably wanted to kill Hunt and me right off, to bind you more closely to him. A brotherhood of blood. Once murder's entered into it, there's no turning back. Of course, he finally got his chance in the cathedral. Two chances, but he bungled them both."

"Shut up, you!" And the man lurched menacingly toward the dean.

Tuckworth held his tongue. Not too far, he thought, not yet. Only just far enough. But time was running out, and quickly. Lightning flashed again in the distance, and the crash of thunder that followed was delayed by a with few seconds. Already the force of the storm was abating. The violence with which it might cover the inspector's escape was slipping by with every moment. The man would be leaving soon, and he would not leave a breathing witness behind.

The inspector paced back and forth. Tuckworth imagined what was running through his mind, the possibilities still before him. It was more than a simple question of flight. There were ends to be tidied up. If he could extricate himself from this somehow, find a way to kill both Tuckworth and Price, with the girl thrown in, then he might yet get out. No one knew who he was or where he'd come from, or so he thought.

Yet he must still be lured by Price's wealth, the promise that had led him into all of this in the first place. "Tell me, inspector," asked Tuckworth, "how will you get to Price's riches while you're on the run from the authorities? I don't suppose a fugitive has ready access to his bank accounts."

The inspector moved quicker than might be imagined, threw himself at the dean and struck him across the face with the back of his hand. Tuckworth sprawled into a corner of the room, landed on his back, and quickly pulled himself up, sitting against the wall. A thin line of blood streamed from his mouth. The man crossed to Tuckworth in one step and lifted him by the collar, throwing him against the wall.

"You shut your face!"

"Don't do that." The voice came from behind them, weak and dry. The inspector looked over his shoulder at Price, who was still sitting on the floor, still languid and dull yet showing now some mark of interest in the scene playing out before him. "Stop that," he said calmly.

The inspector looked back at Tuckworth, then at Price again, then let the dean go in disgust. "Look here, tenderheart," he complained, pointing a thick finger at Price, "you leave the nasty work to me, right? And I'll see you through this."

"Like you've seen him through until now?" Tuckworth pursued, aware of the dangerous game he was playing, the only game left him. "You've only just avoided murder, trailed a dead body across the country—"

"That was his doing," the inspector railed in his own defense, "not mine. Fellow can't get a body dumped in the Thames on his own, he *needs* what help I can give him."

"Does he need help to commit a kidnaping?" Tuckworth went on, pointing at the child in the corner.

The inspector laughed. "Is that what you think? You think we snuck off with that young item? Whisked her away from hearth and home, is that it?" He stepped over to the girl, who until then had looked on impassively at everything going on about her. The man ran his fingers through her oily hair, and she shied, ever so slightly, from his touch. "This here, she's my calling card," the man boasted. "This here's how I got in the door, you might say. Mr. Price, he just wanted protection from you lot, but I seen a better way, a more permanent relationship. So I brought him this sweet morsel. But you think I kidnaped this pretty? Nah, old parson. My first night here, I went out and I bought her."

"Bought her?" Tuckworth exclaimed, sounding more shocked than he intended.

"Aye, right here. You think London's got the clear rights to such things? You think Bellminster ain't up to the world? I bought her, right enough, nor it weren't hard, neither. Just took a bit of barter, and I got a fair price. Better'n fair. A bargain. I'd have paid twice as dear in London."

Of course, Tuckworth thought shamefully. Why not? Why should he be shocked? Yet he was. Bellminster was his home, after all, and it was an awful thing to lose an ounce of faith in your home.

"And that ain't all, neither," the inspector continued. "Don't think our gentleman there ain't above a bit of murder."

"I know how he killed Quarles. He was trying to save Wick."

"Is that all you know? Then do you know what business he sometimes had with Quarles? Oh, not just fetching the darlings. Do you know how sometimes them little ones objected? Decided too late that they didn't like the games old gentlemen wanted to play. Things got a bit nasty then, eh?" He leered at Price. "How many was it you told me, old gent? The ones that ended up in the drink? Three? Four? More?"

Price's face was frozen in horror as he recalled the tortured faces, the dying, strangled noises of the children as they fought against his power. They tempted him to it with their innocence, yes, moved him to the act, but he never meant to harm them. He clapped both hands to his ears as though he might muffle their screams, lose himself to the world that tormented him.

The inspector turned back to Tuckworth. "So you see, old sod, there ain't no help for it. You're in with a right bad bunch o' rogues. Now we've got to get away, and you've got to pay the forfeit." He took a step in the dean's direction. Tuckworth knew the inspector would not shoot him with a search party nearby. The dean crouched and eyed the room hurriedly, looking for any help.

"Price!" he called, trying to pierce the sound of the rain without, to raise his voice beyond the walls. "Price! If he does this, you'll be next! He won't leave either of us alive!"

The inspector struck Tuckworth with his closed fist, clubbing him twice against the head. The dean dropped to one knee, then dived across the room, trying to reach the door. He stumbled and fell and rolled over onto his back, to keep the inspector before him, to be ready for the next attack.

The inspector loomed over Tuckworth as another flash lit the room with a white fire. He knelt down, grasping the dean's throat with his left hand and cupping his right over mouth and nose as he had in the cathedral. Tuckworth tried to breathe, to suck in air, but the inspector's fat hand blocked the way. The dean could feel his lungs begin to burn and spasm for air.

"We calls this burkin'," the man explained, sounding cool and professional. "Won't take long."

The thunder crashed, and suddenly the inspector's grip grew lighter. The dean gasped and coughed, able to find just a stream of air through the man's clutching fingers. The inspector looked confused for a moment, as though he was perplexed at his own weakness. Then he glanced at his side, where a dark stain was spreading against his coat.

He looked up, and this time the gunshot erupted clearly in the room. The inspector flinched, then glared at Price, sitting against the wall with Tuckworth's gun raised in both his hands.

"You lousy bastard," he spat before Price fired a third time, and the inspector crumpled lifeless across Tuckworth's chest.

The dean scrambled out from underneath the man and turned quickly to face Price. It was what he had counted on. Price had killed once before to save Wick. Tuckworth had been trying to remind him of that, to reach that core of humanity he trusted was in the man. That was why he had provoked the inspector so relentlessly, urged the attack and drawn Price into it, thrown his very life into the game, gambling on another man's mercy.

Price sat there now, staring at the inspector, a dull, disinterested look on his face.

"Thank you," Tuckworth said.

Price stared ahead of him into the darkness and muttered mechanically, "You're welcome."

The dean then turned his attention to the girl. She was still where she had been, standing in the corner, her eyes fixed with childish curiosity on the dead man. Tuckworth stood and interposed himself between her and the gruesome shape on the floor, its blood seeping out in a spreading puddle and dripping through the loose boards.

"Hello," he said.

She moved her eyes up to him, but said nothing.

"What's your name?"

In the shadows he could just make out her features. She was a pretty child, though dirty from her travels that night. The dress she had on was plain and mud spattered, her hair flattened by the rain, but her eyes shone out from the dark like beacons, large and luminous, though empty of all feeling. Tuckworth stepped over to her and knelt down, taking her one hand in his two.

"What's your name, dear?"

The girl looked full upon him, unflinching and fearless. "Bit," she said.

"Bit. That's a very nice name for a little girl. Is that short for Elizabeth?" She shrugged, and Tuckworth guessed that she might be five or six. "Well, Bit, we're going to go outside in the rain soon, to find some men out there who will help us. Is that all right?" She shrugged again, uncaring.

The dean remembered and dug into his coat pocket. He pulled out something soft and ragged, and held it out to her. "I believe this is yours," he said.

She snatched the rag doll from him with one hand and cradled it fiercely in the crook of her neck, hugging it with desperate affection, and for the first time she looked truly like a child.

Tuckworth stood up and turned around. Price was still sitting on the floor in the same spot, still staring blindly into the darkness.

"Come along, Price," Tuckworth said. The man did not move. A qualm of fear lurched through the dean like ice in his stomach. "It's over now, Price. Come with me and I'll help you. I'll do everything I can to help you fight this thing."

"Fight," the man whispered.

"Yes, fight it! I'll speak on your behalf to the authorities. You saved my life, the life of this child. You tried to save Wick, and if you panicked after that and made mistakes . . ." The dean paused, unsure what the future might hold for Hamlin Price. "Well, your sentence might not be long, and you might be allowed to serve it here, in Bellminster. I can help you here, Price. We can put a stop to this."

Hamlin Price looked up suddenly, a stern and forbidding resolution in his eyes, and Tuckworth saw once more the supreme command that marked so much of his character. "Yes," he stated. "Of course." And with that, he raised the gun swiftly to his temple and pulled the trigger.

CHAPTER XXXII

BIT

*B*it screamed and ran around the parlor in her pretty flowered frock, while Raphael chased her about on his hands and knees, a lumbering bear, and Lucy looked on, laughing herself to tears at his foolery. The child darted here and there, easily keeping away from her pursuer, until she leaped at last into Lucy's skirts and buried herself there. Her laughter stopped as abruptly as it had begun, and the same sad, grown-up look came back to her. Bit's screams of play were so bright, so different from the screams that cut short her sleep too often.

Two weeks after coming to the vicarage, Bit had become a fixture in the place. She had worked her way gently into Lucy's heart. She was a great favorite of Adam Black, who watched over her antics with his own childlike wonder, and Mary looked to her as a dear little sister already. The only ones to fuss at her presence were Mrs. Cutler, whose ferocious objections to the mess and bother of a child in the vicarage were overbalanced by the ferocious compassion she had immediately felt for the girl, and Dean Tuckworth, who simply believed that the child should be with her mother.

"But I'm telling you," Hopgood informed the dean in his study, where the raucous noise of play easily invaded, "even if we could find her mum, you wouldn't want such a life for the dear. You told me yourself she's seen the doctor, and his report ain't one you'd wish on any little thing."

"Yes, yes," Tuckworth agreed. "I'm sure you're right, but if I could just speak to the woman. I find it difficult simply to take the child in without any recourse to her natural parent."

"One as sold her own child ain't natural. Of course, there's always the Foundlings Home in Morley."

Tuckworth shuddered. As vicar, he had made regular visits to that miserable foundation. The dean thanked the chief constable for his efforts, for everything he had done in the matter, and ushered him to the door leading out to the cathedral.

"You know, Hopgood, if it weren't for you, we might not have saved Bit in time."

"Me?" Hopgood exclaimed in surprise. "I'd say you were the one as did it."

"Well, it takes more than one man to save a life, Hopgood." And Tuckworth thought briefly of the life he had failed to save, alone. "My thanks again."

Tuckworth left the study and went back out into the parlor to sit in his accustomed chair (after first removing Bit's doll and setting it aside on a table). He looked at his daughter with her young charge, and he felt something sad well up inside him, something like a watch ticking irrevocably on, as though this moment was already lost to him.

Closing his eyes, he recalled his farewell to Leigh Hunt that morning, walking slowly with the man across Cathedral Square to see him off in the coach to London, the same coach the dean had taken, so long ago now it seemed.

"Stop worrying about the child," Hunt had told him. "Children are remarkable creatures, stronger and more resilient than we old folk."

"I know," Tuckworth conceded, though he doubted he knew of any child forced to endure what Bit had. "But I'm too old to raise a child again."

"Yet you seem to have done such a marvelous job once. You might try again, you know." Tuckworth smiled, just short of laughter. "I myself am never certain how many children I'm responsible for," Hunt went on. "There seem to be whole tribes of the creatures rampaging about my little house. I can't say that I recall having begotten them all. I am almost certain I didn't. But I *can* say that they have very materially begotten me. We parents often talk of forming our charges' characters, and yet it's our own characters that most profit from the relationship, I find."

What argument could Tuckworth make against such wisdom so kindly spoken? Indeed, what argument did he care to make? The child called out to his sympathies so very much.

"Now," Hunt continued as he hobbled along on his cane, the dean strolling slowly beside him, "I want you to promise that you will write regularly and keep me informed as to our young friend's progress. All my young friends, of course, but Raphael's especially."

"He and Lucy seem to have made up rather nicely," the dean observed.

"Yes, but you know the way won't be easy with them yet. The course of true love, Tuckworth. And then, he's an artist." Hunt clucked his tongue with meaningful concern. "No, it won't be easy."

"It never is easy."

Hunt looked closely at his companion as they walked along, almost come now to the Granby Arms. Something else was troubling the dean. Hunt stopped.

"You could not have saved him, Tuckworth."

The dean nodded. "I know. I know it perfectly well. I'm only concerned that I tried."

"How's that?"

Tuckworth shook his head. "When I look at Bit, and think what that monster did to her, I'm almost relieved that he killed himself and saved us all the trouble of rendering justice on him."

"Yet you had wanted to redeem this monster."

The dean sighed. "I know."

They continued their walk. "It was easier for all of us to see Price as a monster," Hunt observed. "We can hate a monster with little personal provocation. But you saw him as a man, one who suffered from his own desires."

"Was I wrong?"

"Yes, if you want to go about rendering justice in the world. Once we see others as they truly are, as men, it becomes too hard then to be God."

"So it's better to see such men as monsters?"

"Good heavens, no! To see our fellows as beasts and monsters, lesser creatures for us to lord over? That's how Price saw the world."

Tuckworth glanced sideways at Hunt. "You don't offer any simple answers."

Hunt shrugged. "You don't ask simple questions. You know, I think I might try to capture you in poetry."

Tuckworth stopped now, and stared in horror at his companion. "You'll do no such thing!"

"I'm afraid we poets are granted a license to abscond with the characters of our acquaintances. I imagine something slight, ephemeral, but amusing."

"Hunt, if you do this I'll bring you up before the magistrate on a charge of defamation!"

"Now, now. No one will know it's you. I think I'll make you into an Arab chieftain. How's that?"

And Tuckworth laughed now in spite of himself at the memory.

"What is it, Father?" Lucy asked. "You look so wistful."

"Nothing, my dear. Not much." He leaned over and placed his hands on his knees. "How's our little girl this morning?"

Bit turned her sad eyes to him, the eyes that always seemed on the verge of laughter or tears. "Good day, Dean Tuckworth," she said very seriously, before burying her head once more in Lucy's lap.

"And good day to you, Miss Bit."

There was a knock on the vicarage door, and soon Mrs. Cutler appeared to show in Reverend Mortimer. No one had seen the rector for a few days past, and the time seemed to have softened his austerity, for he entered with a glowing smile.

"My friends," he crowed as he entered the parlor, ignoring Lucy's icy welcome. "What a lovely picture of domestic bliss. And who is this sweet creature?" He leaned down to get a closer look at Bit.

The child stood for a moment, being looked at, before making a rude noise and running off to Lucy's skirts again.

The rector ignored this affront with grace. "Dear Mr. Tuckworth," he said, turning to the dean with his smile undimmed, "would you care to take a turn out-of-doors with me?"

Tuckworth stood up. "That's an excellent suggestion," he announced happily. "I was just about to set out on an errand myself, and I'd be grateful for the company."

As they left, Tuckworth winked mischievously at Lucy, who wondered what her father might be up to now.

"A remarkable course of events," Mortimer commented as they walked past the cathedral, the Great Cross now removed and laborers busy rebuilding the floor of the nave. "I understand you managed to coax a few extra pounds out of Lord Granby."

"A few," the dean acknowledged. "Enough to finish work on the floor."

"Excellent! Marvelous! It's good to see you so active again." Tuckworth grinned, but let the rector continue. "You know, this awful business with that man"—Mortimer could not even say Price's name any longer—"illustrates a lesson from which we might all profit."

"And what's that?"

"The strange workings by which God sees His will accomplished. That man was as pure a fiend as ever slunk from Hell, and yet his donation allowed the work to commence on God's house. Not even the devil can stand in the way of the Lord's plans."

"It would appear not."

Mortimer stopped and turned to face Tuckworth. "Yes, but do you comprehend my meaning?" and a nervous quaver tripped over his voice. "In procuring that donation, I . . . we were simply doing God's work. None of that fiend's evil can taint our efforts. Can it."

Tuckworth tried to look sympathetically at the rector. "Mr. Price wanted to be a good man," he said. "That part of him should not be forgotten."

"Your notion of a good man seems out of place, Mr. Tuckworth," Mortimer sniffed, his old manner coming upon him briefly. "Still, it was God's goodness that triumphed in the end."

"I suppose."

"But we should be agreed on that," Mortimer insisted, somewhat emphatically. "If the matter arises as to how we could involve the cathedral in this business, the good that was done must be seen to outweigh the bad."

Tuckworth paused. Even when he was determined to enjoy Mortimer's company, the man could fray his nerves. "Very well, Mortimer," he said at last. "You may report to the bishop that none of this was your fault."

The rector looked offended, but thought better than to say anything. "Then, if we are agreed," and he moved to part ways with the dean.

Tuckworth linked an arm through Mortimer's, however. "Now, you must accompany me. We're almost there."

Mortimer looked confused. "Where? What is your errand?"

The dean dipped his fingers into his waistcoat pocket and took out a folded piece of paper. "Here," he said, handing it over.

The rector unfolded the note, and stopped. He looked at the dean in stunned disbelief, looked back at the note, and muttered, "Five thousand pounds?"

"Yes. I'd quite forgotten about it until Hunt reminded me this morning. He says Price's bankers will have to honor it."

"Five *thousand*?"

"I know," Tuckworth said with a wry grin, pulling Mortimer along again. "That's how I felt when he offered me the money. Let's go deposit it in the Cathedral Fund, and then we can write to the bishop together, you and I, and explain to him how very much good it takes to outweigh the bad."